The Damaged

Received On

MAR 1 7 2022

Magnolia Library

NO LONGER PROPERTY OF
SEATTLE PUBLIC LIBRARY

D0047463

MAR 1 7 2022

Also by Tijan

The Insiders

The Damaged

TIJAN

ST. MARTIN'S GRIFFIN
NEW YORK

This is a work of fiction. All of the characters, organizations, and events portrayed in this novel are either products of the author's imagination or are used fictitiously.

First published in the United States by St. Martin's Griffin, an imprint of St. Martin's Publishing Group

THE DAMAGED. Copyright © 2022 by Tijan. All rights reserved. Printed in the United States of America. For information, address St. Martin's Publishing Group, 120 Broadway, New York, NY 10271.

www.stmartins.com

Library of Congress Cataloging-in-Publication Data

Names: Tijan, author.
Title: The damaged / Tijan.
Description: First edition. | New York : St. Martin's Griffin, 2022. |
Identifiers: LCCN 2021039232 | ISBN 9781250210791 (trade paperback) |
    ISBN 9781250210807 (ebook)
Subjects: LCGFT: Novels.
Classification: LCC PS3620.I49 D36 2022 | DDC 813/.6—dc23
LC record available at https://lccn.loc.gov/2021039232

Our books may be purchased in bulk for promotional, educational, or business use. Please contact your local bookseller or the Macmillan Corporate and Premium Sales Department at 1-800-221-7945, extension 5442, or by email at MacmillanSpecialMarkets@macmillan.com.

First Edition: 2022

10 9 8 7 6 5 4 3 2 1

To my own Bailey!
To all the readers who loved *The Insiders*!

The Damaged

ONE

Bailey

Swish, swish.

The windshield wipers were busy at work this morning. It'd been raining since late the night before, and now there was just a whole dreary feel to the day. Dark and gloomy, matching my mood.

It was perfect.

Swish, swish.

"Are you nervous, miss?"

I wasn't responding, because this isn't how things were supposed to be. I wasn't supposed to wake up in the middle of the night and find the bed empty. And I wasn't supposed to have to be escorted by one of our guards down to the apartment building's gym to find my boyfriend, the guy I loved, the guy who was *so* not a secret from the *entire world* anymore, pummeling a boxing bag so hard that his knuckles ripped open every night. It was not right that I had to stand on the side, waiting for him to fight through his haze before he noticed I was there, and then watch as blood dripped from his hands to the floor.

But all of that was happening.

Because three weeks after there'd been a kidnapping attempt on me, after he had saved me, everything was just, simply, not okay.

To be more frank, everything was shit.

And here I was.

In the back of an SUV being driven by one of my two personal bodyguards, to a school that I used to daydream about attending, while my boyfriend, that guy I had come to love so much, was heading into his own personal nightmare.

Fitz, my guard, clued in on my state and didn't ask again, but his eyes were on me. He saw. He more than saw, and I knew I'd be getting a call from Kash about two minutes after the first chance Fitz had a moment to text his boss that I was not okay.

Because I wasn't.

Today was the day all my dreams were supposed to come true.

Instead, I was a week late going to my graduate program and I wanted to be anywhere except where I was going. And I had no say, because the world found out in a big way I was the daughter of Peter Francis, a tech legend who I'd grown up idolizing until I found out myself, this past summer, that he was also my father.

And then there was my boyfriend, Kash Colello, whose grandfather was one of the richest men in the world, but that came with strings and dangerous alliances with the dark underground of the world. My boyfriend, with his inherited wealth, now that he had come out of the shadows to the world, and whose "coming out" was even bigger than mine because of his connections and his family, was now the ninth wealthiest man in the world.

Life as Peter Francis's daughter, life as Kash Colello's girlfriend, was a whole lot different than life had been as Bailey Hayes.

There were rules and expectations and lots and lots of people watching you.

So no, I was *not* okay.

I had a pit in my stomach the size of the Grand Canyon and no one could tell me not to have it. It was there. It was getting bigger every morning I woke, and it wouldn't stop growing.

But that wasn't for Fitz to deal with, or my new classmates.

I was hoping they had no clue who I was, but I was realistic and knew they probably did. Everyone in our world knew my father, so that meant everyone would know who his daughter was.

"It's a big day today. I'm nervous."

I was lying through my teeth.

The shadow in his gaze cleared. He nodded, the wrinkles smoothing out in his forehead, and while he went back to driving and doing his job, no longer holding a nagging worry, I was still here. I was still not okay.

My phone buzzed. It was Matt.

Naveah. Tonight. I want to hear how your first day went. Hope it's great, sister.

The text from my older brother was helping to ease some of the doom and gloom. Especially because I was pretty sure he'd be sleeping off a hangover from drinking at Naveah the night before. The nightclub was their favorite spot to see, be seen, and to get laid.

I texted back.

Deal.

We drove more, and my phone buzzed a second time. Mom-Boss.

Hope your day is amazing, sweetie!! You'll wow everyone with your brain.

Sigh.

Chrissy Hayes, aka MomBoss, aka my mother. She was being the doting and loving mother this morning, not the feisty, ready-to-commit-murder-and-hide-the-bodies mom or her other alter ego, the party animal.

She had a bigger social life than I did.

Thanks, Chrissy.

MOM TO YOU!

Thanks . . . MomBOSS

Better. You're learning.

We kept driving and my phone buzzed a few more times. Ser:

KICK ASS, BIG SISTER!! FIRST DAY FOR BOTH OF US!

Well, then. I didn't realize my little sister was that excited to start eighth grade. It eased my worry for her, because I knew Seraphina was kind and pure and those friends around her were so not the same.

Slay those other girls, Ser. SLAY.

She might not realize I meant that word almost literally, but I did. She texted back:

Consider them slayed.

That eased my gloom even more. I now matched the outside. It was more dreary, slightly overcast. A bit more than overcast. More like overcast with a good chance of rain. Stormy.

I needed to stop using weather analogies. And then I heard from Cyclone, my little brother.

Cyclone: I finished the robot. What are you doing today? I have school. They're doing a robotics class and I got in. Did Dad tell you? I'm in there with a bunch of older kids, but I'm in. They said the robot sealed the deal. This year is going to be AWESOME!

Cyclone: Aunt Helen said we could all do pizza night tonight. You in? Tell me you're in. I have to tell you about my robotics class. You and Kash have to come.

Me: You bet, buddy, and have fun today! You're right. A robotics class is amazing. I'm not surprised you got in, and YOU'RE going to be AMAZING!

Cyclone: Okay. Calm down. It's just the first day. Did Ser tell you that I grew again? I'm almost as tall as you.

I laughed. He probably was. I was five-six and he wasn't too far beneath me. Even Seraphina had had a growth spurt and was nearing just an inch below me. Though, while it was obvious she could be a supermodel one day, it was pretty clear that I got the short genes and different body structure than the rest of the Francis kids. Matt was tall but lanky. Seraphina already had a little bit of a bigger bone structure than me. I was petite, like Chrissy, and I like to think I had the same feisty Hayes attitude in me. We packed a wallop if need be, but I got Peter's hair and his eyes. We both had honey-brown eyes and jet-black hair with tints of blue in the right light.

The rest of the Francis kids were going to be tall and gorgeous.

And right on cue, as if they all got together and timed their texts perfectly, my little brother's text did the trick. It ripped through the dark cloud. A streak of light shone through. He was a little genius, and he was excited to learn and grow that brilliance. I wasn't as worried about him being bullied, because Cyclone was like me. He'd just hack them, and eventually everyone would learn to instantly fear him.

I loved the little tornado dude.

I'd been at Kash's so much and I'd stayed away from the Chesapeake Estate. I couldn't do that anymore. I *needed* my brother and sister. It hit me then just how much I needed them. There was a whole feeling burning inside my chest, making my heart squeeze. Painfully. After all the scandal that went down, with their mom being arrested for trying to kidnap and murder me, I'd been told that it might be a good idea if I steered clear from the house *and* Seraphina *and* Cyclone.

That was done. The burning just increased thinking about it.

I wasn't staying away anymore.

Me: *We gotta hit up the house before Naveah. There's a robotics class I have to hear about and I need to make sure those girls were nice to Seraphina today.*

Matt: *Sounds good. Do your hacking thing, check those bitches' social media stuff. Can you write a program where if they start talking shit about Ser, their computer gets fried?*

Me: *No, but give Cyclone a couple years. I'm sure he'll be all over that.*

I could hear Matt's laugh in his response.

Forgot. I'm talking to the wrong genius in our family. Too many of you fuckers to remember.

I was almost, and I was stressing the *almost*, in a good mood when I saw we were coming up to the beginning of Hawking's campus.

Gotta go. We're here.

Hawking University was known around town for its football team, but not for me.

All I cared about was that it was where I'd get my master's in computer information systems and then be on the way into my career creating security systems. That said, it was pretty to look at as we pulled up. Hawking was made up of gray brick buildings, most of which looked like castles. The building with most of my classes had a patio that stuck out over the rest of the building, and the roof looked raised, like it was the opening over a grand patio. Weird, but also kind of cool. The front doors were tall enough to cover two floors, and they were made up of metal and painted a dark orange. They looked almost burned, and I was guessing that was a latest trend, too.

Or I was assuming. I had no clue.

But ask me the latest trends for computer spreadsheets, program coding, or websites and I could list off a good two dozen, then give a bulleted list of pros and cons for each new trend, delivering it all with my sharp and snappy wit.

Even now, just thinking about it, I was getting all hyped.

I was almost bright and sunny. Until Fitz stopped the car.

No one deemed me ready, and to tell the truth, I hadn't been. I was a mess, but who wouldn't be? The world knew whose daughter I was, and then the world knew it'd been my stepmom who tried to kill me.

But there were good changes, too: my man and my family.

And all that brought me back to here, because I knew I wouldn't be attending graduate school as simply Bailey Hayes, freak genius brain but cute repertoire. I wouldn't be able to impress anyone with my saved file of memes. Instead, when I walked in there, everyone would know who I was. And not because of all that I just stated but because they knew who my father was, and two months ago I would've been salivating over the fact that Peter Francis had an illegitimate daughter. One who had his brain.

Except that girl was me, so there you go. My dilemma.

I liked being anonymous. No way was I going to be anonymous in there.

God. I sounded whiney.

No more whining. Check.

"You've been registered and everything is up-to-date. Your textbooks were delivered, along with your first week's worth of notes." Fitz kept talking, as if he knew what was bugging me.

Being new, everything was work. Usually I'd have to trek across a campus and make sure all my payments would be going through to pay for my school. I'd have to worry about getting a picture taken, getting my official ID. Textbooks, 'cause you had to be current with what the professor wanted you to have. Then there was the map of actually finding where you were supposed to go, or even just parking.

Kash and my security team went over my safety plan. I had a safety plan! I still couldn't get over that I was someone who needed a safety plan. So I knew the second guard was already inside. Erik and Fitz. Both looked my age or a few years older. Kash introduced us last night. He came around to officially meet me, and Kash told me Erik would be in civilian clothes, meaning he'd attempt to blend in. I couldn't fathom how a high-security bodyguard could "blend" so he was invisible. But they were trying. So I would try, too.

Fitz was about to open his door, and I knew what he would do after that.

I couldn't. That was too much attention.

"Is Erik inside? I'd like to get out on my own."

His eyes met me in the mirror. He knew what I was really asking, and after a second look, he used his phone. It buzzed back a moment later, and I looked through my window to the building. As Fitz answered me, I already spotted Erik standing at the door.

He did look like a grad student. Jeans. Hoodie. He had a bag slung over one shoulder and his phone in his hand. His gaze on me, he pushed open the building's door, taking a casual stance behind it.

He was looking just like the four other students right next to him, but I knew that wasn't the case. He was out there watching me, and I knew as I got to the building he'd somehow find a way to open the door for me. I would have to wait so he could go in first. These rules were stressed heavily to me the night prior. There was protocol and reasons for everything, but mostly Kash said it was all for my safety.

"You're good to go."

I grabbed my bag and nodded to Fitz. "Thank you."

I got out, and as soon as I did, my phone started ringing.

Kash calling.

He'd woken me this morning with his mouth trailing down my spine, a firm hand on my hip, and then a full hour of ecstasy. I expected a quickie for the morning. It was anything but. He'd been in no hurry. There was still that, but there'd been a whole element where it was slow and tender and loving. He kissed me the entire time he made love to me.

My entire body had been trembling from the emotions, and he rubbed a tear away with his thumb at the end. I'd been *that* overwhelmed.

I loved him.

God, did I love him, and somehow he knew the exact touch I needed to start this next chapter.

I answered, my phone to my ear. "You're supposed to be walking into your first shareholders' meeting right now."

Kash came from a powerful, well-connected family. With his grandfather being the evil lord he was—wealthy, powerful, and dangerous—and his mom having been a money genius who left an *extremely* large inheritance, he was a major player in the world. Besides money and power, Kash had his father's shares in Phoenix Tech, since he and Peter started the company together.

Kash had been steadily taking over his father's shares, which my father had previously voted in his stead, and he was also taking over older companies that his mother had started with a similar arrangement. The owners had been waiting for Evelyn Colello's son to step out of the shadows.

A low chuckle greeted me, and it washed over me, my entire body encased in warmth and flutters.

The flutters. I was still affected by just his voice.

"Shareholders can wait. Fitz said you're heading inside. How are you feeling?"

I stopped on the sidewalk, adjusting my bag, and shut the door behind me. The air was warm, sunshine already promising to be high and heavy that day, and students of all ages roamed behind me, around me, cutting in front of the vehicle. More than a few were eyeing Fitz, who could be seen through the windshield.

It was an impressive vehicle, a black SUV, but it wasn't anything more. I could be a normal student just getting dropped off by someone . . . but I was in the back and Fitz was in the front and I could feel their gazes switching to me, wondering who I was.

This wouldn't have bothered me three months ago. Three months ago, I would've assumed I was getting the attention because my tech reputation had preceded me. I would've been trudging from the parking lot, with my own shitty little Corolla in the lot, and I would've been standing in line to get a parking permit so I wouldn't get a ticket on my first day of classes.

But there was no recognition on any of their faces.

I breathed easier. "I'm feeling ridiculous, to be honest."

Another low and baritone chuckle from Kash. "You got this. And you already met Busich and Goa. They'll look out for you."

I pressed my lips tight together.

I'd met them. I hadn't wanted to meet them that way, though. Not in my father's study, with my dad there, and knowing I was already getting special privileges because he was introducing me as Peter Francis's daughter. Busich was the head of all the graduate programs and Goa was the head of my program's department. Two individuals a normal graduate student might never have met, but not me. Another change.

All these changes.

My stomach clenched. My gaze wavered; everyone was starting to circle in on me.

Get ahold of yourself! I could hear Chrissy's voice snapping at me, loaded with impatience and thinking this whole thing was ridiculous. Me, griping about all the "special" things that had happened to me and I knew would keep happening to me. I would've rolled eyes at myself three months ago, but—

"What if you dosed her too much?"

"Bitch . . ."

"Kidnapping and murder . . ."

I swallowed over a knot that was encased in acid and shoved that whole thing down my throat. That happened.

My hands were shaking, but I kept my voice firm. Goddamn, my voice wouldn't give anything away.

"You're right. I'll be all good."

Straighten up, Bailey.

I straightened.

Roll your shoulders back, girl.

I rolled my shoulders back.

Suck it in. Suck it up. And get going. You have a degree to conquer. You're going to earn a master's of science in computer information systems.

I sucked it in, sucked it up, and I was good to go. Hearing my mother's voice smoothed it all away, and I was ready. I *would* be fine.

I changed tactics. "I love you."

He was quiet for a moment. He wasn't buying it, but he said it back, and I knew it was a pass. He'd deal with this tonight, and what "this" was, I wasn't even sure myself. But I hung up with Kash.

I knew he had my back.

I knew he loved me.

Knowing that, feeling that, accepting that, I was ready to go.

TWO

I stepped inside, and there was a greeting line for me. No joke.

Or, well, that was an exaggeration, but Ms. Busich was there, wide smile, her dark hair swept up in a bun. Alongside her were Mr. Goa and two other faculty members and two students. I knew the faculty members because I did my research. One was my advisor, Ms. Wells, and the other was another professor in my studies, Mr. Dvantzi. The students, I didn't know. I hadn't researched them, which said how off my game was. Three months ago, I would've scoured everything I could find and I would've had a hard time not poking around for a list of upcoming first-year graduate students.

"Ms. Franci—"

I stopped Busich with a polite smile. "It's Hayes. I'm still just Bailey Hayes."

She paused, her eyebrows pinched together behind her glasses, then her face smoothed back out. Her smile returned. "Of course. Miss Hayes. Welcome." She gestured to the students. "This is Hoda Mansour and Liam Smith. Both are students in your cohort."

Hoda's face was gorgeous. Big, dark eyes, smooth tan complexion, and lips that were so round they were almost an oval shape. Her hair was robust. It was the only word that came to mind, because there was a lot there. It was smooth and hanging just short of her shoulders, but the volume had me salivating. If she'd had a blowout that day, I wanted to know who her stylist was, and I wasn't that type of girl. Chrissy, yes. My mother would've been all over her, exclaiming over her pedicure and cream-colored nails and the earrings that were hanging and sparkling from her ears. But it was the look in Hoda's eyes that had me snapping to attention.

She wasn't one to be messed with. I saw that right away. A sharp and almost calculating look was in there. I stared back at her with the same look and her lips pressed together in a flat line.

Okay then.

I would toe the line with her.

Liam was almost the complete opposite. Messy blond hair that was sticking in the air, a permanent wave where you could see he pushed his hand through his hair, leaving it where it lay, and as I studied him, he did just that. An almost goofy smile came to his face. Lines around his eyes and mouth were soft, giving him a sleepy look, too. Blue eyes that were smudged with exhaustion or something chemical, but he had a jock's body type. Broad shoulders. His polo shirt cut off on his biceps and they were built, so the guy spent time in the gym.

The two together were not what I'd been expecting. Then again, I didn't fit the IT stereotype either. Looking past them to the hallway, I saw plenty of gangly and awkward-standing guys who did, though, even a girl that dashed past everyone, rushing to our group. Petite. A darker complexion, small lips, and her face was rounder.

I liked her instantly.

"Ah. Yes. This is Melissa Zvanguam."

"Hello." She stuck her hand out, her eyes wide and taking me in.

I knew. I just knew. It was instant, but the starstruck look was there.

If I'd been questioning it before, I would've kicked myself now. The others were keeping themselves more restrained, or they just didn't care, but this girl cared.

And I knew what words would come from her next, in a breathy awed tone. "You're Peter Francis's daughter."

I put my hand in hers and she gripped me tight, gushing, "I am a huge *huge* fan of your father's, and you're going to be in my cohort." A deep breath.

Ms. Busich frowned. "Get ahold of yourself, Miss Zvanguam."

"Yes." Melissa nodded automatically, eyes glazed and glued to me, and stepped back. Her hand didn't disengage from mine, so she was bent forward. "I can't let go of your hand."

Hoda coughed, stepping forward. Her hands were clasped in front of her and the movement tore our hands apart.

Liam was stoned. I was pretty sure. His smile never dimmed or changed. He didn't move at all.

Yep. Stoned. I was certain.

"Ah. Miss Mansour. Why don't you show Miss Hayes the premises, help her get situated."

I was situated. I said it, too. "I had a tour last spring, and I've studied all the maps and layouts. To be honest, I just really want to get to class and get started."

Hoda stepped more to the side so she was half next to me, facing Ms. Busich.

"Yes, well . . ." Busich glanced to the other faculty, which made sense. She was the head of everything. This was a more specific question.

Ms. Wells took her cue and nodded, another formal smile on her face. "Hoda will still show you the more pertinent faculties. Hoda?"

"Yes, Ms. Wells?"

"Bring her to my office after class. Miss Hayes?"

Miss Hayes was so formal. "Bailey. Please."

"Bailey." Her smile seemed a touch more genuine. "It's lovely to meet you. After class, Hoda will show you to my office. We need to go over your program."

I nodded. I had been expecting that.

A meeting with your advisor was normal. The rest of this was not.

"Sounds great. Thank you."

Hoda started the tour with a bang. She marched ahead of me, and I had to hurry up, but she was already going.

"We have twelve students in our cohort. Three are half time. Nine are full time. There's three females. You, myself, and Melissa make up those stats. The rest are guys, and we have two older adults, and when I say *older*, I'm meaning they're middle-aged return students." She passed an open classroom, nodding inside. "Classes on Monday start at nine thirty a.m. Classes on Thursday start at twelve thirty. Each is three hours long. Your advisor will go over the rest of your schedule with you. Here is our personal student lab."

She went to a door and swept it open. It was a bricked room, no windows, just computers. Lots of computers. The printer was set up in the corner, and next to it was an attendant for the room.

"We do use the school's library for extra studying, so if we're not in here, more than likely we'll be in the library. Most are graduate assistants, GAs, but loitering in the extra offices is frowned upon here. The IT department is stressing a cohesive and connected cohort with this program and so yes, that means we're guinea pigs. There was more than the average number of student suicides last year. They've looked at the most isolated programs and the IT program rated high. So there you go. We're being force-fed friends, not that you'll be lacking."

She paused before moving farther down the hallway. "Everyone knows who you are. And after your meeting with Ms. Wells, they'll flock to you. Peter Francis is a god to us." She narrowed her eyes, skimming me up and down. "If you had merited this program on your own, I'm sure you'd understand."

Oh, snap.

My back straightened.

I felt the heat start first in my belly, and it was rolling up at a fast pace.

"Merited? On my own?" I narrowed my eyes. "You think I got in here because of who my father is?"

She went farther down the hallway, her back to a closed classroom door, and stood facing me. "I don't think it. I know it. I work in the graduate office and I was there when Peter Francis called Ms. Busich about you last spring. I'm the one who answered the phone."

That wasn't—My stomach dropped.

Wait, though.

What did that mean?

I got in on my own. This was bringing up concerns from earlier, worrying if I got those scholarships because of me or because of my relation to Peter. I knew who I was. This girl, she didn't. She had no clue who I was, which said more about her than me.

"If Peter called about me last spring, it wasn't to get me a spot. I got early acceptance on my own."

"Your name wasn't even in the files until after that call. *Daddy* got you in. We have a B-average requirement. If you can't hack it in the program, you're out."

Once she stopped insulting me, her eyes went past my shoulders, and this wasn't the first time since we started the tour.

She stepped close, lowering her head. "You know that guy?"

I turned, seeing Erik bending over at the water fountain.

His backpack was on. The bulge was sticking out on his side, and he was watching us from the corner of his eye.

"He's been following us this whole time."

The jig was up.

But she didn't say anything or wait for me to respond. Her hand went to the door and she was going inside.

I stepped behind her and turned.

Twelve sets of eyes turned my way.

THREE

They were gawking. They were whispering. They were staring.

I knew this would happen, so I ignored it all and settled in for my first class.

The professor came in, but he didn't act any differently toward me than the rest of my peers. That was a relief. He came over to introduce himself to me. Brian Zerr. He told me right off the bat that he came from India. I wasn't sure why he told me that, but I noted it and took a seat next to Hoda.

It was after class, after discussing advanced theories of coding systems, that *it* happened.

I was swarmed as soon as class was done.

I wasn't going to remember their names. If they'd had name tags, I would've memorized them no problem, but they didn't, and all the guys seemed to know each other. The university might need to rethink the idea that the IT department was one of the most isolated programs. These guys seemed like long-term buddies, asking about discord servers and if my dad was going to create the rumored AI forum.

One: that alarmed me. Slightly. It also excited me, too.

And two: artificial intelligence was unparalleled and unbarred. The possibilities of that . . . I was kicking myself for sticking to helping Cyclone with his robot rabbit when we could've been reading up on AI theories this entire summer. What the hell. Summer had been wasted, besides all the really great stuff that came out of it, like me getting a family, me getting a father, me falling in love with a scary and dangerous business guy, and you know, the whole *other* other world, like black markets and everything that Calhoun Bastian represented.

Besides all of that happening, total summer wasted.

AI.

Seriously.

That's what these guys were into?

The question was rolling around in my head when Hoda took me to Ms. Wells's office, and once I was in there, I knew we weren't going to be talking about my class schedule, because I'd asked last spring to take on more than a full-time student's load. I could handle it and I wanted to graduate in one year, not two. But seeing the set on her face, I braced myself. She had a round face with light pink freckles, strawberry-red hair that was combed through and styled to rest just under her ear, and a white satin blouse that was a size too small. It was snug, and there was a small pudge forming on her side, but as she shifted and pulled at her shirt to cover it, I wanted to tell her to let it go. Embrace the curve. And I was only thinking that because I was still nervous and worried, but I couldn't quite point my finger on why I felt that way. It'd come to me, or more than likely Kash would just straight-up tell me.

"How was your first day at Hawking?"

I blinked.

That was . . . Okay. Not what I'd expected first. I was going to go with it.

"I'm processing everything."

"The other students don't know about your brain."

Right. My photographic memory, which seemed to be sharpening with each year and not fading.

She picked up a pen, the end digging into her notebook, as she studied me. "They also don't know about your tech skills."

"Okay."

I folded my hands together on my lap, frowning a little. I wasn't sure where she was going with this.

"I'm sure you're aware of the stats, but I'm going to tell them to you anyways. There's one student in your cohort with the IQ level of a genius. There are three students with the IQ levels just below genius. Five students are technical geeks, if that's the term to use. They love computers. They love everything about computers, and their knowledge level is exceptional, but regarding their general IQ level, they are above average, which is typical for students in our department. The remaining three are newer students to the IT department and are here only to secure a job for their family's security. The intelligence levels don't factor into this equation because they're the outliers. They are actually just normal people." She paused. Her eyebrow raised. The pen ground more into her notebook. "Are you following me?"

My nails dug into my palms, just slightly.

She wasn't coming at me like Hoda had, mistaking me for one of those "average" students. Ms. Wells knew my résumé. She was coming at me like I was going to be a problem for her or the department, and I didn't like that. I didn't like it at all.

"Ms. Wells." Shit. Was I going to do this?

I liked professors. Professors liked me.

I wasn't a kiss-ass, but I was the student they never had to worry about or even try to teach. Give me a book and nine out of ten times I could teach myself. But I still needed to pay for the class hours to get that degree, and because of that, I utilized professors. I asked them questions that other students didn't think about. Professors liked that, a lot.

They liked my mind.

This response wasn't aligning with past professors.

I wasn't accustomed to this behavior, and I wasn't sure how to react to it. My father had never been an issue before. But now that people knew who he is, it seemed everything was going to be new for me. My heart was skipping a whole bunch of beats.

My palms were also sweating up a storm, but here goes.

"Yes?" she said.

Oh boy.

I let out a small pocket of air, wiping my hands over my jeans. "You're judging."

"Pardon?" Both her eyebrows were up now.

"You're judging me. I'm not sure if it's because of who my father is, because you probably got an extra call from both Goa and Busich, or hell, even if it's because of who I'm dating"—her forehead puckered at that last one—"but I'm the type of student that doesn't make waves. Being smart, I got teased a lot when I was younger. Like a lot. My cousins went to my school and they helped curtail some of the more aggressive people, but it happened. I'm a loner because of that, or usually a loner. I show up to class. I do the work. I do exceptional work. And I'm the type of student who wants to learn everything.

"I didn't ask my father to make those calls. I didn't ask to have two security guards with me here. Having said that, I know my father made those calls because he loves me, and he's trying to make up for lost time. And the two guards are actually necessary. Who I was before is still me, but who I am now just means I'm going to have extra attention. That's it.

"Those recommendations weren't lying. I read them, each one. I can recite them to you word by word if you'd like, but those letters were also earned. Please judge me on those letters and not on who you think I'm going to be because you got two extra calls that other students don't."

She was silent when I finished, her mouth pressed together. Her eyes never wavered. She was taking me in, like she could sift through my own brain to figure me out, and then with a whoosh, all of what she was thinking disappeared. Her shoulders relaxed. Her eyebrows slackened. There was no more pinch in her forehead.

"Okay." A low murmur from her. She was nodding, and she let the pen rest on the desk. "I started out by giving you stats to let you know that even though *you're* the one genius student, what you've taken on is going to be too much for you, because of the recent events in your life."

What?

I stiffened.

Had I read her wrong?

She leaned forward, resting her arms on her desk, her hands folded together. She lowered her head, still watching me. "But you're correct in your assessment. I started out by judging you based on your father, and I wouldn't have admitted that. I see now that upsets you. I apologize."

Whoa.

Really? A professor who apologized?

"But I'm still questioning if you're ready to take on the load that you asked for this year. You're doing the advanced docket, and that'll put you at finishing next August. It's double the load."

I had no money.

That was the practical reason I wanted to finish as fast as I could.

Kash had money. Peter had money. I was staying with Kash, so he wasn't making me pay rent, but I wasn't comfortable with how dependent I actually was, and there was a difference between earning money and receiving money.

Call it the Hayes pride in me, but I wanted to earn my own way.

I'd been planning on updating computer systems at Brookley Hospital to cushion my bank account before starting graduate school. That hadn't happened, so now I was left to decide between asking for money, getting a job, or holding my breath until I slid through school and got my own IT job.

I was holding my breath through the year.

I leaned forward. My hands relaxed and I rested them on the tops of my legs. "I'm only taking on one extra course this semester. I know first semesters for grad programs are always the hardest and most intensive. Next semester, I'm doing two extra courses, and I'm doubling up for both summer minis."

"Most students want time for a break in the summer second quarter. Are you sure you want to go straight through?" She switched to her computer screen and moved the monitor so I could see what she was seeing. She had my schedule up there. "You're doing one full internship course during your winter break. That's not usually even allowed."

But it was for me. I did the paperwork. I made the calls. I got the permission.

I didn't have the internship, but I had the university's approval to have it early.

I didn't say any of that, because she knew it, too.

"I have to ask you again. Have you *fully* thought about the load you're taking on? You're going to have more responsibilities, being Peter Francis's daughter, and I know who you're dating. You will not have time to sleep, eat, or even shower. As your advisor, I'm advising against this load."

"No."

My response was swift and fierce.

Panic rose up in me, clawing, digging its cold tips into my insides, and I panicked at just feeling how acidic that panic was.

I needed school. She didn't understand. I needed it. I needed it like breathing.

If I was being honest with myself, it wasn't about doing it in a year. It was about being so distracted that I couldn't think, couldn't feel, couldn't remember.

The remembering was the worst.

She saw my reaction. "What is this about? You're looking like you're about to have a panic attack."

Attack.

Memories assaulted me.

"That bitch talked too long . . ."

"Throw her in the back of the van . . ."

"KASH!"

My own scream ripped me back to where I was sitting, and I

physically jerked in my seat. The chair clattered against the floor, and all the while, Ms. Wells wasn't looking happy. A full cloud of worry was hanging over her. And I was back to weather analogies. Lovely.

"I know what happened to you." Her words were kinder. "You need the school in order to deal, don't you?"

I was so tense, but my eyes snapped to hers and I couldn't look away. My chest was imploding, pushing inside me, and I couldn't. Fucking. Breathe.

I got a nod out.

Technology. Computers. Codes. That was my world. Mine. I was comfortable in it. I lived in it. It'd been my life, my security blanket, and it was where I needed to go again or I wouldn't be able to deal. I could get lost in that world, and I needed it. I needed it more than I had realized until just now.

"That's not why I wanted to do the advanced track. I didn't know what would happen to me, but . . ."

She was nodding. She was looking all knowing and understanding, and I breathed easier when she said, "Okay. Let's do this. We'll be fine. I'll help you with anything you need, and I should also let you know that I've been given personal phone numbers for your boyfriend and your father. If I need to use them, I was instructed to use them, but no one else has their numbers."

She thought that was funny. Her top lip curved up.

I grinned back. "Do Busich and Goa know that last part?"

"Not one bit."

That was the part that she liked.

FOUR

I told Matt about my advisor, about my classmates, about everything at Naveah that evening. We were squished into the VIP booth, he had an arm on the back of my seat, and he was turned toward me, shutting out the rest. His friends were across from us, girls around them.

Guy had his arm around one of the girls, sitting on the inside of the booth.

Chester was lounging back, another on his lap.

And Tony—I didn't want to even look. He had tugged a third behind the corner, and I knew she was kneeling, but they couldn't be doing what it looked like they were doing. They were out of eyesight from us, but not from the rest of the club. Though the club was darker than normal that night. Torie came over with drinks and mentioned they had a lighting emergency.

Tony *was* probably taking advantage. So gross.

"It seems intense," Matt was saying, but his gaze kept going past my shoulders. I was at the end of the booth, and he had a perfect view of the tables surrounding the dance floor. I wasn't going to take bets that he was eye-fucking a girl and that soon after he left the table he'd be screwing her for real. It's what my brother did. Even if he said he was going for drinks for everyone, I knew not to believe him. He would go for drinks and *would* bring them back, but the time from leaving to coming back would depend on how long it took for him to get with the girl.

We'd had family dinner with Cyclone and Seraphina at the main estate earlier tonight. Marie was still gone, which was odd.

Marie ran the place. Her being gone, super weird. My mom was there, but distracted through the entire dinner. Kash was still in meetings. Same with Peter, so it ended up being a sibling dinner with their aunt.

The aunt.

That was it.

I didn't know her name. I kept forgetting to ask Kash and Matt. Then she was walking into the room and I expected her to introduce herself. Nothing. She shook my hand when I introduced myself, and stood behind Seraphina with an almost sad smile on her face.

She was pretty.

I remembered the slight heart attack I had when I first saw her, walking behind Cyclone and Seraphina when I FaceTimed them. She looked so much like Quinn, it'd been hard to see her. I'd hoped that effect would go away, but it hadn't.

The hairs on the back of my neck were permanently standing upright the whole time during dinner. It was the second time I'd seen Cyclone and Seraphina in person. Everyone waited, giving me two weeks to heal. They were going to give me more, but I'd had it with everything. I was fine. I would be fine. Let me get on with my life.

But that wasn't the same deal with my two younger siblings. Every time I wanted to go see them, they weren't available. There were lots of family therapist meetings for them, and if they weren't in those, then they were with other trauma specialists or divorce therapists. It was a bit of overkill—bad wording there, but that's what I thought.

Then again, maybe I couldn't judge. It hadn't been my mom who tried to kill my half sister. So tonight I had high hopes of really getting some bonding time in.

And I wanted to hear if they were already talking about AI in there, too.

I was relieved that, by the end of our pizza, he had never

mentioned AI at all, just that the older guys had been super friendly and curious about me. Seraphina seemed happy, too. Lots of smiling and laughing. Matt kept teasing her about the guys in her grade. He kept mentioning an E.J. and she kept blushing. Her whole face was a tomato by the end of the dinner.

The aunt was there, always there.

The official reason was that she was there to help take care of Seraphina and Cyclone, but she was lurking. Sitting. Staring. Actually seeming nice when I looked at her, but I couldn't look at her. I just saw Quinn.

Breathe, babe. Breathe.

I was breathing.

I was fine.

Quinn was not there anymore, and though her sister seemed nice, I had to bail. Matt was cool with it, so we came to Naveah after, and now there were two drinks in for me, three for Matt, and a couple shots for the others.

I stopped talking and waited.

It took a second before Matt blinked, his eyes finding mine again. "What were you saying?"

"Right." I was grinning. "Go. Do your thing."

He was quiet a second, measuring me. "You won't be mad?"

"Matt." I gave him a look. "You've been eye-fucking someone over there this entire time. I doubt you heard a word I said." I nodded again, jerking my head behind me. "Go. Do your thing. Have fun."

"You *sure?* You did have your first day of classes today . . ." But he so wanted to go. I could see it, and I heard it in how his voice trailed off.

Another look from me.

"Right." He laughed, dipped his head down, and knocked on the table. "Then let me out, sis."

As he passed me, his phone buzzed. He checked it before

showing me the screen, saying at the same time, "Sit tight. Your man is on the way."

The text was from Kash.

Heading there now. Bailey okay?

Matt paused, his back turned to me now as he sent a response. Then he shoved his phone back into his pocket. He gave me a last wink over his shoulder, grabbed his drink, and turned to head down the stairs connecting our booth with the rest of the club.

"Francis! What the hell, man?" That was from Guy, his hands lifted in the air, but with a smirk on his face.

Matt just grinned. "You know where I'm going." He motioned to me with his drink. "Watch my sister for me. Her man's on the way."

Guy's eyes darted to me. His smirk never lessened, and he lifted his head up in response. "You know it."

Chester and Tony had both stopped whatever they were doing with their girls. I still wasn't looking at Tony, but I saw Chester lift his head up and glance over his shoulder at Tony before he looked at me.

He didn't say a word. Tony either.

Tony did come back to the table, and to my side. "Can I slide in?" There was no girl behind him. She was heading down the stairs, wiping her mouth with the back of her hand and straightening her shirt.

My stomach rolled over in nausea, but whatever.

I stood up and stepped to the side.

Tony didn't say a word, only slid inside the booth and moved so he was closer to the girl next to Guy. There was a good distance between him and me. Two people could've sat there. Still felt too close to Tony. Guy seemed decent, but I'd seen enough from Chester and Tony. My guard would always be up around them, a fact they both seemed to know, because neither gave me a greeting when they showed. They just came up, nodded to Matt, and did their thing. Guy came up later, a wider smile and an actual greeting for everyone.

No girls. No Fleur, Victoria, or their third friend. Those girls were different than the ones flirting / making out / doing other explicit acts, like the girl who had just scampered away and the two remaining at the table. I was still new to their scene, but I knew that much. These girls were used for one thing: entertainment. Whether it was for flirting or blowing, the girls were used and then told to run off. Once they were done with the girls, the girls had to take off or the guys got nasty.

I'd witnessed it. It hadn't been fun to watch.

But girls like Fleur, Victoria, and their other friend, they were different. They had connections to these guys. Families. Their parents were colleagues, helped each other with charity benefits. They were money. The discarded girls weren't, and so these girls didn't do much to me. There might've been a nasty look, but once they were told who I was, they shut up immediately. In this realm, being Matt Francis's sister lent me protection in that way.

Also being Kashton Colello's girlfriend skyrocketed me above them, too, but I wasn't like Victoria or Fleur. I didn't look at these girls with disdain, just a fair amount of discomfort, because who gives a blowjob next to a booth?

That was a new level of awkward for anyone.

But these girls didn't know that I was the one who might be nice to them. They simply did not talk to me. It'd been like that the first night and every night since.

So, with Matt gone, I sat back in the booth and prepared to wait in silence until Kash showed up. Guy was the only one who might say something to me, but he was firmly distracted by his girl. Her hand had disappeared under the table, and the motion made it clear what she was doing.

Tony was still smirking.

Chester also was nodding, and as I sat there and watched, he took his girl's hand and moved it beneath the table, too. She had to maneuver to one side of his lap so she could do what he wanted, but a second later, yep. Pretty obvious.

I was sitting at the sexual acts table.

Kash couldn't get here fast enough.

It was ten minutes later. Ten minutes where I sat in silence, listening to the music, sipping on my rum and Coke, and studiously ignoring the guys, when a shift in the club happened.

Everyone felt it.

A buzz swept through the club, making everyone pay attention, whether they realized it or not. They instinctively knew someone more powerful, someone more dangerous, someone they should fear was in their midst. It was a feeling in their gut, and whether they acknowledged it or not, they were affected by it. Conversations quieted. People began looking around.

A zap of energy was in the air, and all heads turned as a path opened toward the stairs leading to our booth.

There was my man.

Kash Colello had arrived.

Seriously intense eyes, eyes that were dark and fixed on me, and I couldn't tell from the nightclub's lighting, but I had firsthand knowledge how his usual cognac-brown eyes could go to simmering midnight if he was in the right mood. And that mood was either being pissed off or being turned on.

Based on how his strong jawline was set, and how his broad and defined shoulders seemed rigid, I was going with the first mood. It also didn't help that the lights were flickering and casting shadows that played over his high cheekbones. I still melted on the regular if I saw water dripping down them.

Honestly. They were delicious to look at.

Mix them with his lips, very delectable and kissable and lickable lips—

I was thinking I shouldn't be getting turned on by watching Kash stalking over here, looking like he was going to lay into someone.

I couldn't help myself.

That body, and how he was moving toward us, did things to me.

Another thing I knew from personal experience was that body of his. He was ripped, with barely an ounce of fat on him.

Yes, indeed. Kash Colello was very blessed with some fan-fucking-tastic genes.

He was almost stalking forward, but he was moving with a lithe, predatory motion to him. There was no expression on his face. He was locked down, but he was angry. His eyes were almost glittering. Tony and Chester both sat up straighter. Tony's hand clenched into a fist on the table. Even Guy, who was still wearing an easygoing smile, was wary. His eyes dimmed a bit, and his jaw tightened, but he did it all while grinning.

Kash walked up, his eyes still on mine, lingering, before sweeping over the rest of the table.

The girls had both stopped their ministrations, their eyes glued to Kash, and their jaws slackened.

His gaze paused where the girls' hands were under the table before he growled, "With Bailey here? You serious?"

Tony jerked, slamming into the back of our booth, jostling the rest of us.

The girl's hand jumped back up to the top of the table. She was blinking, looking dazed, but color was coming to her face. Her gaze moved to mine before she lowered her head, her hair falling forward to cover her face.

"She stayed. It's not our problem."

Tony was an idiot. He was talking back to Kash, so he was more than an idiot. He was a moron.

Guy's grin lessened. Then a chuckle came from him as he, too, seemed shocked at what Tony said.

Kash's eyes narrowed, but he didn't move. He didn't lean over the table. His face didn't show anything, but when he spoke,

Tony knew, I knew, everyone knew. Tony had just made a very, *very* stupid decision.

"I had a meeting with your father today."

Those words were whispered from Kash, but everyone at the table heard. And everyone took notice, because Kash was reminding Tony in a very simple way that he was connected to him in a way Tony couldn't touch. He was connected to his family's money.

He was above Tony's family—way, way above.

There was a reason Kash had remained hidden as long as he did. When he came out of the shadows, the entire world took note. They took note of his connections, his wealth, and he was catapulted into being even more powerful than my father—and that said a lot.

Anyone who had ties to Calhoun Bastian should instinctively be feared.

Kash made this point. "His company is going to go bankrupt. He wants me to come in, pour money into the company and save it." Now he moved, stepping closer to the table, his eyes never moving from Tony's.

Tony seemed to suck in his breath.

Kash leaned forward, placing his hands on the table so he was in Tony's space, invading it and pushing him down. "I've not made my decision if I want to save your father or not. Keep being you and you'll help me make that decision."

Keep being a dick. Keep being a douche. Keep just being Tony and Kash wouldn't save his father's company.

Tony's jaw clenched. His hand was still in a fist, but he swallowed. His Adam's apple moved up and down, and air hissed from him as he forced his hand to relax on the table, right between where Kash had put his hands.

I knew that'd all been intentional.

Move in. Force your presence on them. Remind them you

control them. Remind them they are not as dangerous as you
are. These were all moves that Kash was doing. He was reminding Tony of that fact right now.

Tony was the small guy here, and Tony *hated* it.

"Sorry, man."

Tony backed down, but it was visibly costing him.

"Good."

Simple, precise, and a killer shot. Kash switched his gaze to me.

He reached down and grabbed my hand. A thrill went through
me, sliding down my spine in the best way and he pulled me behind him. The path remained open, but then I saw there were
guards lining the way. Kash and I swept past them, heading for the
door. As we passed by the last staff desk, someone stepped back
quickly. I looked up, thinking it was Torie, or someone maybe I
wouldn't know.

Hoda stared back at me, her eyes wide. She was holding a
drink tray in front of her, turned vertically as if to shield her, and
as we both startled at seeing the other, she recovered quicker.

Her eyes moved past surprise to hostility, and then they slid
down to my hand in Kash's and they turned cold.

I didn't have time to say anything. Kash was out the door.
Three steps and we were both sliding into the back of the waiting
SUV. Once inside, the door was shut behind us and I turned
toward Kash to greet him. He greeted me first.

His mouth was on mine.

FIVE

Kash

I needed Bailey.

My body needed her. My soul needed her.

I wanted to hold her.

I wanted to be reassured by her, comforted by her. I wanted her to make the world go away, because right now all I could think was how hard the world was, but there was a need more primitive than the others.

I gave in to that need.

My body was primed, stark desperation strumming in my veins for her, because this day had sucked.

So when I got her in the SUV, I didn't waste time.

The privacy divider was up.

She moaned into my mouth, pressing against me, and I pushed a hand up her shirt. My hand closed over her tit and I pulled. She gasped, her mouth opening, and I surged in there, too.

God. This woman.

She knocked me on my ass the first time I saw her, and her power had only grown. She knocked everyone on their ass, but it was different with me.

I was tuned to her.

When she ached for me, I knew.

When she moaned, it was my high.

When she was moving beneath me, her legs wound around me, her hips trying to pull everything from me she could get, I was addicted. That addiction hadn't lessened. A snap of her fingers, a certain look, a certain sound from her and I'd vanquish anyone or anything I needed to make her ache with pleasure back for me.

I ran my hand down her back, enjoying how she trembled in my wake, and I pushed into her jeans, moving around to her front and undoing her buttons.

"God, Kash."

Yes. I knew. I needed her more than she needed me, and instead of responding, my mouth took control. I loved her warmth.

She bucked in my arms so I pulled her onto my lap.

Our driver couldn't see what we were doing, but I hit the button. He would know to keep driving until we were done.

I kept going, my other hand running down her front, between her breasts, down her stomach, all the way to her waist and around, as I picked her up. Her legs fell on both sides of me. I switched my hands, my fingers sliding back inside, and my other dipped into the back of her jeans, urging her to ride me.

She did. She didn't need any assistance. Her hips were already moving, so greedy, and I loved it. I wanted more.

Her head tipped back, her throat exposed. I bent, finding her there, feeling her pulse skip a beat. My own body was raging. My dick was demanding to be inside of her, but I waited. I always waited. Her first. Always her first.

"Kash," she moaned.

That's it.

That was *it.*

She trembled as I felt her come.

My turn.

I didn't wait for her to come down. I pushed her up, swept her pants down, yanked them off, and then she was back down and

I was surging inside of her. Holy fuck. She was home. My home. My everything.

Her shirt was still on, but my hand moved up, shoving it to her shoulders, just enough. I wanted to feel her against me. She was gone too, her eyes closed. She was lost, and I was getting there.

She began moving with me, her legs tensing, and I relaxed back against the seat, feeling her feeling me.

Jesus.

Christ.

I moved us both, flipping her over, and I bent over, shoving inside, and shoving deep.

"Kash!"

"Bailes." I kissed down the back of her neck, her spine. Her shirt was still over her shoulders, so I pulled it the rest of the way, reaching around and grabbing her breast. I tugged on her nipple, feeling her body shake, then I bent over, molding to her as I kept thrusting inside.

"Fuck, Kash."

She was coming. I felt her.

Soon.

I kept going. Harder. Deeper.

I needed her to come again. I was waiting, holding off.

Come, baby.

So soon. So close.

I felt hers, and with a whoosh she exploded in my arms, and a second later, I followed.

SIX

Bailey

Walking into Kash's apartment, I said, "I saw one of my classmates at Naveah tonight."

Kash was coming in behind me, like he always did. We had guards waiting for us, so the apartment was safe. Kash came in last to have a word with one of them, then made sure the alarm was on. He finished programming it. "You did?"

I went into the kitchen, hearing him following me. "It looks like she works there."

"What's her name?"

"Hoda Mansour."

Kash frowned. "Mansour? We have a Holden Mansour on staff. He works the IT department."

I learned a month ago that my father owned Naveah, but I also learned a couple weeks ago that Kash was in the process of taking it over completely. And knowing Kash, because he knew Naveah was a popular hangout for Matt, and now for me, he would know all the staff names.

"Have you met him?"

"No." He was on his phone a second later. "I had to let a manager go when I came on. He might've been the one to hire her. I'll have Torie look into it. Is she a problem for you?"

This was sticky, so I didn't answer. A second later, Kash's eyes were on me. He finished his text, putting his phone back in his pocket. "So she's a problem."

I was still hesitant, but I said, "I don't know. She's connected in the program, but she looks at me like she hates me. She thinks I got in because Peter got me in."

"What?" He laughed at that.

"She told me, said my name wasn't in the pile of students. Peter called in, she answered the call herself, and the next day my file was on the pile. She's adamant that he got me into that program."

"You know that's not true."

He was moving around me, pouring a drink for me, and then one for himself.

The fact that he poured the same drink I'd been sipping at Naveah wasn't lost on me. It was just a Kash thing to do, but with his, I knew he'd be sipping his bourbon for the rest of the night. I'd never seen him lose control with drinking. He would lose control fucking and fighting, but never with alcohol.

"How was the family dinner?"

"Good, except . . ." Again, I was hesitant.

I wasn't sure if it was my place to question her, but after what Quinn tried with me, I was thinking I should question everything.

He paused, with those eyes that seemed to see through me. "What is it, Bailey?" He said it so patiently, gently, like he knew I needed a little nudge.

It worked.

"What's the deal with their aunt? She's weird."

He studied me a second before he said anything. "Because she looks like Quinn?"

I had put my drink on the table, and now I was wringing my hands together. "I . . . yes. There's a mannerism about her that is Quinn. The same mannerism or something. I *feel* Quinn when she's in the room."

Kash was silent for a beat.

When he spoke, it was low, "Did you tell Matt this?"

Matt was fun. Matt was no drama right now, at least with family. He was trying to forget how he'd had an affair with the wife of the husband that Quinn was having an affair with, and how that same husband had been a decoy in helping Quinn get me kidnapped.

Matt was really trying not to be that guy, again.

So because of all that, I didn't answer.

Kash sighed. "You didn't want to worry him."

It wasn't a question from him. He knew.

I shrugged. There wasn't much else for me to say.

Kash nodded, putting his drink down. He motioned for me to come to him, so I did, and he put his arm around me, holding me, front to front. His head lowered. He rested his chin on my head. "You can always say something to myself or Matt, or even one of the guards. Never feel you need to remain in a place if it makes you uncomfortable."

I fisted part of his shirt in my hand, pressing my forehead to his chest. "Ser and Cy were there. I didn't want to leave them."

That was the gist of it. I could avoid the estate, even though Chrissy was still there. Marie had been sent away. Seraphina and Cyclone were in school now, but I missed my little brother and sister. I wanted to see them.

Kash understood this. His arm only tightened around me. "We'll have them to the apartment one night, or we can do a day with them on Sunday."

I tipped my head back. "Yeah?" Warmth spread through me at that suggestion, all the way to my belly.

He nodded, smiling down, a tender look in his eyes. "I can send Theresa out with Payton for a spa day. We can have Ser and Cyclone all to ourselves."

I wrapped both my hands in his shirt at that suggestion. "Thank you."

He bent down, his lips touching mine, and he whispered back, "I love you."

A full body tingle went through my body. All my nerve endings felt caressed, and my body melted into his. That was still happening at hearing those words, and I said them back, meaning them with every cell in my body. "I love you, too."

Kash picked me up and took me right to bed.

We didn't finish the rest of our drinks.

SEVEN

Melissa and Liam were waiting to greet me the next morning.

Liam looked like he was sleeping standing up. Melissa was bouncing up and down on the backs of her heels, her book bag clasped in front of her chest. Fitz opened the door for me this time. Erik was still with me, just assigned to the car. Kash asked if I wanted a new guard. I knew I should say yes, but my gut was saying to wait and hold off, so that's what I told him. He was fine with it, and now I had Fitz dodging me in the hallways. He was tall, too, but a bit lankier than Erik. He also had dark hair combed to the side, jeans, a hoodie to fit in, and a backpack like the other students'.

However, when he led first into the building, a few students were ahead of me, and he held the door open for all of them. Melissa's eyes were glued to him. Hearts were forming in her head and I swear I could see red and pink glitter bursting out of the top of her skull.

She was in love. So in love that when I approached, her hand clamped onto my arm and she breathed out, her eyes huge. "Who is that dreamboat?"

Liam's eyes opened—so he wasn't sleeping, just stoned—and he looked around me, then grinned. "That's Bailey's security guard."

Screech! Everything ground to a halt.

"Why would you say that?" That came out in a half whisper, half squeak from me, as Melissa's eyes just got bigger, if that was possible.

She squealed, "Really?"

Another burst of bouncing from her.

My gaze was glued to Liam. "What makes you think that?"

Liam barely blinked, that half grin still plastered on his face. "Because the guy's got a gun strapped to his hip. His shirt lifted up when he pulled his bag on him, and no guy has to pull their bag on them. You're a student, graduate or undergrad. You throw that shit on like it's a part of your skin. The bag's not a part of his skin. He forgot to be chill, and his gun showed. Then you walked in and he got all alert-like before remembering his cover, and now he's pretending he's not listening to us, but he's totally listening to us." He lifted his chin up in a nod and raised a finger in the air, a half-cool salute to Fitz. "What's up, dude?"

Fitz was trying to keep with his disguise, leaning back against the wall, a foot crossed over the other and his phone out in front of him. But he was waiting for me; his gaze was on me.

I debated . . .

Then Melissa breathed out, "You mean he heard me this entire time?"

I turned to Fitz. "The jig is up. They're onto us."

He sighed, straightening from the wall, and walked over to us. "Had a lot of eyes on me yesterday. Erik, too."

"Erik." Another breath whispered from Melissa. "He's yummy, too."

My eyes narrowed. This girl was boy crazy.

Liam's grin just turned lazier, if that was possible. "Girl. We're IT. Not a lot of newbies that look like your boys in here that haven't already been around for the last few years, if you get my drift. They know me, and I'm the closest-looking dude like your dudes."

I grimaced. "We're first-year grad students."

"We're IT." Liam said it like it made perfect sense.

Melissa was nodding, so maybe it did.

I growled, "I'm IT."

"Yeah, and we all know about you."

Again. Perfect sense from Liam, except I wasn't getting his wavelength.

"It's fine." Fitz scanned the hallway before nodding to Melissa. "How's it going?"

"Hi." Her cheeks were pink.

Fitz thought it was cute.

Liam just kept grinning that half grin.

I was getting restless. I needed to be working codes, getting lost in that world. "I'm going to the lab."

"Sweet." Liam fell in step beside me, his hand holding his bag's strap over one shoulder.

Melissa fell behind and we could hear her. "How long have you been a security guard? Did you go to school to be a guard? You look young. Have you had to shoot someone? Kill someone?"

The questions kept going, and I glanced back, but Fitz wasn't paying her any attention. He had his finger to his ear and he was talking to Erik, or someone else, his eyes continuously scanning as we went. It didn't seem to bother Melissa. She just kept talking.

When we neared the lab, Fitz touched my arm and passed me.

I'd already stopped, remembering the rules, but Fitz said anyway, "I go first."

He did, and came out a second later, nodding to me. The room had been cleared.

Each of us took a seat behind a computer. I hadn't gone to this class yesterday and there was a new professor to meet.

Melissa leaned over, gesturing to Fitz in the hallway. "Is he going to be out there the whole time?"

Liam leaned forward from my other side. "It's his job. Why wouldn't he?"

She frowned, her little forehead wrinkling. "Because what if something happens to her in here? How would he know?"

Both Liam and I looked around the classroom, but there was

only the one door. No windows. Just brick walls, desks, and computers. And chairs.

"And where would the attack come from?"

She shrugged, turning back to her computer and letting her bag fall on the floor. "I don't know. Maybe one of the other students."

Liam snorted, mirroring her and facing forward. "Then we're her guards and we got it. One shout and that motherfucker is barreling in here, gun drawn. Chaos everywhere. Panic. Screams. We don't want that shit, so on the very low chance one of our own classmates tries to get her, we keep it tight. Okay?"

Melissa and I shared a look.

Neither of us knew what he was talking about, but I lifted up a shoulder. "I'll be fine. He'll still be out there when we're done."

Her head perked up and she grinned. "Nice."

Hoda came into the room then, her eyes searching. Finding me. Narrowing. Then moving clear across the room. The other guys were either already seated or were coming in, and once the hour started, we all sat back and learned the fundamentals of information technology.

It was after class when Hoda came over. She avoided my gaze, only responding to Liam. A few of the other guys were with us, and apparently there was a special eating area for graduate students. It was still a café-style eating area, but it wasn't as big as the undergraduate eating section.

I let Fitz know our destination.

He moved ahead of me, off to the side, but within arm's reach.

Hoda kept glancing at him, but she was more discreet than Melissa.

Melissa was gawking. And that was when I first really felt surrounded by the typical IT geeks, because none of the guys—Liam was the exception—noticed. They were talking about the newest version of Logitech, which was scheduled to come out in a month. Some of the guys were speaking as if they'd already been using it for the last six months, and I tuned in, not because I fully believed them. They were saying they'd been given early review access and I knew that wasn't true. Peter was on the board of Logitech, and the review access did not go to grad students from Hawking University. They went to established professionals in the field. So were these guys bluffing for some reason?

Something clicked back in place with me, and I couldn't hold off a faint grin.

They were bluffing to *impress* the others.

I was walking among my people.

This was my world. I'd been the outcast, now a novice in my father's world and Kash's world, but in this world I was totally a warrior. A kick-ass warrior, to be more specific.

I was thinking this, feeling happy about this, when we walked up to the eating area and noticed the crowd. Or the guys did.

Hoda stopped first, frowning. "What?"

Liam stopped next. His half grin just diminished, so it was a quarter of a grin. He said nothing.

Melissa's eyes never moved from Fitz. Had to give her respect for her devotion.

It was the others' reactions that worried me.

"The fuck?"

"Is there a celebrity here today?"

I didn't know the guys who asked that, but all were watching the crowd, and as we stood there, the crowd seemed to get bigger.

"Those aren't students." This was from Hoda. She took a step forward. "Those are reporters. I recognize a few bloggers."

"Bloggers?" From one of the guys.

The crowd was moving, forming at one end of the court and slowly heading across in front of us. Among the heads moving around, I saw an official-looking older man walking in the middle. A middle-aged woman was with him, and I saw that Busich was with the group.

Someone high up was at Hawking, and it was then that I felt Fitz on my other side. His eyes were hard, focused on the crowd heading toward us. He spoke from the side of his mouth, quietly. "We need to go."

"Why?"

Melissa jostled into me. "Is something going on?"

Fitz pressed a hand to my back, gently but also assertively, guiding me away from the crowd. I started to go with him when my phone rang.

Kash calling.

I put it to my ear. "Hey."

"Where are you?"

Now I stopped, my body almost tipping over from how quick I put the brakes on. "Why?"

Kash's voice was low, insistent, and I heard the urgency. My pulse spiked.

Suddenly, my phone was plucked out of my hands. Fitz spoke into it, his eyes hard and fixed over my shoulder to the crowd. "I'm getting her out of here."

I heard Kash's voice, but couldn't hear what he was saying.

Fitz: "On it. We're moving."

His hand came back to my arm this time, and he began walking me forward, back toward the building we'd just left.

"Hey—hey! Where are you going?" That was Melissa yelling at us.

Fitz ignored her, giving me the phone and still pulling me to the computer building.

"What's going on?" I asked Kash.

Looking back over my shoulder, I saw that the crowd stopped growing, but the not moving part. It was heading toward us, and I say "us" because Fitz and I were thirty yards away by now and that crowd seemed to be zeroing right in on our location. Melissa began trotting to keep up with us. Liam was transfixed by the crowd. Hoda was frowning back and forth, and the other guys were gone. They were either swallowed up by the crowd or had taken off somewhere else.

I'd been looking forward to eating, not going to lie.

Then Kash's words cut through everything. "My grandfather is touring Hawking today."

I felt rocked.

"What?"

"That's him behind you. I want you gone and away from him now," he clipped out, and I could hear sounds from his end.

"Where are you?"

"Coming to you."

"*What?*"

I heard beeping, then silence on his end.

"Do what Fitz said. I'll be there in ten."

He ended the call.

I stared at the phone, turning to Fitz, who was super focused on dragging me out of there. We were weaving and dodging people, and it wasn't just students. Personnel were coming out of the woodwork. Work badges on lanyards and ties were flying in the air as two people rushed past us. A frenzy was taking over. It was unsettling me, right after I just got settled.

A guy started to cross in front of us. Fitz caught his head in his palm, held him as we passed, then let him go.

The guy's mouth dropped open, but we were far past him by the time he had regrouped enough to say anything.

"Bailey! Wait up." Melissa had been caught in the crowd traffic. A group of sorority-looking girls was blocking her way and she couldn't edge through them.

Fitz suddenly drew up short, cursing under his breath.

I saw why, a split second later, when we were face-to-face with Busich, the middle-aged woman, the older man, and Calhoun Bastian. How they got here before us, I had no clue, but there they were. As if they'd been waiting for me, standing in a semicircle. If Fitz and I stepped forward, we would've completed that circle.

A small clearing had formed around them, but I saw a couple of guards moving people backward.

Calhoun Bastian had been all over the local news, so this reaction wasn't something shocking to me. What *was* shocking was that he was here, and I knew right then, as those dark eyes found mine, that he'd come for me.

I swallowed over a knot.

He smiled at me. "Hello, Bailey."

EIGHT

He looked like Kevin Costner, which pissed me off. I love Kevin Costner. He also looked like Antonio Banderas, which still pained me.

This guy, Kash's grandfather, who had dark, penetrating eyes, rich black hair with specks of gray peppered in it, and a jawline that was a box square, didn't deserve to have the looks he did. As he stared back at me, taking me in, oxygen in my chest ceased. I felt him, like I felt his grandson, as if he could read my insides, but I didn't want him in there.

My stomach churned. My insides squeezed, rolling over.

I wanted him out.

Block him.

I envisioned an actual wall coming down in place. My eyes went dead. My mouth flattened. I didn't move, like a prey waiting out a predator that couldn't see them, just waiting for them to pass along.

An approving but calculating smile formed on his face.

The personnel with him blinked in surprise.

"Your file does not do you justice."

My skin crawled.

Fitz moved in front of me, blocking me. He held a hand up. "Excuse us."

Kash had never let me see his grandfather when he came to the apartment. Hotel security, Kash's own security, and the police swarmed within moments. His grandfather had been long gone by then, but the impact wasn't lost on me.

Kash shut down that night, and I'd been fighting to get him to open up again.

Since then, I saw the news. I saw the articles. I read the headlines. Calhoun was in town in a big way, and he and Kash started going head to head. But him coming here, making contact with me . . . A shiver went down my spine.

Kash would not react well to this.

"I'm sorry, I—"

Calhoun took one step, reaching for me. "My dear, I can see why my grandson is so taken with you. You're very beautiful. I can see the kindness."

Kindness?

Fitz shoved farther forward through the crowd, but Calhoun wasn't deterred.

He stepped to the side, where Fitz couldn't block him. An almost sad look came to him as he stared at me, his hands clasped together in front of him. "The kindness must come from your mother."

My chest pinched.

He added, "Chrissy Hayes."

He said her *name*.

My heart ceased.

He knew about my mom.

He kept on, knowing these words would affect me. He was choosing them with purpose. "She had such hardships growing up, the rift in the family, Peter seducing her, and she had to drop out of school to have a child at such a young age."

Rift?

But I knew there were issues. And the rest, including Peter's "seduction."

He was speaking about me as if I weren't that "child."

He had investigated my life and he was letting me know this.

I started to step forward.

It was my turn to address him, but another surge in the crowd happened at that moment. A buzz rose up, and suddenly Kash was in front of me. He was blocking me, and he clipped at Fitz, "Get her out of here. Now."

Fitz took my arm. "Yes, sir."

He began pulling me away.

I dug in, waiting. Needing.

Kash was face-to-face with his grandfather once more. He couldn't do that alone. I needed to be there for him. Kash didn't let anyone close to him, not for this stuff. And as I pulled my arm free from Fitz, we were three people into the crowd. I couldn't look away from where Kash was facing off with his grandfather.

Almost nose-to-nose, he towered over Calhoun.

Both had dark looks, but Kash was so much darker.

There was a calmness to Calhoun, a calm that only years of superiority and authority and power could settle and make so blatant. He stood without moving a muscle, not even an eyelid twitch.

The air around Kash was anything but that calm.

A storm rippled from him, and the crowd felt it, veering away and giving them extra space, but then I noticed, one by one, guards slipped through the crowd. They began to form a circle around Kash and his grandfather. Their backs were to the two and they held their hands up, moving a slow step forward. They were guiding the crowd away, giving the grandson and grandfather privacy, though Busich and the two other staff members were still there. Their eyes were wide, glued to the confrontation.

Busich tore her gaze away to find where I was still standing. Her eyebrows furrowed and she returned to the two, her throat moving as she swallowed visibly.

I couldn't hear what Kash was saying, but I could see his lips barely moving. He was talking and his grandfather was listening, but Calhoun had found me in the crowd. He was watching me at the same time. My skin started crawling again. The hairs on the back of my neck stood up.

As if sensing my discomfort, Fitz moved so he was between Calhoun and me, and he began walking me backward. "Kash will worry. Let's get you to your building."

Calhoun couldn't do anything to Kash. Not there. Not then. There were too many witnesses. Only because of that fact, I went with Fitz.

Hoda, Melissa, and Liam were waiting for us.

Hoda looked sick. Her cheeks had an unnatural pallor to them, and she was holding her hand over her mouth.

Liam seemed only slightly concerned.

Melissa's hand was pressed to her chest. It dropped and she hurried closer to me. "Was that about you?"

Hoda snorted. "Of course that was about her. Did you not see who that was?"

Melissa had no time to respond.

The door opened and Kash swept in. His eyes were blazing. His jaw tight. His face stone.

He was furious.

He didn't say anything. His gaze locked on me, walking to me. He stopped in front of me.

I didn't notice anyone else's reaction, because he bent forward, wrapped an arm around my waist, and lifted back up with me over his shoulder.

"Kash!" I yelped.

He wasn't waiting. He strode forward, through the building. The door was being held open for him and he breezed right through. I saw Fitz coming behind, fighting a grin and failing. He took the door from whoever was holding it, and I could only guess the other one was Erik. The door to Kash's sports car was opened. He deposited me in it, putting my seat belt in place and striding around to the driver's side.

Erik spoke over my door. "Let us drive you."

He was speaking to Kash.

Kash was ignoring him. He motioned to my door, opening his own. "Close her door. I need to drive myself right now."

His mouth tightened, but Erik shut my door.

A split second. That's all it took before he had the engine going and was pulling away from the curb.

Fitz and Erik hurried into their SUV and they were following us.

I was too shocked to start, but Kash wasn't. He *so* wasn't.

He began, speaking low, fury riddling every word, sending awareness through me.

"He showed up."

The venom was almost shocking, but I waited.

"If he had hurt you. If he had touched you." He jerked the wheel and we were merging with traffic and still Kash didn't slow. He swung between lanes, and it would've been reckless if it hadn't been him. Erik and Fitz couldn't keep up. They were two lanes over and three cars behind.

Kash wasn't paying them any attention.

I knew Kash went on his own at times. I knew he was a weapon himself. But maybe we should slow down, wait for the guards?

Before I voiced that concern, Kash kept on.

"He knew you were there. He waited. He staged that whole thing. He knew you met Busich. He requested Busich to be on that tour, and he promised them a thirty million donation. He picked the time. He picked the place. He knew you would go with your classmates to lunch at that time. He knew the path they would take to get there. He fucking knew everything."

His words pierced me.

For Calhoun to do that . . . someone had talked. I didn't even know where we would go for lunch. The other students knew.

"He could've asked staff?"

"Staff go back to their offices. They don't pay attention to who goes to eat, or where, or how they get there. Students do. He has someone in your class on his payroll." He punched the steering wheel, that jaw clenching again, then in a whoosh he eased back on the brake. "Fuck. I'm sorry." He glanced over, worried. "I didn't mean to scare you. I'm just wor—"

"You didn't scare me." But I kept from saying that his grandfather *did* scare me. If Calhoun could affect Kash like this just by getting some information and showing up, I didn't want to know what Kash would do if something actually did happen to me.

I chose to share this concern with him.

He expelled a harsh breath of air, leaning back and forcing one of his hands to loosen on the wheel. "I know."

I stopped, frowning. "You know?"

"I've been ready for him to go after Peter or the family all my life. Half expected it. But you're new. And you mean more to me than anyone, and he knows that now, and I fucked up. I let him get to me."

"You mean more to me than anyone . . ."

I whispered, "More than anyone?"

Kash glanced over, saw how my face was literally melting, and a grin tugged at his lips. He eased back dramatically on the accelerator, but still switching lanes like he was a pro driver, and reached over for my hand at the same time. "You do. You know that."

I was preening now. "It's nice to hear."

His eyes darkened before moving back to the road. They were close to smoldering, and my thoughts were fast leaving Calhoun, fast going elsewhere, to rooms with beds, and then it hit me. "I still have a class today."

Kash's hand tightened on mine before switching to my leg. He slid his fingers to the inside of my thigh, and whoa. Class who?

"I'll make a call. You'll be fine."

That wasn't really my concern. I hated to say this, but I had to. I rested my head against my seat and rolled it to face him. "I'm already a week behind. I can't miss more class time." Not to mention what the others thought about what just happened.

Kash changed the subject, his fingers moving back to the top of my leg. "You mentioned that classmate, Mansour. Was she one of the girls with you just now?"

My head lifted from the seat. "Not the petite one, the other one."

"The bitchy one."

I loved that he saw it right away. I grinned.

He nodded. "I had Torie look into her and made another call this morning. Already they've found out that she lied on her application. There is no Holden Mansour, and every time he's scheduled to work, a Hoda Mansour shows up." He hit the signal and took the exit off to the right. "That's grounds to fire her. Did you want that?"

I frowned. "You'd fire her, just that quick?"

Why did she lie in the first place? That didn't make any sense.

"We fire for less, but lying on your application is a solid base reason to fire someone. It's your decision. She's your classmate."

I let out some air.

"No. I can tell she dislikes me, but I don't want to give her any more reason. I have to be around her the rest of the year."

Kash's hands flexed over my leg. "You mean two years."

"What?"

"You said a year. Your degree takes two years."

Right. He didn't know . . .

I coughed. "The next two years."

He sent me a short frown. "How long's your lunch break?"

I pulled up my schedule and checked the time. "I have another hour."

"You're set on going back?"

I relaxed, more fully grinning. "Stupid school, huh?"

He shot me a grin. "I know a place."

We went to the local Burriotle, and the nationwide burrito chain that had eclipsed all the other competition was filled with students. We should've known that. The line was out the door, trailing down the block and in front of the bookstore next to it. That didn't deter Kash. He made a call, then took my hand as we left his car, which was already getting a lot of attention. Our fingers entwined, he led me toward the door, then let go and switched our positions so he was behind me. His hand was on the small of my back.

He was guiding me inside, and once we had to squeeze past the people in line, his hands went to my hips. He guided me that way, turning me, moving me, and reaching over my head for the door. Once inside, a younger man was waiting for us.

He flashed a giant smile. "Kashton! You've decided to grace us with your presence. Finally."

He had rich, dark black hair, dark eyes. Those eyes fell to me, taking me in with interest, and he seemed to take a step back. He murmured, "Well, then. Now I see why."

Kash reached around me, holding his hand out. "Robbie. It's good to see you."

"And you. And you." He was pumping Kash's hands, but his attention was all on me. Letting him go, Robbie turned more fully to face me, as Kash's free hand went to the back of my neck, his fingers resting around my nape. Robbie was eating me up. "And who is this?"

Kash settled on the back of his heels, getting comfortable. This wasn't a Kash I was totally familiar with, at least not in others' presence, not when it wasn't just the two of us. And Kash seemed unaware of all the customers waiting in line, but glancing back, I saw Erik standing outside the restaurant at one door, and at the other door was Fitz. Both took their positions, backs to the windows and watching the street and the line.

"This is Bailey." Kash nodded at Robbie. "Bailey, this is a friend of mine from my father's neighborhood."

Oh! I took a lot more notice now. He would've known Aunt Judith, Cousin Stephanie, maybe even Uncle Martin. Those names were fictional to me, but I knew that life wasn't for Kash.

I was fascinated in some odd way. Fascinated because Kash never talked about that life, but I knew it was there. I knew he spent time with his family, even though Peter had taken him in after his parents were murdered.

"Come, come." Robbie broke through the line, leading us around to a booth that was being cleaned even as we approached. He stepped aside, motioning. "Sit. Relax. Let me have my staff bring a feast to you both." He winked at me. "I'll be right back."

Kash knew the manager of this Burriotle. I shouldn't be surprised, but I was, and I had no idea why.

I turned to Kash once Robbie disappeared through the back. "Explain, please."

I used his words back on him, and judging by the knowing grin, Kash was aware of that. He turned his back to the customers going back and forth past our booth and wrapped his hand around my neck once more. Bending down slightly, he was creating our own private moment, and his head moved so his forehead was just slightly above mine.

His thumb was rubbing over my neck.

"When I visited my aunt, Robbie was on the block. I didn't go see them a lot—less after I moved in with your family—but Robbie, his brother, and I got into a fair bit of trouble."

I was waiting for more.

He paused.

Oh no. That wasn't it. I raised an eyebrow. "More, please."

He laughed, his hand moving to cup the side of my face, his thumb rubbing over my cheek now, falling to my lips and moving back. "His uncle runs a gym. When I started training, it was with Robbie and Ace. We didn't hang out as much when I stopped coming around, but Robbie reached out a couple years ago. He needed start-up for this place, so I gave it to him."

Both my eyebrows shot up now. "He owns it?"

Kash nodded, his eyes dipping to my mouth and staying there.

"He doesn't manage it. I bought the franchise fee for him and he runs everything else. It's doing well, and I take a cut."

Holy crap. I noticed the customers in a whole different light.

Feeling a little faint, I asked, "Why am I amazed by this? I know who you are, what other businesses you do, and yet you owning the local Burriotle is blowing my mind."

Kash chuckled. "Ace is a big-time MMA fighter. If I hadn't chipped in, Robbie would've needed only to wait another year. Ace would've bought in instead. I got lucky with the timing."

"Does my dad know about this?"

A guarded look fell over Kash, clouding his face. He didn't move away, but I felt him pulling away. His hand slid to the back of my neck again, his thumb holding over my pulse. "No. I did a lot, and do a lot, that your father doesn't know about."

I was hearing a different tone from him. Was that disappointment from Kash? Was that what I was hearing?

"I'm sorry." I lifted a hand, wrapping it around his wrist.

His pulse jumped at my words. His eyes darkened again. "Why are you apologizing?"

"Because, for some reason, that hurts you." I was going with my gut, not really knowing what I was saying until the words were out. "My dad hurt you. I don't know how or why, but he did."

Kash's eyes grew intense. He didn't respond, just held me, feeling my heartbeat, and his eyes locked on mine. I couldn't move.

My other hand went to his chest, resting over his stomach muscles.

They were so tense, too.

He drew me to him, his lips moving to mine in a light and soft kiss before he let me go.

"I love you. Do you know how much?"

He rested his forehead to mine, drawing in a deep breath.

My throat swelled. "How much?"

His hand tightened on mine. "The depths sometimes amaze me. And other times . . ."

My heart began beating faster. "And other times?"

"And other times it scares me."

I wasn't sure what he meant. My pulse was beating an erratic drum in me, so I wasn't sure if I wanted to ask, either.

Then, I didn't have to.

The moment was broken a second later when Robbie returned to the table, but as he sat and talked with Kash, as the two laughed, as we had food and drinks brought over, I was still feeling the effect of those words from Kash.

My whole insides had melted, and he knew, his eyes catching mine and warming. His hand moved to my leg under the table, and like in the car, his fingers rested on the inside of my leg.

It was the best Burriotle I'd ever enjoyed.

NINE

I was listening to my voice-mail and Chrissy's voice played. "You need to call your mother right now. You need to update her on your first few days of school. Dinner was not enough. We didn't get the time to talk like we need to. You need to tell your mother you love her because if you don't, your mother will hunt you down!" She breathed hard into the phone, and I was grinning listening to her. "You got that, my beautiful little genius daughter that I love and cherish and worry about? Call your mother!"

I snorted, because it'd been her who had been distracted during dinner. Not me. I'd been thankful at the time.

"Enjoyed any good burritos lately?"

Now I wasn't so thankful, because calling Chrissy back might've saved me a little from the teasing I'd already endured this evening.

I was at Naveah. It was a couple days later, and that question came to me as I was in the VIP booth, squished with Matt and Guy. No Tony. No Chester. Both absences that I wasn't complaining about.

And I knew the teasing would start, just didn't know *when* it would start.

Tuesday was the Burriotle date.

Someone there took a picture of us, of Kash leaning over me like he wanted to eat *me* for lunch.

That photo was sold the next day.

It came out Thursday. And here we were. Thursday night.

Naveah. My brother beside me. That damn picture was haunting me, and so was Chrissy's voice message.

The club was packed. We had extra club staff at the end of our stairs to keep people from coming up, and since we'd just gotten here, I figured I got my brother for thirty minutes before he'd head off to quench the real thirst that had brought him to Naveah.

I figured I had that long with Guy, too, before he had a girl up here, or two. Both were grinning at me, sharing sly looks.

I flushed, putting my phone away. "Fuck off."

Matt laughed. "I do believe that's the look Kash had, wanting to do that to you."

"I took a girl to get a burrito the next day and what do you know?" Guy piped in, his amusement thick. He winked. "It worked. She got a different burrito within an hour of leaving there."

"An hour?" Matt shot at him. "It took that long?"

I added, "What were you doing before?"

Guy's grin lessened, but he rolled his eyes and gave us both a middle finger. "Fuckers."

Matt jerked his chin up to me. "Where's your man tonight?"

The official answer: "Working."

The unofficial answer: a meeting with Japan investors. Why I wasn't supposed to know that, I didn't know, but Kash let it slip he had to call overseas, and I got a text later telling me not to share with anyone the location of "overseas."

Matt didn't care. He didn't question. He only nodded, all easygoing. "Right on, right on." His hand was resting on the booth next to my shoulder and he bumped me with it. "Fill me in. How's the school thing going?"

Matt barely went to class when he got his degree, so he didn't really go to college. How he got that degree, well . . . I was assuming money had something to do with it, but I wasn't going to ask. Graduate school, what I was doing, was a phenomenon to him.

I got it. I did. He gave me enough teasing, lumping me in with

Cyclone and Peter, that I knew there was a part of him that was bothered by it all. I didn't know why or how it related to him, though I had a guess. And I didn't like what my guess was, but as he asked me this question, I could tell he was genuine in asking. He'd been authentic the other times he questioned me, too, and that was warming my belly in a way no alcohol could obtain.

I smiled at him. "It's going good, actually."

And it was.

I was up to date on my assignments. I thought there'd be more papers, but there weren't. Turns out computer grad school was actually about computers, so the assignments we had were easy for me. I had to put in extra time reading the textbooks so I knew I would get everything correct on the quizzes, one of which we had coming in the morning.

I wasn't supposed to know that, but moving through our student database, I had hit a few extra buttons that I shouldn't have and I got the screen that showed me the complete schedule of pop quizzes in my IT Strategy and Management class. I didn't print anything out. Didn't copy it. Just got one good look at the screen before I was pushed out. That was enough.

I didn't share with anyone that I'd had that peek. I was prepared, because I actually did the readings. Some of the students in the class didn't. They skimmed. Melissa told me her secret was to read the first section, the last section, and every third paragraph the rest of the chapters. Hoda, I didn't know what she did. After I came back from Burriotle, she didn't say anything to me the rest of the day, and it'd been like that for the past two days. Melissa, on the other hand, loved everything about that day and proceeded to share this with Fitz every time he was with me.

The rest of the guys in the class thought Fitz was cool, though only one or two of them told him this. Melissa was the one who told me the guys thought Fitz was cool, because the guys mostly all stuck to themselves. They lingered around a few of their computers. The spokesman was the extroverted "leader" of them,

Dax, but the rest just talked with one another. And Melissa, she was on the in with them.

Me. Liam. Hoda. We weren't.

I hadn't figured out why yet, but I would. It was a mission of mine.

Erik was supposed to come inside with me tomorrow, so I'd see their reaction to him. I wasn't sure if I wanted Hoda's ice to continue or not. I still hadn't said anything to her about Holden Mansour, but she was here. I texted Torie and she looked at the schedule and texted back it was an affirmative. Holden Mansour was scheduled for an eight-to-two a.m. shift in the security room.

I'd only been in Naveah for thirty minutes, so I hadn't had time to even look, but it was during her slotted time.

"Aw, fuck." Guy slid farther down in the booth, his gaze locked on the crowd beneath us.

I looked, and "Aw, fuck" was right.

"Fucking hell." From Matt. He took his drink, slammed it back, and held up the emptied glass. The VIP server rushed over. "Keep those coming, and can we bar those girls from coming up here?"

Bar?

I turned surprised eyes on my brother, until I saw them, too. I'd missed them before.

Victoria, Fleur, and their friend, whose name I recently found out was Cedar Barlow—which, though I'd never share it with those girls, I thought was a cool name. They were making their way up here. Victoria was wearing a slinky cream-colored dress, Fleur had on red, and Cedar was wearing a black one. As they maneuvered up the stairs, I dipped to the shoes, because though I was normally not a shoe girl, I could hear my inner Chrissy Hayes wanting to know.

All of them were wearing the heels with the red bottoms. No surprise there. What was surprising, though, was that all three of them had no jewelry on, but each had some faux fur wrapped around their shoulders. I guess that was their accessory.

Victoria took the lead, a pinched look on her face as she stood in front of the table. Her hair was good. She'd lightened it again, so the red looked like sun streaks of orange. "Guy. Matthew." She didn't look at me, her hand going to one hip and a little purse falling down to rest on its chain over her wrist. "Is Kashton coming tonight?"

Fleur and Cedar were looking at me, *fully* at me. They were doing it for their girl, and both held calculating looks in their slightly narrowed gazes.

Matt's tone was cold. "How would I know?" His hand, the one right next to my shoulder, gestured to me. "Why don't you ask the one who *would* know?"

Victoria's mouth flattened, and she visibly grimaced before sighing, turning her gaze my way. "Hi there, Becky. I didn't see you."

Becky. I rolled my eyes.

I wasn't going to respond to that.

Cedar moved forward. "She asked you a question."

I wasn't going to respond to that, either.

Instead, I picked up my drink and turned to my brother. "Did the music get louder in here? Did you guys say something?"

Matt pressed his lips together, stifling a laugh.

Not Guy. Guy was okay with expressing he was loving watching this showdown. His eyes were twinkling.

Matt shrugged, raising his voice. "Maybe. It's starting to grind on the ears."

"Exactly." I matched him, raising my voice. "Or maybe it's my allergies kicking up. I'm starting to get a headache."

"Jesus Christ," Victoria hissed. "*Bailey.* I'm talking to you."

I turned to her now and grinned. "Oh, hey. When'd you get here?"

Fleur's head was turned toward the floor. Her shoulders were shaking, but Victoria and Cedar couldn't see her.

Cedar threw her hand in the air. "Seriously? You're going to play that game?" Her lips were tight. "With *us*?"

Leaning forward and resting my arms on the table, I said to Victoria, "You usually travel with two others. Where are your friends tonight? You're going alone?"

Her eyes threatened to bug out.

I heard Fleur snort, her hand raising quick to her mouth, and she turned away.

Cedar's mouth was hanging open at me. "Are you seriou—"

I was done playing. My eyes cut to hers. "Use a sentence that doesn't have the word *serious* in it. Do it. I challenge you. Grow your vocabulary. It helps fight off dementia."

Cedar looked ready to scream at me, but her mouth stayed shut.

I was impressed. I thought for sure she'd blast me, but her gaze kept going from Victoria to me and I clued in. She couldn't make a move without Victoria's approval. She couldn't engage me in a confrontation. Her leader wasn't allowing it.

Why? That made no sense.

And to prove my theory, Victoria smiled at me, her tone magically softer. "Bailey. I need to talk to Kashton about something. He's not been returning my calls and I was hoping he'd be here tonight." She glanced to Matt. "Or find out when he will be here."

Kash was freezing her out. Interesting.

Matt's eyes just slid to mine. He only had one eyebrow up now, and I read that look he gave me. He was letting me handle this.

My phone buzzed at that moment. Torie.

Bathroom.

Okay then.

Sliding out of the booth, I said to Victoria, "You want him, you probably should consider the reason he's not getting back to you." Her mouth opened and I beat her to it. "And no, I'm not going to ask *him* about *you*." I nodded to Matt. "Be back. Bathroom."

Erik and Fitz were off shift, so I had two new guards. I hadn't met them, but as one broke off from the line of other guards, I asked him, "What's your name?"

He paused. "Scott." Then he dipped his head and moved forward.

I went with him because I was guessing he knew the plan. They didn't ask where I had to go, and he led the way to a bathroom off the main floor. For once, there was no line waiting to use it, but maybe that'd been put into play already, because he knocked once and stood by the wall. He said, "You can go in."

Torie was leaning against the sink counter, her arms crossed. Her eyes locked on mine.

I cleared the last partition to see where the stalls were and saw that it had all been planned. Hoda stood by the stalls, her head down, her arms crossed tight over her chest.

Torie spoke to the room, "Checked out Holden Mansour's application ten minutes ago . . ." She was scowling at Hoda's bent head before finishing, looking at me. "To find it's now a Hoda Mansour file and the gender has been changed. Male to female. My boss said you get to make the call so"—she leaned forward, but her hips remained resting against the counter—"you give me your call."

Crap. This had progressed quickly.

Hoda's head snapped up. "I don't see why it's her call—"

"It is because my boss says it is."

"Because her dad says it is—"

"Because her boyfriend says it is."

Hoda's mouth closed with an audible clap. She seemed stunned, and I sighed internally because I hadn't wanted to think it, but now I *couldn't* not think it.

"You released that image of Kash and me last summer."

It made sense.

She was here.

She knew who I was by then.

She wasn't happy I was coming to her program.

She worked IT here.

She would've had the skills, and the motivation.

She did it.

I wasn't asking. I knew it.

The guilt that flushed her face told me I was right. Shame flared briefly before she thought about whatever she needed to make it go away.

Guilt. Shame. Then coldness. And anger after that.

Her top lip curved up. "You can't prove it."

Torie snorted. She looked to say something, but I shook my head, quick.

Hoda underestimated me. That was fine with me, because I didn't want to know how she'd react when she knew not to underestimate me.

"Maybe. Probably not. But you did, didn't you?"

She didn't respond, not at first. "Am I fired?"

"What's your issue with me?"

Heated eyes swung back to me and she drew upright, her head falling back. "You mean besides the fact you didn't earn your spot in school? What about the circus you've brought to our classrooms? Or that all the guys think you walk on water because you're related to Peter Francis? Or that you have a seriously hot boyfriend wading into shit to save you, and he carries you out and no one says a word, like his word is god at school. I get it with him being my boss, which I didn't know until now, but at Hawking? It's *hard* to get into that school, and you got in no worries at all, probably no sweat at all. You probably just said 'Daddy, I'd like to go to Hawking' and he picked up the phone the next day and, voilà, you're an incoming graduate freshman at Hawking University by that afternoon. I mean, you don't get it."

Torie's mouth was hanging open, just an inch. She was as shocked as me.

I thought it'd be more. "Jealousy? That's what this is all about? You're straight-up just jealous?"

"My father is a doctor and he works all hours of the night. He's barely home. My mom takes care of us, all of us, and I have eight brothers and sisters. We didn't have it easy growing up. We had chores to do. Every morning I had to get up, help with breakfast, do the dishes before school. Then I had to be responsible for all my siblings, making sure they all had their bags and lunches, and I had to make sure we all got home after our activities. Three girls were kidnapped where I grew up. Three. All just walking home from school. But you don't get that, do you? You probably had drivers taking you back and forth from school and home and your friends' houses."

This girl wasn't with it. There was a screw loose up there. What she was spewing was insane.

Torie's gaze shot to mine, and she knew the truth, but I shook my head again. I didn't want her spilling the truth to the girl who actually had it better than me. She had a stay-at-home mom and a father who was a doctor. Looking after siblings wasn't something I'd gripe about.

I was happy to even *have* siblings.

In that second, I knew I didn't want Hoda to be fired. I didn't before, but I just hadn't decided if I wanted to tell Kash everything or not. He'd fire her no matter what, if he found out about the released image.

But I knew now.

She was here. She was in my classes. I'd have to do projects with her, work closely with her, and I wasn't sure if I wanted to make her a different kind of enemy. At least now I knew what I was working with. Better to have the enemy you know than one you don't, that sort of thinking.

I also knew I'd be getting all the information on Hoda Mansour after this conversation. Unlike her, I was going in prepped and ready. No underestimating for me.

Torie shook her head. "You just look stupid right now." A grunt. "And spoiled."

I hid a grin. She'd taken the words out of my mouth, ones that I wasn't about to say.

Hoda glared at her, then me. "Am I fired?"

Torie rolled her eyes, swinging an elbow in my direction. "Up to her still. But man, if I were you, I'd check my attitude. You do know her dad and her man are connected in town and in the field you're going to be working. You think long term? Might not want to piss off a Francis so early in your game."

Hoda's eyes widened. Blood drained from her face.

She hadn't thought about that, and that told me she was running on pure emotion. All that hatred and nastiness because she was purely jealous, which also shone a light on exactly how spoiled she was, though she probably didn't even know it.

I didn't want to enlighten her.

"No, you're not fired. But like Torie said, stow the nastiness and we'll be fine."

Her eyes burned fire at me before she rushed past me and out the door.

Torie waited for it to swing shut. "She is stupid! She is *stew*-pid."

"She's just wrong, that's all." My phone buzzed. Kash.

At Naveah. Hallway.

I said, "Gotta go. My man's here."

Kash was leaning against the wall, his face turned toward the rest of the club so I got a vision of his side profile. He was lounging back, his hands in his pockets, one foot resting over the other, and for a moment I took him in.

Perfection.

Sensual.

Badass.

Feeling a little unsteady on my knees, I went to him and, knowing I was there, knowing I was watching him, knowing I was coming, those eyes turned back to me. Home. That's what swept up in me. He'd said it before. I felt it now. I almost faltered in my step, that feeling was so strong, so powerful, and it exploded everywhere in me. It filled me up.

I needed a second.

Hayeses didn't cry, but dammit, the proof we did was leaking out of me, and not for the first time.

His eyes turned tender as he straightened from the wall. His hand rose, cupping the side of my face as I stepped into him like I'd been made just for his hand. His thumb wiped away the leak and he whispered, "Hey."

"Hey back."

My voice was hoarse.

He was searching me. "What is it?"

I shook my head, my throat still thick with the feels. "Nothing."

The door opened behind me. Torie came out, and Kash looked up to see her.

He drew me to him, my front to his front and his arm circled around, resting behind my shoulders. "What happened?"

Torie looked from me to Kash. "Your IT employee is a bitch. That's what happened."

I stiffened in his hold.

His thumb moved over my shoulder blades now. "More."

She hesitated again, then moved to the side of us. I turned, my eyes imploring, but she ignored me. "Sorry, Bailes. I can't. He's my boss and he told me to watch out for you when you're here. I have to do my job when it happens here."

"Torie, no."

Her face closed in, her mouth tightened. Her eyes went straight to Kash, not looking at me once as she laid it all out, what had happened in the bathroom.

Kash's body was already tense, but it was cement by the time she was done. "I want her in my office. Now."

"Kash, I—"

He released me as Torie gave him a quick dip of her chin and headed off to do his bidding. His hands caught my shoulders, one moving to tip my head up to his. "No."

"No?" My eyes flashed.

"No." His eyes didn't. They were steady and calm, but there was an undercurrent there. He was pissed off. "My employees don't talk to you like that. Your classmate, I can't do a thing about that, but my employee? Fuck no. She doesn't get the right." His hands smoothed down my arms, going to my hips, pulling me against him.

"I'm assuming you don't want her fired. That's why you tried to hide that from me?"

I nodded.

"Okay." He tugged me back to him. His arms wrapped around me, his head resting against mine.

The situation aside, I was getting heated in the whole physical way. That was going to happen. It was just Kash. Most girls probably felt the same as I did, but the home feeling was still in me. Still wreaking havoc on my senses and whispering words of love and adoration in my head. All that was going on, so I wasn't able to stay firm against him. I was melting, and I wanted him to hold me in his arms just a little bit longer.

My arms slid around him and moved up to his shoulder blades. I held on tight, as tight as I could.

He dipped his head down. His mouth moved over my shoulder, then my neck, my jaw, my cheek, and he expelled a soft breath at the corner of my mouth. "I'll be back. I gotta have my woman's back."

Gah. And those words.

I nodded, my forehead moving against his shoulder.

He cupped the back of my head, pressing a hard kiss to my forehead, and then he was gone. Half the guards went with him. Half remained with me.

I trekked back to VIP.

TEN

Kash was kissing my throat.

Gentle soft touches, caresses, and they were waking me up.

My shirt was lifted and his mouth circled my breast. He was sucking on my nipple. His hand was smoothing down my side, circling my waist, and then *oomph*, I was lifted off the bed, but he only moved between my legs. His arm was firmly holding my ass up, his fingers splayed out, grabbing on to a good chunk of cheek. Then his free hand was pulling my panties down.

I was awake and I was writhing in his arms.

I wanted more.

I needed more.

My legs clasped around his waist. He looked, meeting my gaze, his eyes darkened and filled with lust, and then he lifted up. He slid inside, and both of us closed our eyes at the contact.

His left hand held my hip and cupped the side of my ass as he began to move inside. "My home." Those same words again. Whispered. As if he didn't realize he'd said them. A tear slipped free. It trailed down my cheek. He moved, his mouth catching it, then I arched my back and received a growl in response.

I smiled at the same time I began rolling my hips to urge him on. "Kash." A whisper from me.

He stilled. "Bailey?" His head was next to mine.

I opened my eyes, rolled my head to his, and said bluntly, "I want you."

A primal and raw need flashed hot in his eyes. He moved, his mouth found mine, and it was a hard kiss, almost punishing, then he reared back and slammed inside.

This man of mine. He was always in control, so much restraint. I knew why. I knew the reason he remained, the threat he grew up under, the looming cloud currently over him, but in this bed, I didn't want that from him. I wanted him. Raw. Exposed. Just him, as he thrust harder, deeper, rougher. I was getting him. This was my man. He'd let down the walls and he was taking me on the ride with him.

I wrapped my arms tight around him, my legs raised up higher around his waist.

I was right there *with* him.

ELEVEN

"Your boyfriend is an ass."

I looked up from washing my hands in the bathroom, saw Hoda leaving one of the stalls, and turned off my water. Grabbing the towels, I turned to go, but not before I threw over my shoulder, "Be glad he didn't fire you."

My back hit the door. I pushed it open and stepped out into the hallway.

Going a few feet, I thought I'd see Melissa or Liam in the hallway. I was wrong. Matt was barreling down on me. The guys who noticed him just frowned. The handful of girls in the hallway gawked at him. He was storming my way, his frown fierce. "Did you know about Marie?"

I frowned at him. "Marie?"

"She's gone. Like totally gone."

"She's been gone since we had that family dinner."

Matt's eyes bulged out. "I know! She should be back by now. No matter how long they say Marie will be gone, she's never gone this long. A day, two tops. Not this long. Marie doesn't do vacations. I went by the estate this morning to have breakfast with Ser and Cy, and Marie is still gone. Theresa was there and she was giving your mom the side-eye. You know what that's about?"

I was at a loss for words.

I blinked. "Theresa was side-eyeing my mom? Not your aunt?"

Matt snorted. "Payton's not my aunt. She's Cyclone and Seraphina's, and yes, Theresa was giving your mom the evil eye,

not even the side-eye. I know Theresa. She wouldn't do that unless Marie still being gone was your mom's fault."

"Or she thought it was my mom's fault."

"What?"

I repeated, "Or Theresa thought it was my mom's fault."

"You saying she doesn't know? Theresa knows everything. Her
and her mama Marie. If something's going down at the house,
they know it."

I didn't know why I was getting heated, but I found myself ar-
guing back, "They didn't know about Quinn."

"They knew about Quinn."

"Bullshit."

He stopped and his eyes twitched. Literally. He scowled. "They
knew; they just didn't know they knew."

"That makes perfect sense. They knew but didn't know they
knew."

"You know what I mean." He looked irate, then he stopped
and shifted back on his heels. He reassessed me. "What's going on
here?"

I shot back, "You're blaming my mother for something you
don't know for sure."

I was defending Chrissy, and I swore. "Hold on." I pulled my
phone out and began heading to a corner for privacy.

Matt followed. "What are you doing?"

I turned a corner and settled with my back to the wall. Matt
stood next to me, his back to the students milling past us. Erik was
keeping back even farther, taking point ten feet behind Matt.

I responded, "If I'm taking my mom's back, I'm making sure
I should be." Because one never knew with Chrissy sometimes.
And with that, it was ringing in my ear.

A second later, she picked up. "Well. Well. Well. This is a
long overdue phone call. My daughter has remembered she has
a mother. That I exist. That I was the one who opened my legs
and pushed you out, and it was my womb where you first grew."

She was gloating.

I sighed. "Can you get on with it?"

She laughed, chirping, "How are you, baby? My very loving and so doting daughter of mine? What can your mother do for you, since you deigned to call me today? I should note the date. Put it on the calendar. Make this a national holiday. I could bake a cake. I could *buy* a cake. Balloons. I'm seeing it all right now. A parade, too!"

"Chrissy." I groaned.

"Don't call me Chrissy. I'm Mom." A beat. "And until you do, I've got more in me. I can go all night long, make you miss your next class and everything."

"Don't call me baby."

"Anything for you, honey bunches."

"Chrissy!"

She laughed. "I'm just messing with you. What's up? Are you coming for dinner tonight? That'd be great. I can do this all to your face and in person. Think of the hugs and the patting on the back and the cheek squeezing—"

"Chrissy!" Forget it. I was going back to what I was used to. "Are you behind Marie still being gone?"

Silence.

I waited, my heart starting to pound.

More silence.

Crap. That was the answer right there.

"I just had your back against Matt, Mom. If you were the reason Marie left, call her back," I said with a soft voice.

More silence, then her voice was just as soft. "You called me Mom again." She sniffled.

My head jerked upright. Excepting the time I'd been kidnapped, both times, and when she knew I'd find out about Peter, she never sniffled or even teared up. What was going on? I shot Matt a look. He was right. Something was going on at the house.

I spoke into the phone, "Are you okay?"

A second sniff. "I'm totally fine, honey. Really. Just midlife emotions. You wouldn't know about that yet. And I wasn't behind Marie leaving, but your father told me that she and her husband wanted to go on a cruise, so he arranged for that to happen. That's all."

I tensed.

Something wasn't right.

"Then why is my brother finding me at my school, and why is he so motivated to do that because Theresa was giving you the side-eye?"

Matt moved closer so his voice could be heard. "Theresa doesn't give the side-eye unless it's earned. And she was giving it to you."

Chrissy sighed on the other end. "I don't know why she was doing that, but it's not about Marie. I can tell you that. I didn't even know Marie was going until suddenly she was gone. That had nothing to do with me."

"So what did?" That was from Matt.

Chrissy hesitated again on her end.

My stomach fell. My mom was hiding something. I could read the signs even over the phone.

Enough was enough.

"Mom, about tonight." I held Matt's gaze as he heard me, and his frown was now a scowl. "We're coming for dinner. Six, right?"

Once I hung up, Matt was in my space. "What the hell, B.?"

He called me B. It was the first time I got that nickname from him, so I indulged in a moment to savor it.

My brother had given me his first nickname.

The moment was done.

"My mom's not lying about Marie. I can tell. But she is lying about something. Or she's purposefully not telling me something, something that she knows I would want to know. That means we're going there for dinner. You. Me. Kash."

"Kash is flying to Brazil today."

"Oh." He hadn't told me. Brazil? Wow. "Then you and me." I raised a hand up in a fist. "Team Batt."

The scowl lifted. A grin took its place, a fond grin, and his entire face warmed. He laughed shortly before hitting my fist with his own. "We should use a code name like Team Dracula. It's too obvious, otherwise."

I was having another moment. Team Batt was a real thing, and my brother was joking about it with me.

"You're right. Dracula it is."

He laughed again before tossing an arm around my shoulders, and we began walking back down the hallway. He was taking in everyone. "So this is what a certified nerd building looks like from the inside. I always wanted to know."

Well. Now he knew.

TWELVE

"They're sleeping together."

Kash told me this when I was on the phone with him, as I was driven from school to the apartment. He called to ask how my day was, to let me know where he was flying (which Matt had already told me) and that he would be heading back late in the night. I had just finished filling him in on the rest of my conversation with my brother when Kash delivered this bit of news, and I almost dropped my phone. I was that surprised. He announced it so easily and quickly, and almost lazily, as if he'd known for months and hadn't realized I might want to know.

"Matt and my mother?" My voice might've gone shrill for a second.

"What?"

"Who's sleeping together?"

He started laughing. "Not your brother. *Peter* and your mother."

I didn't let that sink in, not quite. "We were talking about Matt and my mom. You said they're sleeping together."

"Your mom and Peter are sleeping together."

Now I let that sink in, and my stomach was curdling. There was a sour taste in my mouth. "How long have you known and why didn't you tell me?"

Again, no hesitation.

"I've known awhile, but you had other things going on. Also, nothing's going to happen from it."

"What? Why not?" That sour taste turned bitter.

"Because your father is a cheater. I owe a lot to Peter, but I'm not blind. Your father has always had one weakness and that's pussy."

"Kash!" Seriously.

"Women. You know what I mean. And Chrissy Hayes is like her daughter—she doesn't take shit from anyone, even if she's momentarily weakened because her daughter was almost kidnapped for the second time. Hayes women are strong and bounce back, and your mom, she might be forgetting Peter's history for a moment, but it'll just be a moment. Something will happen and your mom will remember that he's not the baby daddy to just her kid."

"You sound pretty sure about this."

"Fact."

"So you're saying that whatever the reason my mom is sleeping with my father, and because he's going to eventually cheat, I shouldn't get worked up about it because it's not going to go anywhere?" Talk about a doom-and-gloom vibe.

"Just being a realist. It sucks for your mom if she's got feelings involved." He sounded hesitant. "For what it's worth, I don't think your mom will let herself go there emotionally. She's too smart, and she's a good mom. She won't want this blowing back on you, especially with what you've gone through. That's my prediction."

"Then why are you telling me?"

"Because you asked what your mom was hiding. Didn't feel right knowing the answer and not sharing with you. And because I love you and I know you're a realist, too. If your mom is doing something with her eyes wide open, which I'm sure you'll assess tonight at dinner, then you'll feel better about it, because you really want to just make sure Chrissy Hayes is okay at the end of all this."

"You sound like you know me."

"You have a big heart, you got a shrewd mind, and I know every inch of that body of yours." A dry chuckle came from him that I swear was acting as a caress, sliding over me. "I know my woman."

My voice was hoarse. "When are you coming back?"

"Probably early morning. You want me to wake you up?"

"You know me, you should know that answer."

Another chuckle, this one echoing the arousal I was feeling. "I'll wake you up."

After hanging up with him, I went home. I had about an hour to change or get ready before Matt would be picking me up, and it'd be Matt's driver. Not just Matt. Both Kash and Peter thought it was a good idea if all of us had two guards on us at all times, at least until the media attention died down. So because I only had an hour, I opted to stay in what I was wearing. Dinner was usually more casual, although that was when Marie was there.

Payton would be there. The Quinn-look-alike aunt. Just thinking about her, I started tensing up. She hadn't said a word last time, but she'd been there. Staring. Always in the background. Seraphina was hanging on her almost the whole time, and Cyclone kept running over to her for hugs, so the two little ones were attached, to say the least. They hadn't been like that with Quinn, so I was trying to tell myself that meant something. Trust the kids. They usually knew. Still, none of them had almost been kidnapped because of her. So maybe I was dealing with trauma, but there was extra trauma that I thought I had processed out of me. Maybe not?

I sighed.

That meant I had shit buried, and I'd read enough psych books to know that stuff would not stay buried. It'd come up.

It always came up.

Maybe I shouldn't have gotten out of counseling so fast . . . But no, I'd been ready. I hated going in there and talking it out with that counselor. Loathed it. Me ending those sessions was a good thing. I felt like I could breathe, once I knew I didn't have to go in and dredge up both kidnapping events. And I really liked not having to see her get quiet and pensive, stare at me as if she could literally read all my haunts and demons, and then write down notes. Those notes. I hated that notebook she had. I wanted to grab it and burn it, but I knew she wouldn't let me. I asked once what she was writing and she told me it was her own code, so nothing would make sense to me.

That pissed me off even more. I wasn't stupid, but she treated me like I was.

And since I had an hour, I did the time calculations in my head.

I'd be in the car with Matt for forty minutes to the estate. Dinner would probably be two to three hours. Ser and Cy would want us to stay after, so by the time we'd be heading back I was looking at not getting to the apartment till ten, and I was being generous with that guess. Matt would try to talk me into going to Naveah, but I couldn't.

I looked through my assignments and there was a whole code I needed to finish.

Maybe . . . I was thinking here, because what I should do now and what I wanted to do weren't lining up. I should do the code, but I really wanted to hack Hoda.

Crap.

If Matt was texting on the phone the whole drive up, I could do the code then, or most of the code. Could I? Yes. I was going to try for it.

That meant I had fifty minutes to hack Hoda and the other ten were for the bathroom and me changing clothes.

I went to the office, settled in, and within a minute I was already running the program to get Hoda's password. First up, her social media accounts.

All of them.

THIRTEEN

Within the hour, I had uploaded my programs to Hoda's Facebook, her Twitter, her Instagram, her emails, because she had five separate addresses, and her website. The program acted like a window. It was a back window she didn't know she had, but I could get into her accounts anytime I wanted or needed.

I could watch her activity.

Was it an invasion of privacy? Yes.

Did I care? No.

She thought I hadn't earned my place. She underestimated me. She released that image of Kash and me, so in the way of us Hayes women, vengeance was totally appropriate here. She screwed with me, I was going to obliterate her if I so chose.

I just wasn't there, yet.

Ring! Ring!

Buzz! Buzz!

Shit. Damn. Crappers.

It was five-forty. Matt was late and so was I.

I ran to the door and hit the speaker button. "I'm late, too. Tell Matt I'll be down in five minutes. I gotta pee." I didn't wait for the guard's confirmation. I let the button go and sprinted to the bathroom. Then I sprinted to the closet and changed super quick. It should be casual at the estate tonight, but one never knew. I threw on jeans and a nicer sweater than what I'd been wearing to school. I ran my fingers through my hair quickly and called it done. My hair could go up in a clip. It'd look like a messy ponytail. That was fine by me. Chrissy would say something, but I wasn't caring at this moment. I could braid it if necessary.

Grabbing my bag, another litany of curses fell from my mouth, because I needed everything to go with me to do my coding in the car. Shit, shit, shit.

My wallet and phone were stuffed in my backpack, and I had my laptop in there. Yes. I was running down the checklist. I had everything I needed. I thought so, anyway. If I didn't, I'd be up later than I wanted to finish my coding, because I had reading to do for tomorrow, too.

There was a knock at my door.

I pulled it open. "Hey."

It was Scott.

He held the door for me, falling in line behind me as I dashed to the elevator that was being held open for me.

Scott hit the parking lot button, folding his hands in front of him as the doors slid closed. "I'll be the guard accompanying you tonight."

I was half-distracted, thinking that I really needed Matt to be texting on the drive there, i.e., not talking to me.

"Huh?"

"Your guard. That's me tonight."

I was a bit slow. "Okay . . . ?"

A faint grin from him. He was being patient with me. "We are taking your brother's vehicle. Both his guards are going. You won't need both of your guards, so Mr. Harkman will remain behind here."

"Oh!" Then I grinned. "Harkman. I like it."

We were nearing the parking garage when I thought of it. "Could you do me a favor?"

He glanced to me just as the elevator stopped.

"I need to do work in the car. It's difficult if Matt's talking. Can you distract him for me?"

His mouth twitched before smoothing back into a blank wall. "Sure. I can do that."

The elevator opened. I was guessing Harkman was the guard standing just inside the garage, because we walked past. He and Scott did a nod thing to each other. I faltered, because instead of the normal SUV, it was a limo.

Matt's guard opened the back door and Matt was there, grinning. He saluted me with a drink in hand. "We're late, sis. Figured we should do it in style."

Guy's face poked out from the inside of the limo. He smiled wide at me. "Heya, Bailey. Guess who's going to dinner with you guys?"

My stomach bottomed out. "Oh no."

His grin only widened. "Oh yes."

I slid inside, or started to.

I paused midslide, with one leg still outside, because Guy wasn't alone.

Tony was inside. He was at the far end of the limo. Guy was on the couch that ran the length of the limo. Matt and I went to the back.

Scott bent down, looking inside, assessing the situation.

He looked at me. "There'll be a vehicle following. I'll ride in that one."

I wanted to ask if I could go in that one, too, but Matt must've sensed my thoughts. He threw an arm around my shoulder, his eyes falling on my backpack, which I was holding in my lap. He motioned to it with his drink. "What's this?"

I was pleading with Scott not to leave me alone.

His mouth only twitched before he shut the door.

Matt's breath was already strong. "What were you doing before this?" I asked.

He just laughed. The alcohol was rank.

His eyes were dilated and lazy. His smile was sloppy. "Partying. What do you think?"

"Partying?"

Both Guy and Tony had glasses next to them, and Tony was in the process of filling his with rum, but they didn't look as gone as Matt.

"Why are you guys here?"

Guy lounged back, throwing his legs up on the seat across from him. He raised his glass toward Matt. "Your bro's been on a bender since last night. We heard you got a visit from him, too."

Whoa. Matt seemed sober earlier.

Tony finished pouring his glass and leaned back, but he was more sipping, with his eyes pinned to me, almost squinting. "The fuck called this afternoon at some chick's place."

Guy started laughing. "He was freaking, didn't know where he was. Totally forgot he had two guards waiting on him."

How much had he drunk between this morning and now? I must've been a pit stop.

Wait. He had breakfast at the Chesapeake Estate this morning. Had he been drinking during that, too?

I stiffened, throwing him a side-eye of my own.

Matt removed his arm from me, shoving to the corner, and he slipped farther down in the seat. He growled, "You both are assholes."

Guy's head tipped back. He just laughed.

Tony rolled his eyes. "Asshole friends that came to pick you up and acted like it'd been the plan the whole time so your babysitters didn't report to your sister's man, and the Great Authority Kashton Colello didn't rain hell down on you. We're super fucking horrible friends."

My stomach was twisting up, hearing all of this.

Matt still growled, looking outside. "Whatever."

Tony snorted before sipping his drink again.

I didn't say a word. Matt was on a bender. Noted. I would be sharing that with Kash, but Tony was wrong. I knew Kash wouldn't be chasing Matt. For one, he couldn't, since he was in Brazil.

I looked at Matt. "Were you drunk at my school earlier?"

Matt froze.

And my second question. "Were you drunk at breakfast, too?"

Matt didn't respond. His head was down. His phone was buzzing, and he was responding to that, not to me.

I looked at Guy and Tony. They weren't looking at me.

"When did you pick him up?"

Neither of the guys spoke up, and that had my stomach twisting all the more.

I leaned forward and hissed, "You should've called Kash. Maybe then my drunk brother wouldn't have been around my other brother and sister."

Tony's jaw clenched, but he still didn't look at me.

Guy was just looking at his phone.

"How bad were you?" I squared off against Matt. He continued to ignore me. "If you don't answer me, I'll take your phone and load a virus to it so you'll never be able to use another phone again."

He continued typing, then stopped. He froze a second before lifting his head. "You can't do that. You're good, but not that good."

My lips thinned. "Try me."

Guy spoke up, his voice strained. "He wasn't that bad in the morning. He called us early, around six. We got him, thought food and family would sober him up, because he wanted to go to another after-after-hours club. It didn't work. He got all worked up about something, demanded we bring him to you, and then we've been at Octavo this whole time."

"Octavo?"

"It's another club in Chicago."

I was going with a hunch here. "One that Kash or our father doesn't own, right?"

I was met with silence. All silent.

I had to sit and contemplate, because what was my role here? I knew Kash used to deal with this, bailing Matt out before *and* after he got into trouble.

I ran down my list of options.

Option one: Blow a gasket that Matt was on a bender and be alarmed at how good he could handle his liquor, because I never once thought he was drunk at school.

Option two: Do nothing and tell Kash later. Let Kash deal with Matt.

Option three . . . I had no clue.

I went with a mix of all the options and I announced it. "Okay. This is what I'm going to do."

All the guys looked at me, each with a different expression.

Guy was mildly curious.

Tony was glowering.

Matt was wary, but there was a "fuck 'em all up" look in his eyes, too.

"I'm going to sit here and do my coding for school. Then I'm going to text Kash later that you were drunk tonight, but you and I both know he won't be flying in to deal with you. And three, if you do anything tonight to scar our little sister and brother, I will blow a gasket." I leaned in close. "You've not seen me blow a gasket. You do not *want* the gasket to be blown. Trust me."

Matt's eyes filled with that crazed look like he was going to call my bluff, but he only raised his glass for another sip—make that a gulp—of alcohol. Guy was back to lounging; he almost looked like he was going to fall asleep. And Tony's eyes were narrowed and fixed on me before I looked at him. He raised his chin up, in a slow way, like he was almost challenging me, but then his gaze slid away to the window. From his profile, he looked pensive.

And me, I set my bag on the floor, pulled my computer out, and did my coding assignment.

FOURTEEN

Cyclone thought Guy was hilarious. That was fine.

Seraphina had a crush on Tony. That was *not* fine.

Matt gargled mouthwash, spit it out, rinsed it with water, and was the best actor I'd ever seen. Really, really not fine.

If I hadn't smelled the booze, I never would've known he'd been drinking. As we ate—it was a spaghetti night—the only person who gave him a long, questioning look was Theresa. Chrissy, no clue. Payton, I was assuming no clue, but then again, it was a repeat of the other time. She said nothing. She kept in the background, only there when Seraphina and Cyclone went to talk to her or hug on her.

Cyclone and Seraphina *really* had no clue. Matt was the most charming and sober acting around them.

That was scary to think about.

He didn't have a great history of being sober—or being drunk, for that matter. Having an affair, getting trashed, and inviting a crap ton of randoms to his place . . . and that was just the highlights I could remember from this summer. His being drunk but acting sober was almost terrifying.

We ate. We bowled.

After, I was right in the time frame. We were in the limo heading back, fifteen minutes to ten. If I'd been worried about how Tony and Guy would act around my siblings, I would've worried for nothing. Both were normal, and both did the mouthwash trick right alongside Matt before walking inside. Tony was quiet, almost competing with Payton for who was the quietest. Matt and Guy cracked jokes, and Guy loved teasing Chrissy.

As for me, I was too distracted with watching Matt like a hawk, while trying to make sure Ser and Cy had no idea I was tense as hell, so I forgot to pull Chrissy aside and talk to her about my dad. I also wasn't sure if I wanted to talk to her about it. Kash seemed sure nothing would come from it, and I still didn't know how I felt about the whole sleeping together thing. So when I did not get an invitation to extend this party at Naveah—where I knew they were going, even though they didn't tell me—I was mostly thinking about what I needed to finish before hitting the bed.

I needed to finish my coding, and I needed to read six chapters. And then I needed to sleep, because Kash was going to wake me up whenever he rolled in. He'd only sent a couple texts and called once before he was loading back onto the plane after his one-hour meeting.

He was in the air now and not within cell range.

I slid into bed around one a.m. My eyes felt like they were bleeding, but I fell asleep with a smile because I knew what I'd be waking to in a few hours.

I wasn't disappointed.

His mouth woke me.

Hard. Demanding.

The bedsheets were whisked away. The bed depressed as Kash crawled more on the bed and his body came down over mine. He still held his weight up, both his arms resting beside my head, but his mouth was on mine. And it was impatient.

I opened for him, and his tongue slid inside. He was tasting me, claiming me. Commanding me.

"Fuck." He pressed down on me, grinding into me, and I felt how hard he was. He was *ready to go.* "I missed you." He whispered those words against my lips, not even lifting away to talk.

I opened my mouth, trying to reply, but he drowned the words.

"Babe, I don't want to wait."

I didn't want to either.

I grabbed the back of his head, my fingers fisting into what little hair he had, and I pulled him tight against me.

I slid my hand down, undoing his pants, and I found him. I wrapped my hand around him, pulling him out and kicking his pants down at the same time.

He helped me, maneuvering, and then a savage growl left him and he was gone.

I was dazed at first.

At first.

Then I heard him ripping his clothes off and I jackknifed up. I was racing him, my heart pounding hard in my chest.

My tank. It was gone. Then my underwear, but I only got a finger through one of the sides, intending to start pulling it down my legs, before Kash grabbed them, and they were gone the next second. I heard a ripping sound and he was back over me, then I felt him, and he was inside me.

Both of us gasped at the sensation.

He stilled. "Fuck."

I agreed, but I could only whimper from my need. It was so sudden, so overwhelming, and I was done waiting. He was pausing, letting me adjust to him, but screw that. I reached blindly for him, my legs lifting around his waist. He caught one of my legs and panted into my ear, "Jesus. I want to pound you."

I was nodding. He felt my response. I was only too eager, and then my legs were raised even higher. He lifted my ass, moving it down and repositioned himself. With my feet over his shoulders now, he reared back, and thrust back down. Over and over. Again and again.

A better angle.

A deeper angle.

He was straight-up pounding me, and I was lifting my hips, going back at him.

I could see him in the moonlight. I was so damned grateful that Kash had insisted on windows no one could see through from the outside, though we could see out. I was so damned glad we didn't have curtains or blinds to block us, because then I wouldn't have been able to watch him, my eyes on him, his eyes on me as we moved together seamlessly.

We were connected.

This was emotional and physical for us.

I felt him inside me, inside my soul, reading my thoughts, feeling my emotions. We were physically together, but it was more. It was so much more.

He kept going and going, and it was rising, and I was gasping, because I couldn't tell where one ended and the other began. I felt like we were one person. And then his hand reached down, pressing to me, rubbing, and I was coming with a scream.

My back arched from the climax's power.

My vision went black. The sensations and pleasure rushed through me, and then I was replete and exhausted, and my man had waited for me to settle before he started again for himself.

He slid in and out, slower, almost torturously, until I nodded and he began moving again. This time for him. This time he was relentless, and I loved it.

I loved him.

I loved that we had this.

I loved that he seemed to want me more and more, need me more and more, because it was the same for me. I was addicted.

I came a second time, just on the heels of his release, as he dropped down and ground into me before gasping. His entire body rested on me, giving me his full weight for a moment. I knew I would only get this from him for a second, and then he kissed the side of my jaw, a feather whisper of a caress, at the same time that his hand ran down the length of me. It went to my hip, leaving a trail of tingles in its wake, and once at my hip, his fingers curled in slightly as he pulled out and went to the side of me. His entire body was pressed to mine, and he reached for my hand, lacing our fingers.

A soft chuckle from him, one that warmed me, and he pressed another tender kiss to my shoulder. "'Morning."

I grinned at him, too satiated to move my head any farther. I turned, just watching him from one eye. "'Morning."

His eyes warmed, and again I was thankful for the moon.

Looking at the clock behind him, it was just past five thirty in the morning, so it was still dark. "How was your flight?"

"Long." He dropped another kiss to my shoulder, his hand moving with mine as he began to rub our hands back and forth over my stomach. "Meeting was good, though. Productive. I'm glad I went."

I wanted to ask, but I was scared to ask, and then screw it. I asked.

"Did it have something to do with your grandfather?"

He tensed, and I knew I shouldn't have asked. Bringing him up always brought this result.

Kash didn't move away. He remained tense, but it was like he couldn't peel himself away from me. He moved more to his backside, his head resting on the pillow beside mine. His side was still plastered against mine. Reaching down, he lifted one of my legs and pulled it over his, and his hands began running up and down the inside of my thigh.

"Yes. I can't say what yet, because I don't know if it'll pan out, but yes. I wouldn't have gone, otherwise."

I rolled my head on the pillow to see him more fully.

"Does that mean that when you travel to another continent for a one-hour meeting, the likelihood it's got something to do with your grandfather is pretty high?"

His top lip moved up. "Very high likelihood."

I nodded. "Good to know. That'll save my questions."

And another one I was a bit hesitant about but still wanted to know.

"Um." I bit my lip. "I want to know how you're fighting him. I want to know—"

I stopped, because he pulled away from me, sighing as he sat upright. He didn't get out of bed, but he sat there. His head folded down and he raised his knees up, resting his arms over them, his hands dangling. He hadn't just pulled away from me. He took his hand away, he took his kisses away, and I was feeling the cold.

My heart hurt.

I bit farther down on my lip, wanting to apologize, but fear was literally squeezing my heart.

What was he going to do against his grandfather? What moves could he make against him? Was he thinking everything through? Was he—

"You can't know."

He stopped my thoughts, twisting around, and I felt slapped again. Not by his words, though. Not even by his tone, because he sounded so exhausted, already too exhausted. I was slapped by the look in his eyes.

Haunted.

Torn.

He had ghosts that I didn't know about. I felt them then. I knew it then: his agony went deeper than anything I've felt. It was a strange feeling, an odd sensation, as if I was feeling someone else's skin over mine but I couldn't see it wasn't my skin. I could just feel it wasn't mine. But instead of shrugging it off, I wanted to reach for it. I wanted to drag it in to me, make it mine, and that's what I wanted to do with his ghosts.

"Who I am. Who I come from. Who I'm fighting. It's already touching you. I have to stop it from taking you over. And it will, so easily. That's on me. That's my burden to bear, and I'm doing it so that you don't carry it one bit. There are things I will do, people I will use, people I will hurt, and I cannot tell you. I tell you, and it's over. You feel that world, and I won't let you. You're in school. You're doing the thing you've been wanting to do for so long. I won't take that dream away from you, and don't make me take that away from you."

A single tear.

I was affected, and I was swimming in emotions, but most of it was just pure love for him. Yeah. He had ghosts. And now it was confirmed that he wouldn't share them with me.

I smiled sadly at him. "I love you, but I won't fight you. I will only say that any burden you have, I carry regardless, because I carry you, too. It goes both ways."

He whispered back, "I'd never let you feel that pain." He leaned down, bracing himself so he didn't fall, and kissed me. His mouth found mine in the sweetest kiss.

I felt an invisible hand grabbing my heart and crushing the life out of it.

He moved to kiss the corner of my mouth before he got out of bed.

He masked his haunts, running a hand down the side of my face. "Can you sleep?"

I caught his hand. "Hold me."

He glanced to the clock. I had an hour before I needed to get up for the day, and he made his decision.

I knew he wouldn't sleep, but neither of us spoke on that, either. He slid back into bed, curling his body around mine, and he wrapped his arms tight. I fell asleep like that.

He was gone when I woke an hour later.

He'd already gone to work.

FIFTEEN

I was on the phone, calling Kash, thirty-eight minutes later.

He answered, "You heading to school?"

"Yep," I replied, sitting in the back of my car, which was being driven by Fitz that morning. Erik was next to him. I tucked the phone more securely between my ear and shoulder and hauled up my bag. I needed to read over one last chapter, so I was hoping to have it ready to go, once this conversation was done. With that thought, I got to it. "Where's your office?"

"What?"

"Your office. I figure you have one that you use, but I don't know where it is."

"You want to come see me at my office?"

I could hear his smile, and that made me smile. "Maybe. I think it's a good idea I know where to find you, and I also want to come see you at your office today."

He laughed briefly, his voice definitely smiling. "I've got a few, but I use my office at Naveah the most. I'm here today. And speaking of, can I pick you up for lunch?"

I faltered.

Did I want to have lunch with my man? Yes.

Should I have lunch with my classmates so I didn't isolate myself from them? Um, yes, but it was only a hesitant yes, because I'd much rather have lunch with Kash.

He heard my sigh. "Thinking your classmates would be okay if I did a drop-by instead?"

That made it so much better. "I'm thinking yes, and if they aren't, I don't care enough to keep you away."

"Sounds good. I'll see you for a drop-by." He paused a second. "Is there something I should be prepped for, why you're coming to see me later?"

"Matt."

He was silent a beat. "Got it. I'll see you later."

With that, I knew that he knew what I had to say wasn't something I could get into with a drop-by from him.

After saying good-bye, I had enough time to read over the last chapter on Structured Query Language. I didn't need to fully process everything, just needed to run my eyes over the text when we brought it up the next day, because we were going to use it in our own systems database.

I couldn't wait.

When we pulled up, Erik got out first. I waited, my chapter done and in my head, and he opened the door for me.

I got out, starting for the building, but today wasn't like the other days.

There was an entire crowd outside the building.

I jerked to a halt at the same time Erik touched my arm.

The crowd just looked like a normal crowd lingering outside a school building before classes started, just larger. There were always students outside the building when we got here. They were going to classes, talking to friends, on their phones, having a smoke, or just stalling before going to class. But when I got out of the car, it changed.

All heads and eyes turned to me.

A buzz began filling the air.

There were groups of girls, the types of girls that looked like sorority girls. I was guessing, but their hair, makeup, and clothes looked like all the latest trends. So, yeah. Total guess there. They surged forward, but they weren't alone. Some athletes, and I was guessing again because of their build. Massive shoulders. Broad. Muscular. Some lean.

Some of the faculty were there, too. Seeing me, they were the ones that got to me.

Goa. Busich. Wells. They were all waiting and coming toward me, each with a set expression on their faces. They weren't happy about whatever was going on.

Wells spoke first, taking an extra step closer as the other two held back. "There's been a development. Did you check your school email this morning?"

Dread had already lined my insides. Ice drenched them.

"No, I haven't had the chance yet."

Wells nodded at my response. She stepped closer, inclining her head as we walked to the building. "Let's talk in my office."

"Miss Hayes." Busich drew my attention before we could start. I held up, waiting.

She dipped her head, regret flashing behind her glasses. Her hands were clasped together. One of her knuckles had whitened. "I am very sorry about what's happened. I already have a call put in to your father, and we will find out who did this."

Well. That didn't sound good.

"I'm not sure what you're talking about, but I will find out. If you're intending to call to get something done about whatever happened, my dad isn't the one to call. Kash is."

Busich was nodding. "Okay. I'll still put the call in to your father, out of respect. We can convene later. We'll give you time with Ms. Wells."

Both Busich and Goa gave me regretful looks before moving away.

"What happened?"

Wells's fingers pressed more against my elbow. "Inside. I'll show you."

I noticed Erik on the phone. As we moved to the door, Fitz joined us.

A couple of the girls called out my name as we passed by. One held out a slip of a paper, shouting, "We're having a party tonight! Come and hang. Check us out."

Erik grabbed the paper for me but stuck it in his pocket as he moved ahead of us for the door. Fitz held me back. We waited. Erik was scanning the inside of the building before he opened the door again, nodding to Fitz. He held it for us as Fitz went first. Then Wells. Then me. Erik came in last.

The inside was a lot less hectic. The crowds had kept to the exterior.

There were looks. More looks than the other days, and I walked around with a bodyguard. Both still dressed as if they were students so there was some blending, but every student in my cohort knew who they were. Seemed the other programs in our building hadn't and they were noticing them now.

There was a new feel in the air. I didn't like it. I didn't want it there.

I ducked my head and walked to where we were going, because it was one I recognized. It was the feeling of being cast out of the ocean. I was a fish flopping on the beach, out of water, out of my element.

That feeling I was feeling was recognition. With it mingled speculation, interest, calculation, and so much more, but the feeling I was zeroing in on was that I was different. I was separate from them.

It was the feeling that they now knew I was no longer one of them. That was the one I hated the most.

My phone was buzzing. I'd put it on silent.

Kash calling.

Erik had just put his phone away. Didn't need to guess who he got off the phone with. I moved to a corner, knowing they'd wait for me and also knowing Erik and Fitz would form a wall for me. I'd have a modicum of privacy.

"Hey."

"You okay?"

No. "I haven't seen exactly what's happened, so I guess?"

"That blogger, Camille Story, released a shit ton of information about you, me, and Matt. She had everything. She also sent her entire blog in an email to the entire student body of Hawking University. It looks like the faculty added were only the faculty of your program."

"Shit," I whispered. "I hacked her."

"I know."

"She must've had more files."

"I know." He added, "She knows about you, so she was smart. Prepared. My guess is she had it on a separate computer, one that wasn't connected to the internet. She got help with the student email list. No way did she get that herself."

"Timing is suspect."

He was quiet a beat. "If your classmate was pissed off enough, I'm sure she could do an easy search. She could find who broke the story on me, reach out to her. You still intent on me not firing her?"

I didn't want to mess her life up. An IT job at Naveah was a good job, and being fired from any job was something that could mess up her life. Maybe not in a big way, but enough of a way to make an impact with her.

Still. I already told her to lay off, so the good in me was saying we needed proof that she was the one to set this in motion. The bad part in me was saying enough was enough and just fire her.

I sighed into the phone. "No matter how it played out, the fact that one of your employees and one of my classmates is our first suspicion on who got this rolling probably says it right there."

"Right. Will you be okay?"

He wasn't fully asking about the leaked information. He was asking about the fallout of Hoda being fired. And my answer was a growl into the phone. "I'll be fine. I'm done waiting. She's going to learn how much she underestimated me."

Another beat of silence before he sighed. "Just be careful. I'm not talking about catfights or whatever cyber war you're going to unleash on her."

He meant me, as in me not getting emotionally hurt. My throat was choking up. "I'll be fine."

"I'll see you later for lunch."

"Okay."

We hung up. I squared my shoulders back, raised my head up, and announced, "I'm ready."

With that said, Ms. Wells showed me everything that was leaked, and it was a lot. It was way more than what was already out there, and it was way personal, with images of Kash and me kissing.

I understood those pictures being put on a blog. Kash was hot news right now. If it weren't me kissing him, it would've been a different girl. But these pictures were of us in his office, and they were current. Like, a few nights ago current.

That had me seeing red.

To make matters worse, these images were intentionally sent to the entire email list of Hawking University.

Camille Story.

She'd gone too far.

She would regret that.

SIXTEEN

Today was another reminder just how new this world was to me.

Going through the day, I was in a daze. I didn't want to be in a daze. That made me feel weak. But I was, and logically I knew it was about me processing everything. My old world to this new world, where I wasn't only visiting. I was in. I was staying.

I was just new.

Not a lot changed in my classrooms, except the normal buzz was quieter. There were a few more sad glances my way. Hoda seemed paralyzed when she saw me, but after one glare, I promised myself that I'd be dealing with her after class. Since then, Hoda had kept a wide berth, which was a good idea. For her.

Liam gave me a chin-up and a "Yo."

Melissa's energy was still there, but she was holding it back. Like the guys, she seemed more sedated, and almost sad.

That struck me, too. I didn't know how they'd react, and to an extent, I still didn't. It wasn't until I was debating if I should even attempt lunch with them or not when I found out. I was in the hallway, just leaving the bathroom. Melissa was quick on my heels, as if she didn't want me to even walk out a door alone. The guys were all waiting in the hallway, which was normal.

Hoda was absent. That wasn't normal.

Liam was at the door, one hand on it, and half turned to look outside.

Erik and Fitz were accompanying everyone. Erik led the way. Fitz fell in step behind Melissa and me. The guys dropped in behind Fitz. At the door, Erik paused, but Liam only gave him a chin-up too, then pushed open the door, and Liam was the one who led the way. His hands were in his pockets. His backpack was on and he was the image of cool and calm together. I caught the amused look Erik gave him, but it was faint and brief. He was half trailing Liam, half walking to the side for a better vantage point on the entire group. Fitz was doing the same, I noticed. He was somewhat observing the guys behind us.

If this wasn't my life, I'd find this whole thing just a little bit ridiculous.

But this was my life now.

It was at the main intersection of sidewalks. They all converged into one giant cement block where the food court building was located, and they'd been waiting. I recognized the girls from earlier. The same one who handed off a flyer was standing up, her gaze set on me and her mouth tightening. She was marching over to us. Most of her friends stayed where they were already sitting at a picnic table, but four or five of them were trailing behind.

"Hey! Bailey!" The girl raised her hand, and her voice matched. She was waving to me. "Hey! Over here!"

Liam let out a whistle and motioned to the girl. She heard. Everyone heard, and she faltered for a second. Her eyebrows pinched together, confused, and that one second of silence was all Liam needed. He called over his shoulders, "Block her."

The guys in my class swarmed.

They literally swarmed, but they just didn't swarm her. They circled where Melissa and I were, leaving us in the middle. Most of the guys were between me and that girl and her friends, but a few were holding firm on the side where Melissa was standing.

They were protecting me. They were shielding me.

Melissa dipped her head and whispered, "Those pictures went out to everybody. We knew who you were and that you're here, but the general student population hadn't. They know now, and you being you, it's big news. There's going to be groups coming out of the woodwork to try to use you, at least for a while. Don't worry. We got your back. Hoda's been put on a list. You don't have to worry about her."

I blinked a few times. "What?"

She moved even closer, her shoulder touching mine. "She's on their hit list. Dax. Shyam. The guys. That's what they call their list of people they want to take down or hurt. We know it was Hoda who gave that gossip blogger the emails for the university. Dax works IT for the campus and he found the IP address for the person who forwarded the list. A file that big, it gets red tagged. That's what he does."

"He red tags file sizes?"

"He's on the computer staff to help maintain cyber security. Last year, we had to download an emergency app because they found a huge hole in the code for the campus internet. It was a whole to-do. Dax was the one who found the hole, and don't tell anyone, but it's because he likes to try his hand at hacking. That's on the DL, of course."

She was whispering and winking, and there was a whole "awe" element to her voice, too. Dax was a legend to Melissa.

I squeezed her hand back. "I really appreciate it." And I did. Some of the need to annihilate Hoda lessened. I was almost more tempted to wait and see what Dax and the guys did, see what their skills were like.

Liam gave another short whistle and proceeded forward.

The guys moved alongside us, not falling back and not going ahead.

I was touched. A couple of the guys glanced over and I mouthed to them, "Thank you." Their chests puffed up and they gave me a chin-down nod.

Liam led the way to where our group ate. It was away from the other students.

Thank God.

After everyone got their food, Erik sat down in front of me.

He glanced around our section, then leaned in. "They're good guys. A bit weird, but good guys." He looked over his shoulder at Melissa. "Your girl seems good, too. Solid."

"She told me that they're going to handle Hoda. They know she's the one who leaked the email list."

I was assuming she also had helped with the current pictures taken. They were from the hallway, when Kash was kissing me.

"Did Kash fire her yet?" I asked Erik.

"She has an official meeting with him at the end of the day."

"I want to be there."

He stilled, eyeing me. "Bailey . . ."

"I want to see his office anyways, and I want to tell him about Matt."

His eyes narrowed. "What about Matt?"

Scott would've known that Matt was drunk in the limo, and I had caught Scott watching Matt more than once when he'd gotten drinks from the bar at the house, too. He didn't know what else I knew about—about the guys picking him up, taking him for breakfast, hoping to deter him from continuing to drink all day.

I was about to say all of that, when Erik spoke up. "Your brother has guards on him at all hours, too."

I frowned. "I know."

"We still report to Mr. Colello, even though he's only hands-on with you."

Oh . . . Oh!

I sat up. "So Kash knows Matt was drinking all day yesterday?"

He nodded. "Mr. Colello knows all of it. He knows stuff you *don't* know."

That had me frowning even more. "Like what?"

A quick clip of his head. "Mr. Colello was briefed on Matthew's situation. I'm also supposed to relay the message he won't be able to drop by today for lunch."

That was disappointing.

Melissa was coming back. Erik stood to help her with the food, putting our orders down, and Liam was coming back. He and Dax did a fist pound before separating for their own tables. Erik returned to his position, conversing with Fitz before moving apart, and both stood as if they were Secret Service.

When we went back for our second class that day, Hoda wasn't there.

She wasn't in the hallways, the lab, even the bathrooms.

Wherever she was, she couldn't hide for long. I would find her.

When we got to the doors, Erik stopped me.

There was a crowd out there, but I expected it. Word was out about me. Now that I understood that, I was expecting things to be more crazy than normal. It would die down. Eventually.

Erik didn't move from the door.

I started to go around him.

He took my arm, holding me back. "Wait."

He had a finger to his ear, listening to something.

His eyes narrowed. He was watching outside.

I only saw the crowd. They were different students this time. I knew I had to deal with it and adjust and get on with my life, because that's just how it was going to be. With that intent, I tried to go forward again, and because of that, I wasn't fully paying attention to what Erik was paying attention to.

I missed the train of SUVs pulling up.

And what was more important, I missed how Fitz was standing outside, and how he wasn't going toward the SUVs.

I didn't see how both Fitz and Erik had set expressions on their faces. Their jaws were clenched and their eyes weren't happy.

But what I didn't miss was how I recognized that black sports car sliding into the very last spot in front of the building. I was happy and thinking Kash was a liar. He did have time for a drop-by. But then he was out of his car and he wasn't coming to me. He was veering to head off whoever had gotten out of the back of the middle SUV and was heading for the building.

Calhoun Bastian.

My stomach fell once again, and ice pierced my chest.

I was having a bad case of the déjà vus.

SEVENTEEN

This day couldn't get worse.

Or at least that's what I thought, until I saw Kash's scary grandfather exit his vehicle, making a beeline for my building. He looked so dignified, too, almost like a diplomat, and he was getting the attention to warrant that impression. Like this morning, I saw Goa and Busich, but unlike this morning, Wells wasn't there. She was replaced by a bunch of other official-looking older people. That's when I clued in on the students. The sorority and jock groups weren't there. They were replaced by more serious-looking students, ones wearing pin-striped suits and dress shirts, or dress skirts and high heels in a nude coloring, so you're still edgy but it's not really edgy.

Calhoun never saw Kash.

It was one of those surreal moments, where you can't believe you're watching it but you are, because it's happening in front of you. It's one of those moments I'd always remember, and not because of my memory but just because it was that awesome.

Maybe this déjà vu case wasn't *so* bad.

Calhoun was looking toward the Hawking staff.

He had this pompous look on his face, straightening his suit jacket as he started for them. He got only a step, but they took the signal and approached. He stopped, his head up, his nostrils going wide as he was breathing this in, and an arrogant smirk was on his face. He was expecting them to come to him, and so he was going to wait and watch them, as if they were beneath him.

Seriously. So narcissistic.

He never took in the crowd. Not once. The way he was at ease with them there, this clearly was something else he was expecting.

He thought they were there for him. To his credit, maybe they were. Maybe the staff rounded them up because the groups were different than the ones congregating earlier this morning, but Kash was cutting right through the crowd, the staff, and going straight to his grandfather.

His face was granite. His eyes hard. His jaw clenched.

He was seething, but he didn't give his grandfather attention.

I thought that's what he was going to do. He didn't. That made it even more awesome, because he cut in. His grandfather's security never stopped him. I didn't know why that was, but only one saw him coming, and his face twitched. His hand dropped to his side, but after a second's hesitation he moved it back in front. He shifted, his face going forward so he, too, wasn't seeing Kash coming.

Then Kash was there, his back to his grandfather, and he was speaking in low tones to the Hawking staff.

To their credit, they didn't look like they wanted to be there. Their faces were reluctant, wary, but resigned at the same time. Seeing Kash suddenly in front of them, his eyes locked on them, they sucked in their breaths.

Then they leaned in.

They were listening to whatever Kash was saying. So was Calhoun, whose face was storming up. It was twisting, and rage was showing—steam could've been coming out of every hole on his face. He opened his mouth, his hand raising, but even with his back to him, Kash knew his grandfather's move. He shifted an inch to the side, effectively cutting him out, and he was still speaking. Low. Calm. Contained.

The staff's heads jerked back when he was done. Their eyes cut to Calhoun, to Kash, and then back again to Calhoun.

Kash spoke, and this time I heard, "You decide now, or I walk. Peter Francis walks. Bailey Hayes walks."

The threats impacted them. One swallowed tightly. Another one looked terrified, her hand shaking at her side. But the head guy, the one in the lead, he was more together, and he looked at Calhoun, extending his hand. His voice boomed out, "It's been a pleasure meeting you, Mr. Bastian, but as you can see, your business is no longer welcome at Hawking University."

Just like that.

Just. Like. That!

He was out.

The crowd hushed, and a surge of volume ripped through everyone, even though most didn't know what had happened. They just knew *something* happened, something big.

Calhoun Bastian was rooted in place.

His fury was clear on his face. The lines around his mouth were white, and he slapped the university staff member's hand away. He grabbed for Kash—or he would have. His hand was going up. Kash turned, as if he was expecting it, but he wasn't the one who stopped Calhoun. It was the security guard who had seen Kash coming. He moved in and merely stood between grandfather and grandson. He folded his hands together, the same Secret Service stance. Then he spoke, a low baritone, but one with patience. "You should remove yourself from these premises, Mr. Bastian." He paused a beat. "For your safety, sir."

Kash stepped to the side, squaring against his grandfather.

He didn't speak. He didn't move again. He was simply waiting for something.

Then Calhoun exploded.

That's what Kash had been waiting for.

Calhoun looked from the security guard to Kash and back, then back to Kash, and his restraint vanished.

He didn't say a word. That was the scary part of it. He simply lunged for his grandson, but again he was blocked—*by his own guards*. His own guards! Not even the one that moved in the first time to block Kash, but the other three around Calhoun. One barked a command. The door to Calhoun's SUV opened. The three guards caught their employer and half carried, half guided him to his SUV.

Into his SUV.

They closed the door.

The SUV took off; the one before it, too. The last one waited.

The first guard looked at Kash and I heard Kash's one word. "Stay."

The guard nodded, moving to the driver of that SUV. They exchanged words, and then that SUV moved on, too. The guard remained, stepping back onto the sidewalk, but waiting.

Those guards, Calhoun's guards, were Kash's. Not Calhoun's. They worked for Kash!

And now Kash was coming to me.

I realized it with a jolt. I'd been watching the guard, and then he looked at Kash and I looked at Kash, and Kash wasn't as contained now. His face wasn't granite. The seething I saw in his eyes was all over his face, and the crowd felt it. People moved back a step. The path was cleared right up to me, and he turned, said something to the university staff. Their gazes moved to me, back to him, and they nodded. The man shook Kash's hand before all of them left.

Kash was coming my way, striding over in a few steps.

He reached forward, his hand grabbing my arm, and he led me briskly and with purpose to his car. The front passenger door was opened. He was not messing around, and he set me inside, waiting while I quickly pulled my feet in. Then he was rounding the car for the driver's side. Calhoun's guard shut my door. Erik and Fitz descended on Kash, listening and getting orders.

Erik nodded, and both he and Fitz hurried away.

Kash's hand went to his door handle but didn't open it. He spoke over the hood of his car to Calhoun's now ex-guard. I couldn't catch what he said, but the guard moved away. He disappeared into the crowd of students who were still lingering. A third of them were watching the guard that was heading into my building. The rest of our audience was gawking at us, some with phones pointed at us, others with their phones pressed to their ears.

Kash took a pause. I couldn't see what he was doing, but then the door was opened. He was inside, and he didn't say a word before he pulled away.

I knew he was furious.

I was bracing myself, because I didn't know if he was mad at me, mad I was there, or just mad at his grandfather. I was guessing the last two were definites, but I wasn't sure about the first and I was holding my breath, waiting. A sick feeling was in my gut.

He waited until he was on the freeway before starting.

His voice was low, back to being controlled, but he didn't look at me. "I knew he was coming to your school today. Knew he was going to make a move to approach you again. I knew all this because those guards on him work for me. He knows about the one, but I gotta make the decision to pull the rest or risk him figuring it out and executing them all." He swore, and it was savage. He punched a button on the car's phone.

The dial tone filled the car, and then it was ringing.

"Boss?"

Kash was grimacing as he spoke. "Pull everyone. I can't risk him doing anything to you guys. Everyone, Connor. Everyone."

A moment of quiet on the other end, then, "Got it. Disperse, or new job location?"

"Disperse, except you and Monty. Both of you come in. I want you at the estate."

"Got it, boss." Another beat, and then we could hear his smile when he said, "Have to say it was a pleasure holding him back from you today. I'll send the word and we'll dump him. He'll get picked up within minutes, but the guys will take off and wait for your new orders."

"Good."

The call ended, and without blinking, Kash was filling me in. "I had six men guarding Calhoun. He thought they were a gift from a family friend. They weren't. They were sent by me, and through them, I was told his plans for today. I've known about his plans for the last week, and even before that. His stop at the apartment was not announced to his team or I would've been told that ahead of time, too."

He flashed his turn signal, smoothing his car over two lanes of traffic and onto the exit ramp.

I was half taking in our surroundings before he started again. "I didn't want to lose my guards on him, but he upped his trip today. I had to move in, drop my news to your school, and he would know that the first time might've been a coincidence but the second time was not. He would've known. I had to burn six guards I had on him. The trip to Brazil was a calculated guess and a move to strike a better relationship with who I think he might pull a brand-new security detail from. It's a guess. He won't trust anyone else from this country, since your father and I are the two people who most want to be aligned with, not aligned against. I guessed at who he'd approach, just didn't know it'd be so fucking soon."

A nerve was pounding. A vein stuck out from his neck. He was speaking again, the car sidling up to a stoplight. "My grandfather wanted to hurt me through you, so he was moving to hold a claim over your school, and then therefore over you. After he thought that would be cemented, he wanted to see you again. That fact alone had the sole purpose to scare you, to let you know he could get to you whenever *he* wanted, wherever *you* went. I took out both those options because I told your university that if they accepted his thirty million donation, Peter

Francis would pull his seventy million donation that they were set to receive later this month. Like I said before, money aside, they do not want to align against myself or your father, and that was them choosing. They chose our side."

The light turned green and we moved forward.

We weren't going to the apartment. I recognized our surroundings. We were going to Naveah.

Kash was still speaking. "I lost one of the edges I had on him today. I don't know if my trip will work out to give me that same edge on him, so that means after we go to Naveah, after I fire your classmate, after I shower with you, I have to keep making moves on him. I have edged out ahead of him and I cannot lose that. I could lose you, but that won't happen, because I know his last play and that will be to hurt you."

We were slowing, turning in to the basement parking lot of Naveah. Kash stopped talking until he had parked. The door leading to the elevator inside opened and two guards were standing there.

Kash ignored them and turned to me. His eyes were glittering and fierce. "He wants to destroy me, even more now, and the one way to make sure he shatters me is to touch you. I will never let that happen."

I was breathless, my stomach was in knots, and I was reeling all at the same time—and yet I wasn't. I knew Calhoun was coming for me, but seeing Kash in action today changed everything. It all got a bit more real, a bit more surreal, and I reached for his hand.

I had to touch him.

He grounded me.

As soon as my fingers grazed his skin, I felt the roots sink into the ground.

I felt stronger.

I also had a feeling I was getting a few more guards.

I whispered, "I believe you."

Some of the fierceness lessened, and a softness came over his face. His hand lifted, cupping the back of my head, and his fingers slid through my hair. He tugged me to him. "I need to kiss you, then I'm going to fire your classmate. You can watch if you want."

I would be delighted to watch him fire Hoda.

EIGHTEEN

Torie greeted us as we stepped off the elevator. She was wearing a black Naveah staff shirt, black skirt, and pumps, holding a clipboard. She flashed me a smile. "Hey, girl." A professional smile formed and she cleared her throat. She straightened, and I could see the actual employee slide into place. "Miss Mansour is waiting downstairs in the lobby. Should I give you a moment before showing her up?"

Kash's hand was behind the small of my back. He ushered me in first, as our two guards followed us. One took point outside his office door. The other remained by the elevator. Torie moved ahead, opening his office door, and we followed inside. Kash's hand touched my back, keeping me in place, and he moved close behind me. He said over my head, "Give us five. Erik is downstairs. Have him walk her up."

Torie winked at me before leaving.

Once those doors were closed, the club's music was faint, but still there.

Kash was at my side, his hand on my chin, and he was turning my head. "I need more." His meaning became clear as his mouth touched mine, and anything I might've thought or felt about him having Erik show Hoda up to her firing was wiped away. The usual heat and need and desire took over, and it wasn't long before standing and kissing me with his head tilted wasn't enough. He groaned, taking over. Tugging me back to his office, he picked me up, sat me down on his desk, and was between my legs within one second.

Then his front hit mine, his hands were into my hair, holding my head, and his mouth was opening over mine.

Jesus.

I was swept up. My pulse was racing, my blood pumping, and I was panting as his tongue slid inside to meet mine.

One second.

Two.

Thirty.

The kiss kept going.

My legs were wrapped tight around him. Our chests smashed together.

We were doing something, or waiting for something. I was trying to remember, but I forgot everything.

I was unbuckling him, not remembering where we were, when we heard a discreet knock, followed by the elevator arriving.

Kash tore himself away from me, cursing as he did. He barked out, "Hold."

There was absolute silence outside the door.

Not in here. I was breathing loud and ragged, trying to gather myself, still on his desk. I was half-sprawled over it, and Kash was breathing almost as hard, a few feet away. I watched him, literally watched as he closed his eyes and a wall fell over him. He'd been there with me, right there. Needing. Living. Feeling. Then a knock, the elevator *ping*, and I was sitting here, cold from the loss of him, and a stranger came down over him. He was pulling on his mask and his face turned granite again. He was hard, and he stared back at me. A flicker of heat speared me from his eyes before he came back to me.

He straightened out my clothes. He pulled down my sweatshirt. I hadn't noticed when that went up.

He buckled my jeans. I hadn't realized those were undone.

He was brushing some of my hair off my shoulders, and I saw the top button of his pants was undone. I put it back in, and he paused at my touch, his forehead coming to rest on mine. His chest rose, held, then fell back, and he cupped the back of my head. A kiss to my forehead, and he murmured there, "One hit isn't enough."

I knew what he meant, but I tipped my head back. "I think you mean a drug."

His eyes were dark, holding mine. He was all serious. "No. I don't."

I got his meaning, and I swear, the oxygen left my lungs.

We need air to live.

I *so* got his meaning. "Oh." My throat swelled up.

His eyes were starting to smolder, so he pressed one last kiss to my forehead, then to my neck, before he picked me up and walked me to his couch in the corner. It was in the dark and he'd only turned on one lamp in the entire office, the one on his desk, so it was possible I could sit where I was and Hoda would never even know I was there. I didn't know if that's what he intended, but he deposited me down, leaned over me a second. His mouth twisted in regret before he straightened and went back behind his desk.

"Okay."

The door opened, and just as Kash was pulling his chair out, Hoda entered the office.

This wasn't a Hoda I'd ever seen before.

Her shoulders were curved in. Her head down. Her face pale. She wore her sleeves over her hands and she was tugging at the corners of each of them. She was almost shuffling in. Her hair was in a simple braid that started at the base of her head and trailed down to where her hair ended, just beyond her shoulder blades.

"Sir," she started, her voice tentative.

He didn't waste time. "Why did you lie on your application?"

Her throat jumped. "Sir?"

His gaze was intense on her. He didn't sit, but he didn't speak or anything. He was waiting for her. He also didn't explain his question.

"I . . . uh . . ." She lifted her head, blanched, and looked back down.

He spoke. "The timid look doesn't suit you."

Her shoulders straightened and she looked up. "I lied because I didn't think I'd get the job as a woman. I knew someone who worked here before. They said the hiring was a joke, that I could apply as a man, show up as a woman, and they wouldn't even notice. So, I did it. I was hired on paper, with my résumé, and when I showed up, they didn't question me."

Kash's eyes narrowed. "Those staff members are no longer with us."

"I know." Her voice was clearer.

Kash leaned back against the wall behind his desk, his head lowering, but his eyes remained on hers. He crossed one ankle over the other and motioned toward her before his hand went into his pocket. He was the image of relaxed. But his eyes weren't. I saw the heat running behind the mask he had in place.

"I saw the tape. I heard *her* voice."

Her eyes widened. "You can't have video in the women's restrooms."

"Who said I did?"

Her eyebrows pulled down. Her head lowered an inch. She was thinking, confused. Then she stiffened, and she jerked back up. "You tapped my apartment?"

"You called the Camille Story blogger in the hallway of your building. Your building is owned by a subsidiary of Phoenix Tech and there is security in all Phoenix Tech buildings. It took a moment to locate the video, but we got it, and we have your voice on tape telling the blogger that you will send over the list."

She was thinking, her eyes locked down. "'The list' could've meant anything. I could've been calling about my grocery store list."

"You could've, but we also found your email, where you sent the link for where she could download the Hawking University student emails. I've had staff look into it, and you were thorough. You didn't just send the main email that every student is given. You looked into second and third emails for students, especially students in your program. You added certain staff members onto the email. You wanted to make sure everyone knew about who Bailey Hayes was, including who her family and her boyfriend are. You wished to humiliate her, though I don't know why you would want to make an enemy of her."

She was seething. "You have no proof of any of that. If you did, you obtained it illegally. I can fight you—"

"You're fired as an employee from this nightclub, and we can fire you on the simple grounds that you lied on your application. We have copies of your first application, and the changes you did yesterday, and we have you on video making those changes. I have not asked Bailey to search, but if I did, she would be able to find proof that you were the one who released that image of us months ago."

She was standing so rigid. Her chest was heaving. "You're lying." She spoke through gritted teeth.

"No." Fuck. He almost sounded sorry for her, as if he pitied her. "You have made enemies where it was very foolish of you to do that."

I'd had enough with being quiet. If she didn't know I was there, she was about to. I stood up and spoke from the corner. "Did you tell Calhoun Bastian where and when we ate lunch?"

She jumped, half screeching. She hadn't known I was there. She'd been so focused on Kash. Whirling, a hand to her chest, she fell back a few steps. "Oh my God! What are you doing—" She saw my face, and got right. "No! I would never do that. Out you in a stupid email, yes. But not Calhoun Bastian. Jesus. How stupid do you think I am?"

"Are we talking on a scale from one to ten?"

Kash snorted.

I took a step forward. "Why the email? The university isn't going to kick me out. They know who I am."

Her eyes rolled to the ceiling and stayed there. She muttered, almost speaking to herself. "Because your dad is seriously powerful, and rich. And your boyfriend is even wealthier. And he's got a huge, scary enemy. I wanted others to know you were there. I wanted them to either hate you or stalk you or try to use you. I didn't care. I just want to make it such a hassle to have you be a student at Hawking University that they have to ask you to leave the premises."

I waited, because there must've been a better reason.

She stopped talking. A calm settled over her, and I was guessing that *was* the reason.

"You're an idiot." I shook my head. "They'll lock down the building. I'll come in the back, stay in the building, and leave another way. More security guards will be there for me. That's it. That's all they'll do. They're getting a seventy-million-dollar donation from my father. You think they're going to *kick me out?*"

She was, and she was seeing it. Her mouth slackened. "Oh."

"Right." Kash had had enough of this conversation. He tapped his phone. "Escort Miss Mansour from the premises and give her a list of buildings within the city she's banned from."

She gulped. "What?"

"It's within our right to ban you from any premises and locations where we feel you are a threat, and unfortunately, that's your apartment building. You have the weekend to vacate your place. You're no longer in our employment, and I'm half considering encouraging Hawking University to expel you. Five of your graduate scholarships and two of your loans have been pulled. If you remain a student at Hawking, you'll need to find other funding."

She *really* hadn't thought anything through.

She whispered, "Fuck."

Kash didn't care one bit. The door opened. Erik was there. He took her arm, and Kash said, "Walk her to her locker. Give her a box for her belongings. Once her locker is cleared, walk her to the street. Call her a car."

Erik guided her out of Kash's office.

The door closed, and I could only gape at Kash. Even *I* hadn't thought about all of that. "Her apartment? Her scholarships? Shit, Kash."

He spared me a look, but he wasn't messing around. He tapped some buttons on his computer, picked up his phone, told them he needed an hour. Putting the phone back in the cradle, he walked around and took my hand. He was leading me to the back of the office. "The apartment was necessary. She knows now who owns her building. She could stage an accident, try to sue us, and most companies settle. I'm sure she'd get some money out of us. As for the scholarships, I was pissed off. Still am."

He opened a door in the back and flipped the lights on.

Kash led me into a bathroom. He moved to the sink, turning the water on before coming back to me.

"Her life is not over." His arms slid under my armpits and he lifted me up, sitting me on the counter. He moved between my legs again, his forehead coming back to mine as his hand slid down my chest, settling between my breasts and staying there. "But she has the means and capability to come back and hurt you. She can't do what you can do, but she still has IT skills. The first blow I strike against her has to sting or I risk having her coming back and doing worse to you. I cannot risk that, not after what she's already done."

He stopped, staring at me, the wall gone, and I was seeing his heat, all of his heat. He whispered, bending to kiss the side of my mouth, "I have bigger and badder battles coming. The long-term war is my grandfather. I can't get pulled away dealing with someone being petty and trying to hurt you because of whose sperm helped birth you."

When he put it like that, okey dokey.

NINETEEN

Kash

"It's nice to hear you're alive after all."

It was the twelfth call I'd taken over the past three weeks from business partners who had found out that Evelyn Colello's son was alive after all. Business partners who had worked with my mother, half of whom had never sold her share, and it was mine to claim if I wanted in. The other six had been bought out, and a team of lawyers was accounting for the loss of those shares right now.

"Bad time?"

Lifting my head, seeing Peter in my door, I said good-bye to the newest business partner I'd found out about that morning and hung up the phone. "Come in."

Peter glanced around, holding two coffees in hand. "I heard you were using the Naveah office. This your 'daytime' office?"

I motioned to his extra coffee. "That for me?"

"It is. Black. Plain. Boring." Peter pretended to wince as he handed it over, then he took a seat on the other side of my desk. He finished scanning the room. "Your dad used to use your other office, back when he and I were the majority holders at Phoenix Tech, before everything got big."

And "got big" was an understatement. They grew that company to be one of the leading companies in cyber security. My father went on to lead the business end while Peter took over the computer end. It'd been a match made in heaven. And he was right. I'd taken to using my dad's old office at Phoenix Tech headquarters a week ago.

Taking my coffee, I sipped it and waited.

Peter came. Peter never came without a reason.

He sighed, looked at me, and there it was. The reason. He reached behind him and pulled out a file he'd stuck in the back of his pants. It was an odd habit, but he did it often over the years.

I noted, "Briefcases can be used as weapons, too."

He shrugged. "You know I hate those things."

Not unless there was a computer in it. His photographic memory wasn't the only thing he'd given his daughter. Both needed their computers on hand or they felt naked. They got twitchy, anxious, and the second you gave them a laptop, both settled down. It was uncanny.

"What am I going to see when I read this over?" I skimmed through the papers. "This is an order of protection."

He nodded, sipping his coffee. "Against your grandfather, on behalf of my family. My entire family. That's the summary of all the orders."

Okay.

I tossed the papers on my desk and sat back, studying him more squarely.

His eyes twitched, enlarging before he clamped down. "What?"

He was guarded now. Good.

"What are you doing?"

"What?"

"What are you doing?"

"With what? I'm helping. I know you have a lot on your hands."

"Have you checked in with Matt?"

He frowned, his eyebrows dipping again. "Did something happen?"

"He was on a bender recently." I'd reported this to him, or had my team report to Peter's team. I knew he would be notified, and I was now seeing that he didn't listen or read his team's reports.

"He was?" He jerked forward in his seat. "Did something happen? Is he okay?"

"He was on a bender."

"You just said. Did you stop him?"

"Why would I?"

This was what I'd been worried about. I was at a crossroads, and I had to choose.

Bailey. Her face on the sidewalk as my grandfather pulled up. That image flashed in my mind.

I chose.

"You're fucking up."

Peter flinched, his head snapping back.

I kept on. "You are my superior with age, with years, with expertise in your field, but you are completely fucking up when it comes to your family."

Peter closed down. A nerve was ticking out.

I'd pissed him off. I was about to piss him off more.

I leaned forward in my seat, knowing my eyes were dead as I delivered the rest to him. I should care, but fucking hell, I couldn't.

"You are not grasping that things have changed. I am no longer in charge of watching your family. Matt is fucking up. He went on a *bender*. He hasn't done that in weeks. If I were to guess, I'd think it has something to do with Quinn." Peter stiffened at her name. I ignored it. "I know you are sleeping with Bailey's mother again, and Bailey knows this."

His mouth slackened. "She does?"

"I don't think Bailey's talked to her mother about it. I don't know if Bailey even has an opinion on it. She was almost kidnapped, four weeks ago. She refused counseling two weeks after. She started school a week later, and since starting school she's been targeted by my grandfather twice and has been targeted by one of her classmates for the sole reason that her father is Peter Francis."

"What?" He jerked forward. His hands dug into the chair.

"I get reports from the security teams. I get reports from all of your accountants. All of them. I get reports from your assistants. I get reports from your publicity team. I get fucking reports from everyone, and in the middle of all of that, I am finding out about another company my mother was running in secret, once every second day. I am also spearheading a war against my grandfather, and this is a battle that you don't seem to give one shit about." I rested my arms on the desk. "You *should* give a shit about it. He comes in and wins, I'm dead."

Peter winced. Again.

I ignored it. Again. "He comes in and wins, Bailey is dead, or *worse*." His face closed up, and I was content to let him sit on that, think on that. "It's not escaped anyone's attention you shipped Marie off for an extended vacation. Why?"

He didn't answer, his face shifting away.

"Peter."

He remained quiet.

"On Matt's bender, he had breakfast at the estate. He no ticed, even while drinking. He went to Hawking and shared his revelation with Bailey. She shared with me. She's gone back to the house, something I know she's in turmoil about, because she wants to see her little brother and sister but she does not want to see a Quinn look-alike there, and especially one standing in the back and lurking."

Now Peter looked up. His nostrils flared. "Payton does not lurk."

Why those nostrils flared on that point was something I would tuck away and turn over later. "She makes Bailey uncomfortable, and because I know the second reason for your visit, I'm just going to give you my report. Your daughter is still struggling. She loves school, something I'm assuming you understand, but she's not keeping it together. She's acting like she is. She's convinced herself she is. She's not, and it is killing me that I am unable to give her the attention she needs from me."

Those nostrils had calmed, and his Adam's apple moved up and down before he coughed to clear his throat. He ran a hand down his tie, then leaned forward in his seat. "Those restraining orders are a wake-up call."

I sat back. "Restraining orders won't do shit against my grandfather."

"But they're paperwork. Paperwork is—"

"Not currency my grandfather adheres to. He is in bed with corrupt government leaders. He's here. He's attempting to battle me in old-school ways, buying up shares in companies he thinks I want, trying to get shares of companies you and I both own. He's trying to get to Bailey for the mere fact to scare her. He has not clued in, either, that I'm not playing that way. I am taking a page from Bailey's playbook."

Interest sparked in his gaze.

"I'm letting him underestimate me, but there'll be a time where he realizes he's losing. He'll get angry and he'll explode. I'm trying to cover all bases so when he does explode, everyone I love is safe."

Peter let my words sink in.

I hated this. It made my stomach churn. He had helped raise me, but there were facets of Peter that were not there. Being monogamous and being proactive in areas outside of technology were two that he struggled with. It was unfair of me to expect him to know how to physically disarm an attacker or, if need be, to pick up their gun and shoot them in the head with it. I wasn't asking that of him.

He let out a deep sigh. "What do you need from me?"

"I need you to be a father."

His eyelids shuttered. He looked as if I'd struck him.

"Check in with Matt. That bender happened for a reason.

Make it right with him. Check in with your daughter. She needs a father right now, and I know she's walling off her mother, and I haven't approached that topic with her yet. I looked into her schedule. She overloaded herself so she would finish within twelve months."

"What? That's too much, even for her."

"Exactly. Figure out why, and tell me." Though I had a strong guess as to why. "Then help her as her father. She just got you. Let her actually have you."

He gestured to my computer, my desk. "Is there anything else I can help with?"

I wheeled back my chair, but just watched him.

He waited.

"When I have reports sent to you, read them or listen to them and move on them. I send them to you for a reason."

He let that digest before clipping his head up and down. "Got it. You sent another one over this morning. I'll listen to it on the way to check in with Matthew."

That was it.

He came.

He tried to help.

I schooled him on how he wasn't helping. And now we would see if he did.

Now he left.

If I were to guess, I wouldn't be surprised if Bailey shared that she got a surprise call or visit from her father.

My phone rang.

"Yeah?"

"Kashton?"

This was a call I never wanted to take.

"Victoria."

She was hesitant, but then asked, "Can we meet for lunch? There's something I need to talk to you about. About . . . about your grandfather."

I looked at my screen, seeing the latest report that one of my private investigators had sent me. It was the amount her grandfather was in debt to my grandfather, but I highly doubted this was what she wanted to talk to me about.

With that, I knew what I would do, and I knew I wouldn't tell Bailey, and I could only hope it didn't come back to bite me in the ass.

"Sure."

TWENTY

Bailey

A week passed, and I fell into a routine.

Kash woke me up every morning, and after I fell back asleep, fully satiated, he left for work. I woke forty minutes later, went to Hawking. Hoda wasn't there for the first three days. Rumor was that she found herself having financial problems. She got that sorted out, but I'd taken to sitting with Melissa and Liam. We ate at the same place for lunch every day, and because of that, other people and staff took note. It didn't take long before my class-mates' pictures were being put on a couple social gossip blogs. Camille Story had remained quiet, but she was on the list for me to hack. Again. She was slippery, though, so I wanted to wait and figure out the best way to go at her.

Matt came over twice. He didn't ask about Kash. He asked about school, and he had a look in his eye like he wanted to talk about something else, something important, but both times he never brought it up.

I was biding my time before I pushed to get answers from him.

I worried he would close up to me, so I wanted to wait until the right time.

I needed answers.

If he was going to Naveah. If he was going to see a new woman.

If he was going to the Chesapeake Estate. But mostly, I wanted to know what was bothering him.

Until then, lots of studying. Lots of coding. Lots of reading.

I wanted to get ahead with my classes, so that meant even more reading and even more coding. Melissa dropped a hint that there was a big internship opportunity coming up. She looked at me as she was talking about it, got all squinty, and then clammed up. I asked Liam later about it and he told me that Phoenix Tech always offered a first-year graduate student in our program at Hawking an internship. That internship sometimes led into a job.

I understood why she clammed up.

Liam added, "Though I don't think anyone will get too excited about it this year. It's pretty obvious you'll get it."

But he didn't know, and I didn't know, and I realized then that I hadn't heard from my father for almost three weeks. And I further realized I was okay with that. As for Chrissy, she'd been quiet, too. She had texted a couple mornings ago.

Checking in, sweetie. How's everything going?

I didn't respond to her. I didn't know why, but as soon as I put the phone away, my mind was moving on to other things.

I was leaving our afternoon class when my phone started ringing.

Torie calling.

Melissa was with me. We were both watching Hoda, who'd been back the past two days. She stuck to herself, only talking once with Liam, who walked away, looking annoyed. Melissa asked what the conversation was about but he didn't say. He just got that same annoyed look and left us, too. So we were standing, eyeing Hoda, who was sitting at a table in the hallway, acting as if she didn't know we were mostly glaring her way. But she did, and we knew she did, and we were still doing it anyway.

I answered, "Hey, Torie."

Hoda's head snapped up. Her eyes jumped right to me.

"Bailey," she breathed into the phone. "Tamara called, and her man broke up with her. We need a girls' night, stat."

"Torie—"

She overrode me. "Kash gave me the night off. I'm calling in reinforcements. Get over to our apartment in an hour. You got any girlfriends from school?"

I opened my mouth.

Melissa had heard. She piped up next to me. "She totally does! Me!"

"Well, whoever you are, get Bailey and your asses to our apartment. Just let one of those hottie guards know you're going to Torie's place. Now, I have a question. Are you the type of girls who want food *before* drinks and dancing? Or are you the Taco Bell *after* drinks and dancing type of girls?"

"Uh . . ." Melissa looked clueless.

I took the phone back. "We'll bring something to tide us over—"

Melissa grabbed the phone. "No! Drinking. Dancing. Taco Bell. That's what we're doing tonight."

Torie chuckled, still sounding all smooth and seductive but I was wondering if this was how she was, off duty. "Add in shots, and I'm not talking shots where they can be added into the drinking section. Shots get their own category. Trust me, Tam will be hurting a little less by the end of the night."

She hung up.

I turned to Erik. He was the closest. I didn't say a word. He nodded before I could. "We know her place. We'll get you there."

"You're off duty soon."

"Scott and the new guys know it. You're covered." He looked at Melissa, then back to me. "Are we giving your friend a ride to get ready, too?"

Melissa's eyes got big. "That would be amazing."

I guess we were now, and I didn't mean that in a snarky way. I meant that in a belated, I-feel-like-shit way, because I hadn't even thought about offering. I was glad Erik did, and I felt his eyes on me as I was thinking all of this.

"Where are you going?" Liam had migrated over after the call.

Melissa shot straight up. "Girls' night. You're not invited. And I hope we go to Naveah at some point." She leaned into me, her side brushing my arm. "That would be *amazing*."

I gave Liam a grin as we started to head out. "This'll be awesome."

He grinned back. "Have fun."

We went outside and got in the waiting SUV. The guys all sat in the front while Melissa and I were in the back.

"Where to?"

Melissa gave him directions to her apartment and my phone was buzzing as we started going. Kash.

You're with the girls tonight?

I reiterated about Tamara.

That sucks. How was your day?

He asked the same thing every day, once I got into the vehicle. And it always had the same effect; pure golden warmth washing through me.

Day was good. Did you catch any more Calhoun moves and counter them?

I asked every day. This was another routine I'd fallen into.

Every day. I'll be working from the Naveah office tonight if you're there.

My heart fluttered.

I'm sure that'll happen. Torie said dancing.

And Naveah was one of the hot spots to dance at in Chicago.

If you go to Octavo, tell me. I know the owners, but I want extra security on you if you go there.

Me: *Okay. I'm sure we'll stick to Naveah tho.*

Kash: *Still.*

Me: Okay. Love you.
Kash: Love you. Have fun tonight.
Me: Please don't work so hard.
Kash: I won't. Love you.

I noticed Melissa watching me as I put my phone away.

"What?"

She had a weird look in her eyes, one I'd never noticed before. She shook her head, her mouth twitching. She kept looking at where I'd stowed my phone away. "Nothing."

I saw the grin. I also saw the fight to keep it back, and I rolled my eyes. "He's my boyfriend."

"He's one *hot* boyfriend."

Melissa's grin was wide. It kept widening until we got to her place.

She lived in a cute smaller apartment building that housed ten units. There was a buzzing system. The front door was locked, but once we got inside, the only other security was the apartment door. As we walked in, two doors opened and I was staring at two elderly residents. One was a man wearing suspenders, a stained white muscle shirt, and baggy jeans that were only held up because of the suspenders. His hair was a mess, with two days' worth of beard on his face. The other resident was an older woman. Her hair was wrapped up in a fancy up-do, dyed black, and she had a heavy dose of makeup on her face. Her mouth had eight coats of red lipstick and there was an equal number of coatings of blush on her cheeks. Unlike the guy, she was dressed to impress. A suit jacket and skirt, both a lavender color with white lace fringe. She was just missing lavender high heels. She had pink fuzzy slippers and cotton between her toes.

She was getting a pedicure.

"Liss, who's this?" From the woman.

"This is a classmate of mine!" Melissa was bouncing, still grinning, and her elbow jostled me. "Get this, Esther. We're going drinking, dancing, and Taco Bell. I'm going on a *girls' night.*"

The alarm faded from Esther and her smile softened. "You deserve it, Liss. You're a good girl. A night out having fun is something you should've been doing for ages." Her sharp eyes went to me. "You take care of our girl. You hear?"

I opened my mouth.

Melissa got there first, saying, "No. We're totally covered. Bailey's got guards on her at all times. I thought it was only three, but we got in her car today and I saw she had a driver too, so four. It was two before, but this week's been four. We're safe. Totally."

Esther's eyes had started to wander, but at the mention of my guards, they were razor-sharp again. "Four?"

The guy harrumphed, "*Guards?* Why the fuck you need guards?"

"Harold," Esther hissed. "Language. They're still young."

"Excuse me." His hands went to his suspenders and he arched his back, then bellowed out, "Four *fucking* guards? Why the fuck you need *four fucking guards?*" He aimed a glare across the hall. "That better for you, Est?"

She sucked in a breath and looked to be counting under her breath. After a bit, she nodded at me. "You keep her safe or you'll deal with us. Don't care who you are. We'll get to that another time, and why you need four guards, but I got bridge tonight and need to head out of here."

Her door was closed and Harold guffawed. "Don't know why she's in such a hurry. She's only walking to A2. It's the building next door. We're the B building. And she don't need to dress so hoity-toity. Only does it to rub it in the other ladies' faces that her husband was a banker. I know she does it to piss Gail off. She's married to Henry, who once made a play for Esther. Esther wasn't having it, but she doesn't want to quit bridge. You play bridge, and you learn it's the social hour around these parts for us. Every Friday night together. Damned ruthless over there sometimes." He took a beat and focused on me. "Why do you need guards on you?"

I was sensing a pattern, so I didn't even try to speak.

Melissa stepped up. "Because she's got a hot and rich boyfriend, and her pops is Peter Francis."

At that, Harold's eyes widened, and he even stepped back a foot. His hands flattened over his chest, the suspenders smashed in the middle. "Peter Francis?" He paused again, his eyes narrowing on me. "Know the boy who came out that was being half raised by Francis. Kashton Colello."

Oh, crap.

I swallowed. "That's him."

"I follow the sites, know who his grandfather is." He took in Erik and Connor, who hadn't changed shifts yet and were standing just inside the apartment building door. Fitz was outside. "You need more guards."

Connor and Erik both looked away. I saw both their mouths curving up as they did.

"Okay. Alrighty. Seems you'll be fine and safe tonight, Lissy girl. You have fun. Don't sleep with any of those guards down there. Those kinds are married to their jobs. You deserve a guy who'll be married to you. Treat you right." His gaze went to Esther's door a second before he harrumphed again and disappeared inside his own place.

Yes. I was seeing why they didn't need more security.

I asked, "Are all your neighbors like that?"

She laughed, leading the way up to the third and last floor. Her place was above Esther's. "Most. One of the apartments on the back side is where a couple of developmentally disabled adults live, but they're sweethearts. A fire alarm went off one night and I met them then. They were worried about everyone. They had staff with them, taking care of them."

She showed me in, and it was a quaint apartment. The kitchen was still in the fifties era. In the dining room was a metal table with red tile on top. Her living room had modern couches. The television could've fit in a box; it was tiny. But she had a full desk setup *set up*. Four desks, one chair to wheel between all of them, and each desk had a different computer screen on it. The girl was pimping her own tech. I approved.

"Take a load off. I have wine in the fridge, if you want some. Do you need to change before going out?"

If I was remembering how Torie and Tamara took care of me before my dad's welcoming-Bailey-to-the-world party, I remarked, "I think I'll be good."

"Suh-weet! Give me a second. I can get dressed super quick."

I grinned to myself. "Amazingly quick."

She heard me and shouted, "Girl! Amazingly quick. You got it."

TWENTY-ONE

Kash

Griogos Maragos's picture was on my desk, staring up at me.

I got the report from my men. I knew how in debt he was, and not just to my grandfather. He was in heavy with the Bennetts and the Marakovs, both Mafia families. If you want to be stupid, sign up to owe them. He had payoffs to senators, mayors, commissioners. And I hadn't gotten into what he was doing with his daughters. I knew there was more. There was always more. What was found, what had been done on his behalf, was always just the tip of the rest to come. There was a glacier underneath it.

I was going to bury him with this.

And his granddaughter was in my backyard. She was friends with someone I considered a brother, a pain in the ass for the woman I was already head over heels for, and she'd been calling me, texting me, and all-around being a nuisance for me.

Was this what she wanted to get ahead of? Could she have known I was going after one of my grandfather's biggest assets, who was her grandpapa? It made sense to me. I couldn't say if it would've made sense to her. Or was I jumping the gun and she was calling because of other reasons?

I didn't know, but I knew I had to deal with her. I had to bring her in, converse with her, put her on a string. And if need be, I would reel her in. We may even have to take a trip overseas.

I wasn't used to thinking about someone else's feelings when it came to business. It was black and white to me. Bailey was good. Everything else about me was in the dark. No gray.

But, Bailey.

I had to think of her, but even as I thought it, I rejected it. Bailey could not know. If she knew, she'd react a certain way. She might whisper something, or squeak something, if Matt cornered her. And he would. If his sister was acting strange, his ass would be up in her face making sure she was okay and finding out what was going on to make her act off.

Matt, he couldn't hold a lie. Not like this. He'd want to rub it in Victoria's face.

I couldn't risk it, and that whole sensation of feeling off balance myself returned. I was not used to this.

I could protect.

I could shield.

I could do what was necessary to enforce that protection. But considering feelings and emotions and being sensitive about someone else was totally new territory to me.

This was where I was.

I loved Bailey, but I had to do things that might hurt her.

Ripping into Griogos Maragos had factors that could touch on her, but I had to get it done. No matter the consequences.

I had his quarterly taxes for the past twenty years.

I had images of each of his children, bastard or not. I had their net worths, their spending habits.

I had the names of his current wife, his last wife, and his two mistresses.

I also had the bank account he thought no one knew about.

Every third month, a quarter of a million dollars was deposited into it.

Every third month, the day after that money got put there, he got a visit from Calhoun Bastian.

I had the locations for each of those visits, too.

What I didn't have was any video or audio recording of those meetings. They were always set too far away for any listening device to get close.

I either needed to go on a hunting trip or I needed to hire a better private investigator. The ones I had were the best in the world. I knew this because no one knew I had worked with them. No. One.

That meant I needed to go hunting.

First up, lunch with his granddaughter.

I picked up the phone. "Victoria, let's do lunch tomorrow."

TWENTY-TWO

Bailey

"Men suck."

Torie announced this to the world while standing on a table in a seriously scary biker bar, holding a shot in the air. I knew this already, because she had burped that confession to me in the bathroom, jerked her clothes in place, fluffed her hair, touched up her makeup, and strode out of there like she was on a mission to save the universe from an impending alien attack. Also at the table was Tamara, or Tam as she was sometimes called, and she was three sheets to the wind.

We had started at Torie and Tamara's apartment, where they finished dressing, saw that I hadn't changed, and proceeded to "make me up" (their words) for a night of drinking and dancing. I was wearing skintight jeans—my compromise because a miniskirt was not my thing—and a halter collar tank top that fitted me almost like a glove. My hair was in a braid. I had makeup on, makeup that shined and glistened and made me look like I almost belonged on a magazine cover.

When they started reaching for the jewelry, I stood my ground. I've never been a big jewelry person. It was my nonwoman card. Chrissy always gave me the same look they were giving me now, whenever she tried to gift me a bracelet. She knew necklaces were always out, but sometimes I broke down and took on a brace-let, until those started feeling too constricting. So bracelets were out, too.

But the pumps. I had the best pumps on. I hadn't had much practice, but I was enjoying the whole wavering effect. Made me feel like I didn't need to drink. I was already on a roller coaster.

So I *looked* like I was three sheets to the wind but was not, while Tamara actually was and didn't look it, not one bit.

I was thinking the heels were the main reason I wasn't drink-ing as heavily as the rest of them, but they weren't noticing. When we showed up, Torie's eyes got big, taking in Connor, who said he'd stay for another shift. So it was Scott, Connor, Grand, and Row. I just met Grand and Row that night. I met Connor previously. He was the guard Kash pulled from Calhoun so in my mind, Connor was epic.

Tamara saw the guys and said, "Cool! We got four sober cabs standing right here. Babes, we can drink!"

We started with wine at the apartment. Coupled this already with dancing.

Went to a pub, had beer. Coupled that with dancing, too.

We were now in the biker bar, and you guessed it—we drank and danced.

It was around midnight when Tamara had an idea. "Hey! We should check out that new place. Octavo."

Torie loved that idea. So did Melissa.

Connor and Scott, not so much.

I knew Scott better, so he shot me a look and I remembered Kash's warning.

"Uh. What about Naveah? We can end the night there."

"Girl! No way." Tamara was shaking her head, and she pointed at Torie—or where she thought Torie was. Torie was on the south side of the table. Tamara pointed to the north side of the table, where Melissa was bouncing and beaming. Tamara thought Melissa was Torie. Neither Melissa nor Torie realized this. And Tamara kept on, "She works there already so much. We go there and she'll be roped into working. I know it."

Melissa was nodding. "Let's go."

"We know you."

That came from someone *not* in our group.

The guys both stiffened.

That was my first clue.

Then a louder, "Talking to you."

I turned around.

A couple girls were there. Biker girls, or what I assumed were biker girls, since they were in leather corsets and skintight jeans like mine. Their hair was done up and they had a solid layer of makeup on, too, heavier than Torie and Tamara. They weren't too far from me, but the second time they spoke, Connor was there, an arm out so they couldn't come closer.

They turned hostile eyes on him. "We just want to talk."

"We want to know why a stuck-up bitch like her is here." Both she and the other one turned on me at once, as if it was rehearsed. "Why you here? This is our place. These are our guys."

Torie heard that. So did Tamara. And both were pushing their way around the table to me.

"You back off, honey." That was from Torie. She liked using endearments when she drank, or so I'd learned that night. "We come here too, and she ain't like that. She's not after your men."

"She has two guards here."

Tamara snorted. "You're dumb, too. She has four! Just the other two are by the door."

Oh. That did *not* go over well.

The first one got red in the face.

The second just launched. Claws out, a howl, and she was over Connor's arms, almost reaching me. Her hand grabbed my hair before Connor had her up in his arms. He turned, saw her hold, and had her hand out of my hair in the next blink of an eye. As he moved her away, Scott waded in and Grand and Row were there.

Scott moved the other "friend" along with the one Connor was carrying.

Row and Grand were ushering us out of the biker bar.

As we went, I caught sight of the other customers. Most were grinning, enjoying the show. Others didn't give two hoots. A few guys were watching us leave, eyes locked on me as if they knew I had no business being there.

A weird sensation started in my belly. It was growing as we moved outside.

In another world, one where I never knew Peter Francis was my father, I would've enjoyed going to that bar. I would've enjoyed cutting loose as I saw a few other Hawking students doing.

Maybe in another life I could've been one of those students, there to have fun without four guards and without two locals recognizing me and starting a scene so I'd have to leave. Not that person.

But I am Peter Francis's daughter, and now we were outside and being hustled to the SUV and my chest was burning because I knew I'd never be that girl again.

That was done.

I could never not be Peter's daughter. I could never not be Kash's girlfriend.

Life being anonymous, pushing to fight my way up, claw my way up, was done.

Connor and Scott came out, unmarred and unscarred, and climbed in.

Scott turned around, took in everyone, and paused on me. He decided for us.

"Take her to Naveah."

Tamara didn't need to worry about Torie wanting to work.

As soon as we got to Naveah, Torie let out a loud whoop,

grabbed whoever's hand was closest, and surged past the lines. She wasn't done when we got inside. She kept going, all the way straight to the VIP booth. Following behind Tamara, because Torie had grabbed Melissa's hand, I slowed, seeing who was already there.

Tony. Chester. Guy. And Fleur and Cedar.

Guy saw Torie and lit up. Chester saw Melissa and turned carnal.

Tony saw Tamara and dark interest sparked.

The girls saw me, and both of their lips curled up in disdain. Well. Too fucking bad.

Guy was already out of the booth, with his arm around Torie's shoulders, by the time I got there. She was doing the introductions. When she got to Fleur and Cedar, both looked Melissa up and down, picked up their purses, and slid out of the booth.

Fleur was the spokesperson. "We can see where we're not welcome."

"No! Stay!" Melissa tried, a friendly smile there, because bless her, she wasn't jaded like the rest of us. That made my heart ache.

Melissa shouldn't be here. Not in this club. Not at this booth. Not with these people.

Torie and Tamara knew the score. They could handle themselves. But Melissa was bright and light and innocent. Fleur turned to her, her gaze locking on, giving Melissa another once-over. "I don't think so. They just let anyone in here now, don't they."

Enough!

A switch was flipped in me, and I'd had it.

"Why do you still come around? If you're here, you look miserable. Every time. I've never seen you smile."

She flinched as if I'd slapped her.

Cedar waded in. "Maybe it's because *you* joined the group." She sent a scathing look at the guys. "And trust me, we smile plenty when you're not around."

I shifted, leaning closer. "Really? Because I could get the security vid. I could look for the past hour or however long you've been here, and I'm pretty sure you had the same piss-ass look on your face the whole time. Do you even like these guys? Why are you really here?" I skimmed the guys with a look. "Is it because of their connections?"

Melissa's eyes were huge this whole time, and at the mention of "connections," she visibly swallowed. I watched in real time as she realized she was no longer in a safe crowd. I hated seeing it. We weren't surrounded by our classmates, guys who adored her and secretly would jump at the chance to date her. It wasn't even how it'd been at the biker bar or the pub before that. Torie and Tamara were good people, but they got where they were by crawling and climbing up by their own nails.

Melissa was a puppy that had somehow found herself in the middle of a pack of rottweilers. Three of them were foaming at their mouths.

I was one of them.

I felt it in my bones then. I smelled it in the air. I could see myself from an outside perspective on our group. I hadn't been one of them this summer, but now I was.

I'd lost that puppy innocence. Then again, maybe I never actually had it?

"Are you seriously giving us shit because we don't smile enough?" Fleur snapped at me.

"It's not the smile. It's the fact you sit here with the guys and you act like you hate every second of it. You're leaving with a snide comment that's a dig at my friend, but mostly me, and I just can't help wonder why you even care?"

I felt a presence behind me. He was coming in, and fast, and a second later, a body was pressed against my side. An arm was draped over my shoulder, and I heard Melissa suck in her breath on the other side of me.

Matt drawled, his head leaning down to grin at Fleur and Cedar, "Ladies. My sis has a good point. You used to put out, at least. Now you know not one of us is going to marry you, you both act like you got permanent sticks wedged up your asses."

Cedar hissed, "Matt!"

He looked at her. "We've had years of friendship, so I get why you're sticking around. It's what you do. What you've always done, but winds changed this summer when I learned I have a sister. You still want to remain in the group, get with the program and stop being such a bitch."

Fleur's eyes narrowed to slits. Her smile turned acid and she stepped in close to us, her voice lowering, but we were able to still hear. "That's funny. Kashton asked Victoria for lunch tomorrow." She focused on me.

Kash and Victoria. Lunch.

Bile rose up in my throat.

It was a slightly intimate setting. Lunch could stand for so many other things. Lunch with a friend. Lunch with an enemy. A business lunch. But those words coming out of Fleur's mouth, with the malice in her gaze . . . I knew this lunch wasn't just nothing.

It meant something.

A wave of sickness washed over me.

"Kashton loved Victoria." She cocked her head to the side, her smile almost turning pitying.

That was the worst part. Her sympathy.

"Kash used to be almost obsessed with her. They dated, you know. They had a good thing going between the two of them. Vic thought for a while he was going to propose. They were like that. No matter who's come after her, it's always been her. Kash knows it. Vic knows it. Everyone in our group knows it. You think we hang around the guys for nothing? No, Bailey. We hang around because no matter how many Discard Girls there are, there's only us and the guys. That's how it is with our families. This society. It's pretty small up here. Sometime down the line, each of us will marry one of them, and if not them, then another like them. Some things *don't* change after all."

She was lying.

Had to be.

I was thinking. I was remembering. Those girls weren't the same as the others.

But no. Not Kash. Not Victoria.

I wanted to vomit, and my chest felt like it was being ripped open by two bare hands, and every breath I took in was laced with arsenic.

I wasn't just feeling sick. I was really going to be sick.

She and Cedar strolled down the walkway and I tried to hold it in. I did.

It was going to spew out of me, so clamping a hand over my mouth, I started to take off.

A hand clasped my arm. "This way." Torie was pulling me from Matt. She saw what was happening, and she was dragging me behind the VIP booth, to a door I never knew was there. She knocked on it, looked up at a corner, and the door opened a second later. We were through into a dark hallway, but there was a restroom right there. A bright red neon sign hanging over it.

She pushed me inside, and then it was coming out of me.

I was on my knees and vomiting, wondering how the hell all of this had happened.

My hair was being pulled back, a clip put in it.

Torie went to the sink.

The water was running.

The whole time, I kept emptying.

Then she slid down the wall next to me, a towel in her hand. "What a night, huh?"

She gave me a pitying smile when I was done and lifted my head, and handed over the towel.

I took it, pressed it to my face, and settled back against the wall on the other side of the toilet. "Men *really* suck."

TWENTY-THREE

Torie disappeared, then returned with a small bottle of mouthwash.

I grinned. "Thank you."

She nodded, her eyes hooded. "Gotta warn you." She motioned to the hallway. "Your man is out there."

I closed my eyes. Crap.

She continued, "And I'm saying 'your man' because I'm not his employee right now. I'm your friend. This is girls' night still, so saying all that, you want me to try to get rid of him?"

My stomach was still uneasy, but I shook my head. Taking a shot of the mouthwash, I waited, swished it around, and spit it out. Torie handed me a bottle of water, too, and I rinsed my mouth. When everything was done, I looked at the door and sighed. "I need to talk to him, and to be fair to him, I don't think I was sick because of what they said about Victoria."

"Good." Her eyes flashed. "Because you shouldn't be. That girl's a bitch. No way in hell do you need to worry about Kash and her. Like, ever. *Ever* ever."

I laughed. "Thanks."

She grinned. "Okay. I'm going to head back out. We'll watch your girl, too. I know Tamara is wasted, but I'm not too bad. I'll quit drinking from here on out, since you were the sober one, and the guards are all gone."

"Matt's are out there."

Her head popped up. "Oh. You're right." She pulled the door and said over her shoulder, "Give me a buzz. I don't know how I'd do it, but if you need me, I'll come up and help with whatever. Burying a body. Fighting zombies. Whatever. I'm here for you."

"Dinosaur outbreak?"

She rolled with it, her grin spreading. "Then we better make saddles to throw on a couple of triceratops, because we're too late to imprint on baby raptors."

I barked out a laugh.

"See ya." She gave me a wave.

I nodded to her, waiting, because I knew my guy.

She opened the door. He was in the hallway, leaning back against the wall opposite, his head down, his eyes on me. His hands were in his pockets, and he looked relaxed. Looks were deceiving. As soon as she cleared the way, he straightened, and the look that he swept over me was primal.

I sucked my stomach in, waiting.

He came in, strolling like he was stalking his prey.

I tried to ignore the tingle that went through me, putting all my senses on high alert, but it was there, and then he was in the bathroom. The door closed and the room shrank. It was just him and me. We were sucking in all the air.

I backed up without realizing I was doing it, until I hit the wall.

He stopped right in front of me.

I whispered, "Hi."

Those cognac-brown eyes narrowed. His head tilted.

His cheekbones seemed even more chiseled, if that was even a possibility.

His jawline seemed even more square, and strong, and why did I feel like I was in trouble?

I didn't know, but I felt it, and I flattened my hand over my stomach, feeling all the flutters there. But it was more. I'd just been puking. I should not be turned on, but I was. An ache was settling between my legs.

That was for him, because of him.

I let out a sigh. "Oh boy."

He relented then, whatever he was doing. A small grin eased some of the intensity. "You were sick?" He moved in so only two inches separated us. His hand raised. He smoothed his hand over my forehead, tucking some of my hair behind my ear. Then his hand fell to the back of my neck and he tugged me to him.

I closed my eyes, feeling his touch become comforting.

I grabbed his shirt, my own hand taking hold, and I melted against him. Feeling how tight his body was, the strength there, some of the ache left me, but it was there. I think it was always going to be there.

"I feel better now."

"I saw the tapes. What'd Fleur say?"

I recited it verbatim.

Anger flashed in those eyes of his, then he damped it down so they were only smoldering. "Victoria's family knows my grandfather. I'm following an angle to him. That's why I asked her to lunch and why I think she's been trying to get ahold of me. I'll find out more tomorrow."

I bit out a harsh laugh. "I'd hoped it was a lie."

His hand curved around the back of my neck. His voice murmured next to my ear. "It's not, I'm sorry. But it is work-related and . . ." His chest rose, held, and lowered again. His fingers slid through my hair, pulling, tipping my head back so I could see his gaze. "I'm sorry I didn't tell you ahead of time."

That sucked.

"It's work-related?"

"Yes. Very much so."

If it was work-related . . .

What could I say or do? Nothing. A whole big, fat nothing.

It didn't quite feel right, but I had to accept it. If that's what Kash said, that was the truth.

I flattened my hand against his chest, feeling how tight it was, his heat, and I felt his heart there. "Okay. I'll deal, but it'll suck."

His hand smoothed out from my hair and ran down the length

of my arm. He moved more firmly against me, into me, and we both stepped back to the wall. He was right there, pressing against me. Then his hands rose, resting against the wall on each side of my head, and he was all around me. Trapping me there.

"You going to tell me the real reason you were sick?"

My stomach rolled.

I lied. "That jealousy we just mentioned?"

His eyes went flat. "Try again."

I frowned. "I don't know what you're talking about."

He lowered his head. His forehead almost rested against mine. He breathed out, "I know it's not about Victoria. What's really going on?"

The same sensation slid through me, the one I felt walking out of the biker bar, and other images flashed in my mind.

Talking to the counselor they sent me to.

Telling Kash I didn't need to see a counselor.

Driving to school that first day.

Hoda accusing me of getting in the program because of Peter.

Hoda giving that information to the blogger.

Hoda giving another picture of us.

Me not telling Kash about that picture.

Just Hoda in general.

The crowds at school.

Knowing Camille Story did another blog post about me, about us.

Knowing every single student at my school saw that, and read that, and I was now a walking target.

I had four guards now. Not just two.

All those memories and images and words assaulted me. One after another.

But I swallowed over a lump, tried for a smile, and lied again. "I'm totally fine."

Kash shook his head. "You're lying through your teeth."

A ball was in my stomach, and it began bouncing around. It

was competing in an Olympic volleyball match, pinging all over me, racking my insides with punches and hits and bounces.

I was lying, but I drew in a ragged breath and I closed my eyes and I rested my forehead against his chest.

"I don't know what it is, and I don't want to find out, because when I do, I know I'm not ready to deal with it."

Kash's body softened. The tension vanished, and he cupped the back of my head again, his head lowering so his cheek rested against the side of my temple. His voice was a whisper. "Okay. But you will have to deal eventually, and I'll be here."

I grabbed ahold of him. Both hands fisted in his shirt, I tucked my head to the crook of his chest and arm and tried to burrow into him. My throat was full. I couldn't say anything more because that "it" was right there, threatening to break open and spill out. And I knew I couldn't handle it.

Not yet.

We heard a soft knock at the door.

"Hell." Kash lifted his head and barked, "A minute."

A second knock.

He cursed under his breath but pulled away and went to the door. Opening it, he stood there. "Someone better be dead."

Someone said, "We got a problem. VIP."

"What is it?"

There was silence.

I lifted my head, saw Scott there. He was handing something to Kash to look at, and a second later, Kash handed it back. "Give me a minute."

Scott nodded.

Kash stepped back inside. The door closed, and he turned, staring at me.

I was waiting.

He didn't say anything.

"What is it?"

"My guess, your classmate friend called in reinforcements. The guy from your class is in a heated confrontation with Matt right now."

I jerked away from the wall. "Liam?"

Kash nodded, his mouth flattening, but I swear, I couldn't tell if he was pissed off or trying not to laugh.

"Liam's here?"

"So is my very recent ex-employee, along with one Camille Story."

Kash waited a beat.

I connected the dots. "That blogger?"

He nodded.

I frowned. "Wait. Why isn't Hoda banned from the premises?"

"She is." His jaw clenched. A vein stuck out. "My guess is that's why she brought her own reinforcements."

I swore. "Camille Story."

Another brief nod from him. "If it were me, the whole lot would be kicked out, but these are your classmates. What do you want done with them?"

I swore again. "I want to see what this bitch looks like. That's what I want to do. I want to go home and I want to hack the fuck out of her."

He stared at me. A beat. Then a smile spread. "There's my woman."

I grinned back.

He brushed his lips to mine, then we went out to deal with both of them.

Kash was at my back.

TWENTY-FOUR

Liam was more having the confrontation with Matt.

Matt was more not doing anything.

Not quite true. He was smirking and half grinning, two hands on the table behind him, and he was half sitting, half lounging there. There was a lot of "half" with Matt, but not with Liam. He was fully in Matt's face, fully angry, and no one could argue otherwise. As we approached, Liam's arms had been spread wide in the air, but then he pointed a finger in Matt's face, and that's when the "half" of Matt ended.

The smirk vanished. So did the half grin. A scary glare formed and his eyes narrowed as he stood slowly from the table. He was now squarely in Liam's face, and Liam registered it. He paused, the finger still pointing in Matt's face, but he moved back a step and swallowed. He lowered his hand, and it was the right move.

Matt's glare lessened, and the side of his mouth went up in a half smirk, but his eyes remained hard. Liam had messed up.

Hoda was a few feet behind Liam, along with two of the guys from our class—Dax and Shyam. Both were looking around, nervous, shifting on their feet.

The woman next to Hoda was not what or whom I expected Camille Story to look like. She was petite, with the fairest skin I've ever seen and strawberry-blonde hair that was nearly white. She almost looked albino, except her eyelashes were black. She was wearing a pale pink sweater hanging over a white top, and white slacks that were baggy and loose. There was a slit up the side of the leg, showing a full thigh. They were the type of pants that truly could be pajamas or could be mixed with a nice sweater, like she was wearing, and be classy and chic.

The girl had fashion sense.

She had a row of three braids that ran the length of one side of her skull, then fell down. The other side of her hair was loose and curled lightly.

She was in the know with the trends. That was for sure.

Before she saw Kash and me, her lips were parted. She was watching Matt like she couldn't memorize his face fast enough. Her eyes were dark and hungry, and sharp.

If I hadn't already known she was smart, I would've known for sure then. Those eyes weren't missing a thing—unlike Hoda, who was standing next to her, half hugging herself. Her arms were folded in front of her, but slightly loose, so she was cupping her elbows with only a couple fingers. Her gaze was wide and looking panicked.

Melissa was off to the side. She wasn't a part of Matt's group. She was standing a few feet forward and away from Torie and Tamara. But Melissa was also not standing with our classmates. Her eyebrows were furrowed. She was biting her lip, and her head was bouncing from Liam to Matt and back again. Her body shifted as her head moved, too.

Camille's entire demeanor changed when she saw us. She was the one who saw us first. Everyone was focused on Liam and Matt, but her eyes went from sharp to panicked. She paled for a second, her mouth clamping shut, and she jutted back a step. She bumped into Hoda, who was jarred, threw her a frown, and moved aside as she reached to rub her elbow. Then Hoda clued in. She followed Camille's gaze to us, and her reaction was a twin of the blogger's.

Kash didn't move, though I felt his intensity ramp up a notch. His hand touched my hip, and he fitted me back to him. My entire back side was plastered to him.

"Yo." Matt noticed us, and he resumed his half-leaning stance.

His eyes remained alert, but everything else about him was relaxed, and he almost looked like he was bored.

Tony. Chester. Guy. They all remained sitting in the booth.

Everyone quieted after Matt's greeting.

They were waiting for us to take over whatever this was.

I frowned. What *was* this?

Liam snapped out, impatient, "Melissa sent out a nine one one to the entire group chat: 'Nine one one, I'm at Naveah.'"

"What?" Melissa squeaked. "I did not."

"You did. Nine one one, Lissa. So we scrambled who we could, and we're here, and this guy is all in Melissa's space. He's crowding her, making her uncomfortable. We show up, and I'm here demanding to know who this guy is, and not one of your staff will call the police."

I looked at Melissa.

She flushed, hanging her head. "I meant to say 'Four one one, I'm at Naveah'! In like an excited thing, not a nine one one that I need help. 'Cause I don't, and I didn't." She motioned to Matt. "We were just talking, Liam."

Liam growled, "You were squished so far down in the booth that you were a slide away from going under the table. He was all over you, and leaning in your space."

I looked at Matt and raised an eyebrow. "You were hitting on my classmate?"

Matt's smirk turned into a rakish grin. "She's cute and I'm single." He shrugged. "Why not?"

Liam's face got beet red. "She's cute and you're single and why not? Why not? *Why not? Who* are *you?*"

Matt straightened again, some of the bored look fading as he narrowed his eyes. "Bailey is my sister."

Liam's eyes bulged out. His mouth closed, before falling open again.

He knew Matt was now Matthew Francis, and then he closed his eyes. A curse left him. I couldn't hear it, but I saw it and could read it. Regret tightened his face. He swung his gaze to me. "I didn't know."

My brother equaled Peter Francis's son. That's who Matt was to Liam, but Liam didn't know that Matt didn't give two shits about our father.

I stepped away from Kash. "It's fine."

Liam rolled his eyes upward. He was gripping the back of his neck and cursing more, staring at the club's ceiling.

I frowned at the same time that Melissa moved to Liam's side, touching his arm. She was saying something to him, and then that moment was done. They moved aside.

Matt turned to me. "Your friends are interesting. We should have them out more often."

I threw him a dark look.

He meant "interesting" in the way that a wolf would play with its food. Melissa, Liam, Dax, even Hoda—they weren't on the same level as Matt and his friends. They were less jaded, more pure in their world. If they mixed with us, we'd ruin them. I knew it, and gritting my teeth, I hated it. I should've fought against coming to Naveah. Torie and Tamara fit in both worlds, and if we had stayed away, this wouldn't have happened, but I saw the spark in Matt's eyes.

He was interested. His gaze swept back over Melissa, and I saw where his interest centered on.

"Shit."

Kash moved up against me again, his hand on my side, anchoring to me.

It was his turn.

He spoke over my head. "Camille Story."

Matt's head snapped to attention, whipping to the person Kash was talking to.

I frowned at that. Matt had dated the blogger, but he answered my question when he stepped away from the table. "You've changed," he said. His tone was confused. I couldn't tell if he appreciated the change or not. Then his face clouded over and he growled, "Get the fuck out of here!"

He didn't like the change.

At his tone, Chester, Tony, and Guy were no longer amused bystanders. All three slid out of the booth, taking Matt's side, and all three were glowering at the girls. I'd never seen Guy without some sort of grin on his face, but I was seeing it now, and he was menacing.

I remembered the first time I had met Tony and Chester.

They'd been intimidating then, and that same air was moving around them again.

Melissa and Liam both stopped talking, feeling the change and cluing back in to the next exchange happening.

Hoda cursed, her hands darting to her mouth then falling back in front of her.

Camille blanched as she lifted her chin up. "I came in for assistance, with a friend of mine."

"Fuck whoever you came to assist. Get out of this club. You were banned long ago."

Chester drawled, "I'd leave. You've done pieces on all of us."

Tony's face was glacial ice, as was his tone. "Or stay. Have a drink. Let's get to know one another." His eyes were mean, and Camille paled all over again.

A man was coming up the aisle toward the table. He paused, his gaze sweeping, and that's when Kash moved.

He set me aside and moved around me, his hand lingering on my stomach. He waited, not stepping away, and I looked up.

His gaze was on me. He said one word. "Stay."

I nodded.

He turned toward Camille and Hoda, his hand leaving my stomach.

At Kash's movement, everyone paused. All eyes went to him.

Camille looked like she was watching a dragon rise up over her in real time. Hoda's gaze was on him too, her head cocked to the side, and she was back to biting her lip.

Kash motioned for the man, who was wearing a business suit. He was older thirties, dark hair swept to the side. Lawyer. His entire walk and how he was taking everything in, no-nonsense and brisk. Nothing fazed him.

Kash raised his head up. "You have it?"

The man climbed up the stairs to where everyone was. He reached inside his jacket and pulled out a stack of papers. He looked between Hoda and Camille and asked, "Which one?"

"The blonde." From Kash.

The man nodded. "Yes." He handed the papers to her. As soon as Camille's hand closed on them, he said, "You've been served."

Hoda gasped.

Camille couldn't pale any more, but her hand started shaking.

The lawyer guy didn't care. He released the papers and stepped back. "You are being sued. See you in court, Ms. Story." He nodded to Kash and left.

Simple as that.

Matt started laughing. "Couldn't figure out why you were waiting. Now I get it."

Chester and Tony gave Kash appreciative looks.

Guy laughed. "Savage."

Kash's glare ripped into Camille Story. "You and Miss Mansour will leave the premises. Now."

That was it, too. No other words. No chiding or threats or anything. He didn't explain what was in those papers. Nothing. Just "You need to leave," and the dismissal was almost as humiliating as her getting served in front of everyone. Either way, she'd been stupid to come here and she knew it.

Her face changed so it was beet red. She was steaming.

Since she didn't move right away, Kash motioned to Connor. "I want them out. Now."

The guards descended.

"Hey. Wait a minute . . ." Liam was frowning. He made a move to help them, but Kash severed him with a look.

"Miss Mansour and Miss Story have both been notified that they were banned from these premises. Both broke that order."

"But they came because Melissa sent out a nine one one call. They were trying to help—"

Kash cut him off. "You came. Your friend came." His eyes moved to Dax and included Shyam. "And a third showed. That was enough."

The girls hadn't moved. The guards hadn't pushed it.

Kash clipped out, "Remove yourself or my guards will remove you."

Hoda's eyes sought mine. They were seething, and, her mouth tightening, she stormed out. Camille hesitated, her eyes sweeping over Matt, and a flicker of emotion was there. Brief. Then gone. Matt saw it, and his eyes went cold.

Some of the red had left her face. More of it left again at that flicker. Without saying a word, she followed behind Hoda. The guards moved with them, following behind until the crowd swallowed them.

Then it was just Liam, who was standing close to Melissa, and Dax and Shyam.

Suddenly, no one cared that they were there.

Matt still eyed Melissa, but he yawned and turned to me. He flashed me a grin. "I'm hanging out with you more."

I muttered, "Great."

He motioned to the dance floor. "Gotta go do something. Be back when it's done."

Guy barked out a laugh, hitting Matt's shoulder as he passed by, heading for the stairs.

Tony, Chester, and Guy all slid back into the booth.

Guy snagged Torie's hand, pulling her with him.

Chester motioned for Tamara to join their side of the booth.

Dax and Shyam moved in closer, both eyeing Kash warily. Liam was watching, too.

Kash didn't care. He moved back into me, pulling me to his chest. Ignoring everyone, he dropped his head to mine and said in my ear, "You want to hang with your friends a bit?"

I didn't. I wanted him, and I pressed against him to let him know.

He chuckled. "Right."

Taking my hand, he said to Torie, "I'm taking her."

Torie nodded and turned back to Guy. That was the end of it.

Kash stepped aside. It was my turn now, and I moved toward Melissa, still holding Kash's hand.

I asked her, "You okay?"

She nodded, her eyes lowered. "I'm so sorry. I didn't mean for any of this to happen. I really meant to hit a four and not a nine. I was just excited to be here, you know?"

"It's fine. It worked out anyways." I looked to Liam. "Can you get her home?"

His nod was short, and he was still eyeing the guys behind us in the booth. "I got her."

Melissa gave him a small grin before saying to me, "I really am sorry."

"It's all fine."

As dramatic as the night in Naveah had started, it was ending on an almost disappointing note. No big scene happened. Melissa, Liam, Dax, and Shyam left shortly after. Melissa went to say 'bye to the girls. As soon as they left, Kash didn't waste time.

He slung an arm around my shoulders, and we left through that back door. He didn't wait like Torie had. It opened immediately for him and we were through. He took me home and did as he had promised.

It was a good Friday night.

TWENTY-FIVE

Kash

I was leaving Phoenix Tech for lunch with Victoria when I heard my name being called.

I saw her on the sidewalk, and she was alone.

"Chrissy."

Skimming, I also saw there were no guards with her. That wasn't good.

"Where are your guards?"

She was giving me a stone face, then snorted at my question. "Where are yours?"

She was right. Some days I didn't travel with them, and most days I preferred driving myself, but I had security measures in place. She did not.

"You should have guards with you."

She jerked up a shoulder. "I wasn't a target before. Don't know why I would be now."

"Who Peter spends time with in bed is always considered a target."

She flinched. It was brief and barely there, but it was there. Her eyelids fluttered a second before she got herself under control.

Bailey's mom was tough and hard-core and sometimes a pain in the ass. But she was Bailey's mom. I knew only part of her story, why she was who she was, why she'd instilled in Bailey the idea that Hayes women don't cry, but I knew there were still secrets to be unraveled. Just wasn't my place.

Yet.

"Tell me your reason for finding me."

Her head moved back slightly. "Right." The lines around her mouth tightened. "You're Mr. Badass now. Don't got time for civilities with the mom of the girl you're bedding."

I almost blinked. "I would, if you gave an indication you gave a fuck about that. And Bailey's a woman, not a girl. She's not a girl I'm 'bedding.'"

"Right. Business." She put her hands in her pockets, faced her shoulders more square against me, and raised her chin. "My girl's not been taking my calls."

I hadn't known that. "You want me to talk to her? See the reason?"

She studied me. "You'd tell me if you found out the reason?"

"Only if she was okay with that."

Her mouth flattened. "Then why'd I stand out here an hour to wait for you?"

I shrugged. "Felt like wasting an hour of your life."

She went still, her eyes glued to me, and then she burst out laughing. "Shit. You are the enforcer for the family, aren't you? Peter's talked about you, but I didn't see it till just now. You're the husband and Peter's the wife. You're taking care of business so he can dink around and do what he likes."

I scowled. "If that's your analogy for a marriage, I can see why you never married." I didn't let her feel the burn from that. I pushed forward. "Peter was given room to do what he does best. He's an inventor in the cyber world. His family has the money it has because of him, and he continues to grow Phoenix Tech every year."

"Right." She continued to stare at me steadily. "And you're not making money?"

"I'm maintaining right now. It's what one does in war."

A slow blink from her.

I saw it then. A flash in her gaze.

"That's the real reason you're here," I said. She was worried about her daughter. I eased back a bit. "Bailey is safe. I've doubled the guards on her and I have secondary security measures for her, ones she doesn't even know about."

"Spent the last week reading up on your grandfather. He's a scary guy."

"Yes. He is." She got no reaction from me. It was knowledge that I'd grown up knowing. I didn't quake to my bones anymore. He'd get that reaction from me only if he got his hands on Bailey, and that was never going to fucking happen. "You got another reason for finding me?"

Her head had lowered during the conversation. It rose again. "You told my daughter Peter and I are sleeping together."

"Yes."

Her eyes cooled. "Why?"

"Because I knew. Because I love your daughter. Because the reason for her to know came up, so I shared." Okay. I wasn't going to play this game, and I wasn't sure if Chrissy was there to start a game or not, but I really wasn't going to let it start. I moved in a step, lowered my head, and spoke softly enough to show respect but hard enough so she didn't think I was babying her. "I have three priorities in life right now, and these are not in order: Protecting the Francis family. Destroying my grandfather. And loving your daughter."

She jerked back a step.

I kept on, not taking the time to wonder which got to her. "If you want to know my thoughts on your daughter, I'll give you the ones you're entitled to. I'm worried about her. She doesn't talk about almost being kidnapped. She's trying to bury herself in schoolwork and she's not pushing to see you guys as much as she should, as much as Bailey before the last kidnapping attempt would. Have I shared these concerns with her? No. I'm giving her time, because she seems to need it for some reason. But am I always there, always worried about her? Fuck yes." It was my turn to raise my chin. "That settle you at all?"

"You two seem to be getting serious, quick."

I felt that one in my gut. "Seems like, yes."

"Bailey doesn't handle things moving too fast. Never has. She needs to be eased into things."

That was another hit to my gut. "You warning me?"

"Yes." No blink. No reaction. She wasn't lying. "She's going to freak at some point, but hold on."

Right. Hold on, because the storm I knew was coming wasn't the only storm coming.

I nodded. "I will."

She nodded too, and began to back away, her hands still in her pockets. "Take care of my girl. If she keeps avoiding me, I'll have to come around. I'll be able to get in if I do?"

I grinned. "I'm thinking yes. Would be an idiot who'd bar the mother of the woman he loved when that mom was coming around to check on her."

She grinned back but didn't reply. Her head ducked as she turned away, and she moved to an SUV that I knew Peter had either given to her or was letting her drive. Maybe there was something more permanent about their sleeping arrangements than I'd originally thought.

Then I stopped considering it, because I had a lunch to get to, a lunch I knew I'd have no appetite for.

TWENTY-SIX

Bailey

Rolling over in bed, I picked up my phone and saw my mom was calling.

I hit Decline, like I had been since Kash told me she and Peter were sleeping together. I didn't know how I felt about that. I didn't know if I could feel a certain way, so I was avoiding. Chrissy would be able to spot me being fake in two seconds, so avoiding was the better option.

And rolling the rest of the way out of bed, I didn't have long.

Three days ago, Kash had lunch with Victoria, so I was also avoiding her and her minions.

I was avoiding Matt, too. Or I was avoiding Naveah.

I stayed in the apartment all weekend and I hacked. I studied. I did coding. I was in computer heaven.

Melissa called on Saturday night to invite me over to Liam's for pizza and the latest gamer console that had come out. Dax and the guys were in their own heaven, but I didn't go. I didn't want to ask if Hoda was attending and I didn't want to put them in the situation where they felt they had to choose one over the other. So, again, I was avoiding.

The only person I wasn't avoiding was Kash, and that was because he came home after lunch. He had a dark and intense look in his gaze as he made his way through the apartment. He picked me up, took me to bed, and he laid claim to me for the rest of the day. The way he was doing it was as if he needed to either brand me into his skin or brand himself into mine. I wasn't altogether complaining, since he made me see stars three times that day.

This life we had was working out just fine by me.

He was a workaholic. So was I. So he'd go and work. I could do the same.

He'd come back in the middle of the night, wake me with his mouth between my legs, and I was purring within the hour.

But it was Monday now and I checked my phone right before hopping into the shower. Melissa.

Today is Peter Francis day! Are you excited?

A second buzz.

I mean, you probably aren't since he's your dad and all, but we're excited. I can already feel the group buzzing. That's how it always is whenever someone from Phoenix Tech comes in. Oh hey. You want me to grab you coffee? I was going to stop at Bucks since it's a treat day for us.

Today was Peter Francis Day.

Jesus. Shit.

I raked a hand over my face.

I wasn't ready for this day, but I typed back.

Me: Whatever that has the most espresso. I don't care. Just load it up.

Melissa: On it! I know exactly what to get you. See you at school!

The !! All the !! So many !!

I was already hoping this day was done and I hadn't gotten into the shower yet.

When I got to school, I got a surprise. I was *invisible*.

I loved it.

People did not give one crap about me.

Melissa hadn't exaggerated, which was also a nice surprise.

They *were* buzzing. There was extra energy in almost everyone, professors, even Busich and Goa, as I spotted both in the hallways. Like everyone else, they didn't blink an eye at me. Not once. There was extra security in the hallways. I recognized some from the Chesapeake Estate, but a few had on Hawking University apparel, so I was assuming the university had kicked in with its own security, too.

When I walked into the computer lab, Melissa shrieked. She almost flew across the room to me, my coffee in hand. "Here," she breathed, pushing the cup to me. "Have you seen him yet?"

My phone had buzzed a few more times this morning.

Kash checking in, like he usually did.

Another call from my mom.

There were two texts from Peter.

I'm going to your class today. Did you want to ride together?

And

I'd like to speak with you before your class. Wait for me outside.

That'd been it.

I hadn't replied to the first one because I didn't get it until I was halfway to the university. And the other . . . I murmured something to Melissa. I didn't know what it was, but it appeased her and she went back to her computer.

I sought out our instructor, told him Peter's request, and he nodded. "Yes. Yes, indeed. Go and wait. We're going over a few items before he comes in, but I'm sure you've already read them, so you won't miss a thing."

Like my advisor, my instructors were quick to realize I was ahead in the class. I knew word got around among the professors about my photographic memory, and after the first week of watching, making sure I didn't take that gift for granted and that I read ahead, and read ahead a lot, all of them eased up on me. Not that I'd been worried. But there was a stereotype of gifted people purposefully pissing away their talent.

I wasn't going to do that. Ever.

I'd lived on the other side, with a single mom who worked double shifts four out of seven nights a week. She worked. She suffered. She sacrificed.

Setting my things down at my normal computer, I took my coffee and phone and went to the hallway to wait.

Hoda was coming in as I was leaving.

We both stopped.

"Oh." Hoda's surprise closed down, her eyelids shuttering. "Sorry." Liam was coming in right after her.

He stopped, stared at me, a slow blink. "Sorry about being an ass Friday night."

"You weren't an ass to me."

"It was your man's place. Your brother I was mouthing off to." He crossed his arms over his chest and gazed down to the floor. His jaw clenched. "I'd be massively stupid to piss off the Francis family. A guy like me, I don't look like a computer person. I look like a jock. I *was* a jock. I was supposed to go pro, until I blew my knee out in a basketball injury. Thank fuck it happened early in my undergrad so I was able to process and get smart. Computers are the only other thing I'm good at, so I don't want to fuck up my future a second time." That tic again from his jawline. "I'm sorry. Can you relay that to your man and your brother?"

"Kash didn't pay attention to you on Friday. He knows you exist. He knows everyone in the room behind us. But what you did Friday night didn't even filter in with him. He's got bigger opponents to demolish. I'm not saying that to be a dick. Just reality."

Liam grinned at the word *demolish*.

"And as for Matt . . . He liked you."

His grin vanished. "You serious?"

I nodded, sighing a little. "Matt's got a warped idea of fun. You made that night fun for him."

"He's got his eye on Melissa."

"He does." It was what it was. "I tell him to back off and he'll take it as a challenge. It's gotta run its course. All I can say."

He nodded, his eyes thoughtful. "I get that." He squinted at me, his head cocked to the side. "That mean we're going to see more of your brother?"

"Yeah." I grinned.

He grinned, too. "Then I better figure out how to handle a future billionaire playboy."

My stomach shrank a little at that phrase, but it was true.

It was something that'd been on my mind, but I hadn't been really giving it much attention. Money. Matt, Seraphina, Cyclone, They all had trust funds set in place. I knew Matt was already getting money from one of his. Peter had money. He had a lot of money. But there'd been no mention of any of that money coming to me.

I didn't know if I wanted to broker that conversation. I didn't know if I even wanted any of his money.

But I grew up poor. Both Chrissy and I were staying in places where we weren't paying the bills. We were getting access to transportation, food. We could pick up a phone and call for anything to be delivered to us. But it wasn't our money.

That meant something to me, and I knew without even talking to my mom that it meant something to her. I didn't know how she was handling it, but she had a job she could go back to. Thinking of that, I didn't know what she was doing. I should know this, but the thought of talking to her about it made my head start swimming. Waves of pressure forced me back down and I gave up the thought.

As soon as I did, I was able to break the surface again. I didn't feel like I was drowning.

That brought me back to me.

Anything could happen.

Kash could decide he suddenly didn't want me. I could get cast out. Chrissy could get cast out. Peter could decide he didn't want us in the family after all.

These were all probably not going to happen, but plan for the end of the world. That's what Hayes women did, because we'd had a few brushes with the end of the world.

My pride wouldn't let me ask about money. I didn't feel right with that option.

So that meant option two. I needed to get a job.

"Bailey."

I sucked in my breath. I hadn't realized he was there, until I saw my father striding down the hallway toward me. Guards were positioned at the ends of our hallways, with a few standing between him and me. People, other students, other professors, other staff came out and stood there, watching a legend in their world walk by them.

I got it.

There was still a little of a fangirl inside of me. She'd been in there since I was little and I grew up worshiping Peter Francis, like everyone else here. He had opened so many doors in our world.

Now that I knew he was my father, and he was sleeping with my mother, it clicked in. I knew what my feelings were on that matter.

He drew abreast and I shared those feelings. "Don't hurt my mother."

He stopped abruptly, his face tightening. He smoothed down his tie. "What?"

"I wasn't sure how I felt about it. It's why I've been ducking her calls. But now I know. I'm worried, and I'm feeling some daughter claws coming out. I know you're sleeping with Chrissy. Kash said it won't work and that Chrissy knows the score. The score being that you're weak when it comes to women. Do not hurt my mother. Just don't."

Peter's gaze skirted around us and he stepped closer. "Bailey."

I moved back, but I lowered my voice. I didn't want this spread, either. "Let her go if you're not serious about her."

My throat was burning.

I didn't want to question why my throat was burning.

He straightened. "What if I *am* serious about her?"

"Then go to therapy. Get your problem in check and *never* hurt her." I held up a finger. "That's the key part of this whole thing."

His face was still tight, but his eyes softened. "Okay. I will."

The burning eased up.

"Just like that? You give in? You're going to therapy?"

His eyes zeroed back on me. "If you go, too."

"What?" I took a step back, hitting the wall behind me. I hadn't seen this turn coming.

"I'll go to therapy if you go back to therapy, too."

My throat started burning again. "Is that why you wanted to see me? To tell me to go to therapy again?"

"No. I wanted to talk to you about the internship at my company. I can't offer it to you, since you're my daughter."

Damn. Dammit. That hurt more than I thought it was going to.

I averted my eyes. "That makes sense." Because of course it did. Of course. I'd been foolish to think for a brief second that I was a shoo-in. There hadn't been a lot of thought put into it. A lot of other things had been happening, but one time I'd considered it.

I shouldn't have.

Just like that, I was back to the first few years. Always applying for a job or an undergrad internship with Phoenix Tech and never getting approved. They gave me scholarships, but no job. No commitment.

I *still* wasn't good enough.

I wasn't looking at him, but I muttered, "Okay. That's fine. I can get an internship somewhere else."

He didn't say anything.

I jerked my head up, still not fully seeing him. "We done here?"

He flinched.

I saw that.

His face got a twisted look on it, and he spoke funny. "I guess.
I'd like to have lunch with you. You haven't been around lately.
Ser and Cy miss you."

I flinched this time. "I miss them, too." But Payton was there.

"I do have another matter I need to talk to you about, but
we can do that at lunch. You'll have lunch with your old man?"
Peter's eyes warmed.

He meant to be teasing, but the pain still sliced me.

"I'll have lunch with my old man."

He smiled. "Good. I'm looking forward to it."

It truly was Peter Francis Day.

We walked into that room and the lesson stopped midspeech.
I'd started to get used to the attention. I hadn't realized until just
then, but it barely fazed me when all eyes came to Peter and me.
He had a hand on my shoulder, a loving smile on his face, and
he squeezed briefly before walking to the front of the lab. The instructor was all smiles and welcoming. Everyone was welcoming,
even Hoda, though she was more reserved than the others.

Dax. Shyam. They were gazing at my dad as if he were their
dad.

He gave a speech, one that was motivating and moving all at
the same time. He talked about a few new programs he'd been
key to creating and how Phoenix Tech was hoping to work
on even better programs in the next year. He talked about how
they were close, and they had exciting new opportunities as well.
Everyone was aware they employed undergraduate interns. I
knew this. He was excited to announce that they not only had
a slot for their usual graduate internship but actually had slots for
two graduate interns.

"As I'm aware you know, we always reserve a graduate spot
for a Hawking student. This year, that's the same plan." He extended a hand toward me. "And I want to make sure to clear any
confusion. We'll not be offering one of those internships to my

daughter, Bailey. What else I want to be clear on is that there are two spaces open, but only one is reserved for a Hawking student. That means the other could also go to a Hawking University student or it could go to someone from the other graduate programs in the nation. This is a first for Phoenix Tech, but I am very excited to see the entries."

He remained, answering questions.

It was explained that our final project in the class would be our application for the internship. We were told to download the instructions, and when I clicked on my link, a separate attachment loaded. It was a note to speak to my instructor at the end of the day, since I would have different guidelines for the final project.

While everyone was going over their own instructions, Peter waited in the back. We were released to start working, but it was really an unofficial option for a one-on-one with Peter Francis.

My classmates took the opportunity.

I sat.

Liam turned in his chair by me. "It's *amazing* that your dad stuck around all morning."

I grinned at him. "You're spending time with Melissa."

He winked before he got serious. "Is this weird for you? Him being your dad and all, and such a big inspiration to everyone here?"

I considered it, glanced around, saw evidence of how he was inspiring.

I shook my head. "No, because I'm one of you guys. He was my hero until I found out he was my father."

"He's not anymore?"

I was eyeing my dad and shrugged. "It's just different. That's all."

"Sucks though, you can't be considered for an internship."

I stopped eyeing my dad and turned back to my computer. My back was turned to the rest of the room. "Yeah. Sucks."

My stomach churned with how much it sucked.

Liam kept on. "Thought for sure, since they said there'd be two openings, one would go to you."

I had, too.

My shoulder was stiff, but I still shrugged. "It's fine. I'll go somewhere else. It's all good. It's better if I earned it, not had it given to me."

"You know . . ." He had lowered his voice, leaning even closer.

I looked over.

His gaze was knowing. "I've seen your work. Sitting next to you, it's hard not to watch you. You do it almost seamlessly. Don't break a sweat, and your work is quality. Why he won't let you into Phoenix Tech is stupid. Your dad ain't that much of a genius if he lets you go somewhere else. I know you think none of the students know, but I noticed. I know Dax has noticed. He's asked questions about you. Hoda, too."

"Hoda?"

His grin was knowing, too. "Why do you think she's so jealous? She thinks you got all the breaks. Iconic father. Genius brain. Looks. Your guy. People like you. But now she knows you have actual talent."

They don't know.

None of them know.

The summer.

The break-in.

A hand over my mouth.

A whisper in my ear: *"They're going to think I raped you . . ."*

A rushing sound was filling my ears.

A pounding was starting behind my forehead.

My vision was starting to blur.

None of them knew.

Liam's voice was beginning to circle around me.

She didn't know shit. Neither did he. None of them did.

None of them knew shit.

That's what I knew.

None of them knew shit.

That's what I learned.

None of them knew shit.

"You are a problem . . ."

"Jesus! Bailey!"

None of them knew shit.

"Bailey. Honey." That was my dad.

"Once you're gone . . ."

Fingers were on my hands.

None of them knew shit.

They were trying to pry me away from something.

None of them knew shit.

My stomach was churning.

Churning.

Churning.

None of them knew shit.

"Bailey! Stop it."

I was ripped away and yanked out of whatever I was in.

I was being held back.

Two of my nails were split down, half off my finger. I was shaking, and my hands were completely white except for the blood. White and red. I was barely standing.

I looked up. Peter was holding me, his eyes concerned. "Bailey—"

I shoved out of his arms, grabbed my bag, and hightailed it out of there.

I was in the hallway.

I was running almost blindly for the bathroom.

I needed to get ahold of myself. Clear my head. Clean my hands. I hit the door running and collapsed inside. I couldn't go to the sink. I was on the floor. On my knees. I was shaking so much, I couldn't stand up.

I kept trying.

I'd push, and I'd fall.

Again.

And again.

And again.

Then I gave up, except I pushed back so I was blocking the door. There. Curled on my side. I moved into a ball and I let the storm hit.

I gave in.

TWENTY-SEVEN

Kash

I parked at the school and I was sprinting.

Cameras were there. Press. I knew Peter was visiting, so I wasn't surprised word had leaked. He and his daughter at the same place—that would hit gossip sites all over. I was distinctly aware of Erik running to meet me, except he ran past me. I tossed him my car keys and I was through the door when I heard my car's engine starting again.

I didn't need to ask.

The guards were waiting. They pointed me down the right hallway, and halfway down was a crowd. A few of Bailey's friends were there, kneeling at a door. Peter was pacing. Seeing me, he stopped and pointed at the closed door. "She's barred herself in there."

His voice was panicked.

A couple of others heard him and twisted around, surprised.

I was guessing he'd kept it together until he saw me. It was what Peter did. He held it up, then I came in, and he let it all on my shoulders.

This . . . this was on my shoulders. Bailey was more mine than his. I nodded to him, knowing I was grim, almost as grim as him. "I got it. Take off."

He didn't.

"Take off, Peter."

He nodded, but he was still hesitating. He was torn, his eyelid twitching as he looked at the closed door.

"Peter."

"I was supposed to take her for lunch. I was going to tell her that she's already getting job offers from companies but they're waiting for me. They're doing it out of respect, or not to piss me off. I was going to offer her a job today, and now she's in there, and she's holed herself in there." His voice hitched. "*My daughter has barred—*"

"I know." I didn't have time for this shit.

"You don't. You didn't see her . . ."

Fine. He needed an explanation. I'd give him the truth. Whoever got this, I'd hunt them down if this was leaked.

I stepped close and I got in his face. "She was kidnapped. By your wife."

He stopped.

Everyone stopped.

My words echoed, and a pin could've been heard if it fell.

I knew my tone was ragged, but my God, he was keeping me from my woman. I couldn't contain that. "It was only minutes, but she was taken. She heard them. She knew that, in that second, she was dead. That shit's never happened to you. Cy was taken, too. Neither was gone long, but it didn't matter, because in that moment, they were both *taken*. They were helpless. And they both knew they were going to die. Thank the fuck Christ that Cy was too young to remember, but she does, and she's not dealing, and I knew this was going to happen. It's good it's happening now. That means the inner wheels are working and she's getting closer to healing than I thought."

Peter was like a ghost, staring back at me. Haunted. He blanched. "You think this is *good* it's happening?"

"She's gotta break down before she can stand up. This is

good. Now, if you can get *your* shit together, I need to see to my woman."

He nodded quickly and hurried back a step. "Right. Yes. Right."

I moved past him.

"Kash!"

I paused.

"Take care of her."

I kept to the door. "That's the plan."

I took a second to identify the people at the door. The guy and girl from Naveah. I didn't have a brain like Peter and Bailey, but I could pull up information if I really needed it. Details were fuzzy, but I remembered their names. Melissa and Liam. There was a woman, too.

I focused on the woman, a brief recognition flickering. "Professor?"

She nodded. "Her advisor. Ms. Wells."

That would explain the two calls I got, one from Peter and one from someone I didn't take time to answer. She had my number.

"Right." I gestured to both of them. "Move."

"We think she's—" the guy started.

"Move!"

He did, not giving a shit I'd barked at him. "We think she's on the ground. We can't tell, but—"

"Shut up," I growled, kneeling down. And I listened.

I could hear her.

Fuck. I could hear her.

She was sobbing. And shaking. And they were right. She was right on the other side of the door.

I motioned to the closest guard. It was Connor. "You got tools?" I gestured to the hinges. "I want this door off, now."

He had a hand to his ear, moving away.

It didn't take long before they located a janitor, who came rushing in with the right tools. I stepped back and we watched him work. If it were another day and another place, I'd give

Connor shit about never not working. The guy was on all day and night. But I didn't, and instead I just made a note to look into his file and his time clock.

The door was done in record time.

Connor, Fitz, and the janitor helped to lift it clear.

Bailey was curled in a ball, her arms wrapped around herself, her body as white as a sheet. I stifled a curse, ignored the gasps from those who saw her, and bent in. Gathering her in my arms, I motioned to Peter. "Cover her. Your coat."

He took it off, tucking it in place so it wouldn't fall, and then we were striding out of there. Everything else would work itself out. Just needed to have my girl in my arms.

We were clearing the door. I expected a crazy scene, and there was one, but I paused at seeing Erik walking up from my car, which he'd pulled back to the curb.

His face was set in stone.

At that, I knew.

My arms tightened around Bailey, feeling one part of me settle at just having her there, but the other part twisted up at his face.

I *knew.*

Peter was with me, and he braked behind, seeing Erik. Our guards were fanning around us, lining up so they were a wall and giving us a modicum of privacy.

Erik glanced at Bailey before looking at me. "Quinn made bail."

"*What?*" Peter exploded. "That bail was set at ten million. She's a flight risk. Who did that?"

I'd been waiting for him to act. I knew a strike was coming.

Here it was.

Erik told me, "Calhoun Bastian."

See? I knew.

TWENTY-EIGHT

Bailey

I woke.

It was dark.

My head was pounding.

I could feel the dried tears on my face.

The memories started coming back to me. One after another. They filled my head.

I lost my shit.

Straight-up. I completely lost my shit.

Fuck, fuck, *fuck*.

The door opened. Light shone in.

Kash was coming into the bedroom, a bottle of water in hand. "Hey."

My head was still pounding. I groaned, rolling to the edge of the bed. I was in my sleeping tank top and underwear.

The bed depressed as Kash sat next to me, taking my hand and placing a couple of painkillers in it. "Take those. Drink this." The water was next. I popped the pills in, swallowed, and my throat was parched, so I drank half the bottle before handing it back to Kash.

"What do you remember?"

God. He was being sympathetic and kind, and that was making

me lose my shit all over again. I could feel the emotions clogging my throat, but I forced myself to chill out. Stop. Clear the head. Shove that crap back down. I wasn't going to crumble again. No way.

My nostrils flared as I forced air back out—that was the effort it took to stop the waterworks from having a repeat show.

"I remember the bathroom, and losing it."

He shifted, putting the water on the nightstand next to me. His hand came to my back. "You feeling nauseous at all?"

I shook my head.

"Pain?"

"Just a headache."

That was enough.

Kash had an arm underneath me and I was flipped over in bed, then hauled back so I was on his lap. His back was to the headboard and he was cradling me. My head was against his shoulder and chest, and he was rubbing a hand up and down my thigh.

I felt his lips press behind my ear before moving down to my neck, then my shoulder. He moved my tank top strap aside, lingering where it had been resting over my skin. "Fuck. I love you." A beat later: "Are you okay?"

My throat clogged up. I nodded.

I couldn't speak for a second, remembering what had happened.

His arms flexed around me before he was turning me.

He rolled me to my back and loomed over me. His gaze was dark, serious.

"What happened?"

God. It washed over me again.

I closed my eyes, trying to shove it back. I needed to hold it at bay.

My voice came out raspy. "A panic attack."

His eyes flashed. Fierce. "Why?"

I shrugged, looking up at him. "Trauma?"

His mouth flattened. "You know what I'm talking about. What brought it on?"

I looked away. This hurt. This was me being vulnerable in a way that sex could never make me feel exposed. I was raw on a whole other level.

I said, "I was triggered. I think. But who knows what brings those on sometimes. Might've been the mix of Peter being at my school. Or Liam talking about how great my life is. Suddenly I was back in my bedroom. That guy was pushing me against the wall, telling me an attack was coming."

It was there again, pushing to be set free. It was in the back corner of my mind.

I couldn't let it out. I did, and it would take over.

He eased me back, a finger pushing against my stomach. "Are you okay?"

His words were so soft.

He was looking at me with such tenderness.

I was almost not able to handle him looking at me that way. A girl could cry, seeing love like that looking back at her.

His hands smoothed up both of my sides, a trail of warmth and shivers coming after.

"Let me in." He pushed on my hip. "Tell me more."

I sighed. My hands went up his arms, curling over his shoulders, then moving to his neck. "I lost it."

My lungs were rattled.

I told him what I could handle telling.

"I applied four times for one of their undergraduate internships. Got turned down every time, and I shouldn't have. I was one of the best of the applicants, but I was rejected *every year*. Got the scholarships, but not me being in their building, learning from them. I was back there, feeling that same way and listening to Liam talk about how great Hoda thought my life was, how cool it was for me to have Peter Francis as my dad . . ." I had to stop. My throat was shrinking, as if a piece of bark had been pushed in there. "All I kept thinking was that they didn't know shit. Over and over again. And then Quinn was in front of me." I shuddered. "Heard her voice. Felt when she drugged me. It all went black."

I was trembling again, remembering.

"I came to and Peter was holding me. I was bleeding. Then I bolted. I didn't want anyone to see me like that, and I wanted somewhere safe so I could regroup, get control of myself."

I lifted my eyes, and it took effort. My head was encased in cement, and I could barely see him through the sludge.

My voice broke, whispering, "I felt you pick me up, and that was it for me. I knew I could disappear completely. You had me. You'd take care of me."

His hands sank into my hips at my words. He closed his eyes. "Shit." A hiss from him. He bent forward, his forehead resting against mine, and he raised a hand to cup the side of my face. "I'm struggling here, because what you need to hear and what you want to hear are two separate things."

I eased back.

"What do I need to hear?"

His eyes slid to mine, looking raw. "You cut your counseling too quick."

Oh. Oh no.

He was right. I did not want to hear those words. I began to ease away from him, but his hands tightened, holding me in place.

"You gotta talk, B. If not to a counselor, then to me, and if not me, then someone."

"I *have* talked to you—"

"Not enough." His words were gruff. "Not enough. You gotta talk more, and you need someone to guide you there, to really get all that crap that went on during the kidnapping. You need help shoveling all that shit out. I can be here. I can be a listening ear, hold you, kiss you, make you feel and think other things, but I'm not a pro. You need someone who knows trauma, and you've been traumatized. I heard how your voice went soft when you said the word. I felt your pulse skip a beat. Nothing wrong with admitting to being traumatized."

Nope.

Hands to his chest, I shoved out of his arms and slid across the bed.

I wasn't fast enough.

He snaked after me, grabbing me, and he hauled me back in his arms.

"Let me go!"

"No."

He just held me in a cement hold, but he didn't pull us back to the bed. "Okay. If you don't want to talk in bed, we'll talk somewhere else."

We were up and moving, and we were going to the shower.

I relaxed slightly.

He turned the water on, set me on the counter. "It's not going to be that type of shower, babe."

Babe. I gritted my teeth. "I'm not liking the use of that word right now."

"Don't care."

He was taking his clothes off.

My shirt was off.

My underwear next.

He lifted me back again, carrying me into the shower. He backed me all the way against the wall, the water coming down on us, and he lowered his head so he was staring directly into my eyes. "I see you're dealing, but you're not. You're barely treading water. You're submerging yourself so much that you don't even know you stopped breathing long ago. Bailey." He sighed, a caress of his breath against my face. He lowered his forehead to mine again, his lips brushing over me. "I need you with me. This fight against my grandfather, it's the hardest thing I've ever done. He's making moves every day. I'm countering him, and that's just business. I gotta tell you something, but you can't freak. You can't panic. You have to promise me that you trust me. Do you trust me?"

Oh God. What happened?

But I was nodding without even thinking about it. I did trust Kash. I trusted him more than I trusted myself.

"Good." His thumb rubbed over my cheek. "He posted bail for Quinn."

I stiffened.

Feeling that, he said, "That's his first move that he scored a hit. His first *personal* move."

"Aren't they all personal?"

I lashed out those words, but I was reeling inside.

Quinn was out. Quinn was free.

Quinn could do it all over again.

I began to pull away. "I have to go—"

He moved me back against the wall.

"No! Kash—" Another try.

His hips helped to anchor me this time.

"Kash, stop it. I have to go—"

He buried his head in my neck. His hand went down to my hip, and he lifted it as he moved between my legs. "No, babe. You're not going. You're not running." His other hand went down my other hip, and he lifted that leg, too.

I was completely suspended in the air, being pressed against the wall, and I felt him at my entrance.

But he didn't move in.

I wanted him to move in.

"Kash." His name was a plea from me. I wanted him. I wanted him to make me forget.

The panic.

I couldn't deal.

It was rising.

It was threatening me.

It was choking me.

I gasped, searching for his mouth at the same time. "I need—"

His hand raised up, catching my face, and he paused, his lips over mine. "What do you need?"

What did I need?

Fear was shoving through. Desire was stomping it down.

Hysteria was there, trying to climb up. Inch by inch.

Pleasure, as he began dropping kisses down my jawline, pushed that down, too.

I was in a state of upheaval. One side pushed. The other side pulled. So many emotions were swirling, fighting, and then I latched on to his head.

I pulled him back.

I made him look into my eyes.

I told him what I needed.

Me.

I decided.

"You said this wasn't going to be that kind of shower."

His eyes darkened. "I wasn't intending it to be. Clothes got taken off and I wasn't fully thinking things through." He waited a beat, though he knew. He knew. "What do you need, B.? I'll give it to you." He bent in, a tender kiss to my mouth. "I'll give you anything in the world."

"You want me to talk? You talk."

He tried to pull away.

My hands held him firm. My legs wound tighter around him.

I added roughly, "I want to know every move your grandfather is making. I want to know every move *you're* making."

His eyes were hot and smoldering. "Sometimes I make moves spur-of-the-moment. Can't run all of them by you."

"Then run what you can by me. I want to be a part of it. It's the only way I'll beat what's inside of me."

I had to know.

I had to be prepared.

I couldn't have another hand over my mouth, a voice whispering in my ear that men are going to break in.

I couldn't take another pinprick that makes the world go black.

I hated the rough hands, the rough handling.

The drug in me.

No more of those moments, so that meant I had to know instead.

He was studying me, then nodded. "Okay. Deal." He nipped my lips with his, and I felt him grin against them. "What else do you need?"

I reached down, found him, wrapped my hand around him, and moved over him. "What do you think?"

That said, he pushed inside at the same time I sank down.

He gave me exactly what else I wanted.

I pulled a shirt over my head later. "How bad was it, really?"

We were both getting dressed after the shower, and my stomach growled the introduction to a composition by the next Bach prodigy. Kash lifted his head, grinned at me, and patted my tummy. "I'll order pizza. You need food."

It was after one in the morning, but Kash didn't care.

It'd been a while since I ordered pizza after midnight.

He walked past me, his own T-shirt falling down to mold so perfectly and so yummy over his backside. "Bad, but not many were actually there. Only a few."

I trailed after him to the living room. Both of us had pulled on sweatpants, and they were heaven on skin. If I could find the same sweatpants, looking like jeans, I'd buy the entire company in stock. Genius.

"What do you mean? Who?"

I was asking about my meltdown. Kash was trying not to answer my questions. It was annoying.

"Your buds. Your advisor. The guards. Peter."

I frowned, braking in the middle of the living room. "That's a lot."

He threw me a look, grabbing up his phone. "It wasn't. Really. And who cares. You're human, Bailey. The shit you went through, you were gonna crash. If you think you weren't, you're only fooling yourself." He waved his phone in the air. "Pull up some psych text on trauma, read it into that head of yours, and you'll know I'm right."

Shit.

He was right.

Still.

Annoying.

I grabbed some water, and thinking on it a second, I poured a glass of wine for myself. Kash wouldn't want one. Taking both beverages into the living room, I curled up on the couch and settled in. Kash ordered the pizza, went to the door and let the guards know, then came back. He paused before me and took in the wine in my hand. "Put it down."

I did.

He scooped me up, depositing me so I was on his lap. Then he reached for the wine and handed it back. His arms wrapped around me and he nuzzled into my neck. "Better."

I relaxed back into him. He was right. Much better.

"There's going to be a banquet at the end of your semester. Peter talked to me about it. He wants to invite all your classmates and announce the internship winners."

Okay. Not as much better anymore.

Kash slid a hand under my top and it splayed out over my stomach. His thumb started rubbing back and forth. "He'll be pissed I'm telling you, because he wants to do it, but you gotta know."

My breath was suspended.

He nuzzled just behind my ear. "He's getting companies interested in you."

"Other internships?"

"No. Jobs. They already want to make a job offer, but they're waiting so they don't piss him off. You weren't going to get the internship, because your dad was going to offer you a job at lunch today."

That's why he wanted to go out afterward.

"Oh my God."

He kissed my jaw. "Whatever you decide, congratulations, but I need to inject my two cents. I think you could write some program like your dad. I think yours could blow his out of the water, and I think you could be your own boss. That's what I'd do, but it's not my decision. It's yours."

My bank account was seriously dwindling. A job would help cushion that.

I'd already laid so much at Kash's feet to deal with. I'd figure the job out later, but I turned and met his gaze. He grinned. I grinned. We were both grinning, and I knew we were both happy right then and there. That was important. That was good.

"I love you."

His eyes grew tender. "I love you, too."

There were words to say. I wanted to know more about my meltdown. Kash was going to avoid it, but it was because he knew that wasn't a good experience for me to relive. But I was okay with it.

In that moment, warmth seeped all over in me, and I didn't think it was the wine.

TWENTY-NINE

We were no longer newsworthy.

With Quinn being released, her face was front and center on every news program, every magazine, and every blog I saw. News of her impending divorce from Peter Francis was the second story trending on social media. There were still mentions of Kash and me, but it was mostly Quinn, then Quinn and Peter. Because of his connection, because he'd slept with Amanda Bonham, whose husband had had an affair with Quinn, Matt was getting a lot of attention on the gossip sites as well.

The affair world was going round and round.

I was happy. Things at school got a lot more manageable. Not so many people lingering outside the building. We could go for lunch with two guards again.

So things were getting relatively more normal, and that word was subjective because my "normal" would never be what it used to be. That extended to my classmates, too. I worried how they'd react, my first day back after the meltdown, but nothing was said. No one acted differently. The only odd thing was that Hoda seemed less hostile, but I was still avoiding her, so I couldn't be certain that was true.

It wasn't until the next Friday, when Melissa was leaving our last class with me, that my suspicion was confirmed.

Erik had the day off, so Scott was walking behind us. Fitz was in the car, and Liam was going ahead of us, as he'd taken to doing since that first trek to lunch with everyone.

"Kash"—Melissa blushed saying his name—"didn't tell you?"

"Tell me what?"

"He lit into your dad that day. You know." She moved closer, her head ducking. "The bathroom incident."

That was *her* phrase for it. Now I knew.

"Your dad was freaking out, saying, 'My daughter has barred herself in the bathroom,' and he was getting hysterical about it, but also kinda pissy about it. Like it was Kash's fault or something. Then suddenly your guy rounded on him and was like, 'She was kidnapped. By your wife.' And I swear to God, everyone stopped what they were doing. It got eerily quiet in the hallway, but he didn't care one bit. He went on talking about how you and some-one named Cy had been taken, and it didn't matter it was only a few moments, because you were taken. You were helpless, and you knew you were dead.

"When he said that, something happened. I don't know what. I don't think he noticed, but I looked back and Hoda was standing just inside the lab's door. She heard, and her eyes were so big, they could've swallowed a bat if a bat had flown at her. You weren't here the next day, but she came in different. Me. Liam. All of us. And Ms. Wells. Her, too.

"I guess just hearing about you being kidnapped was enough. The dangers you deal with . . . It all got scary real, and you're no longer the cool and exciting Peter Francis's daughter to us. You're Bailey. You're one of us, and I don't want to lose you. Not like that."

She cursed under her breath. "Not that you're not one of us, but you know. Or. Maybe you don't. I'm messing this all up. I'm just trying to say, all the dangers, the reasons you have these guards in the first place, got really real for us. We're in. You're ours. Dax. The guys were pissed about what Hoda did to you. They were just mad before. Now they're scared. We're all scared." She looked at me, stopping in the sidewalk. "We're all scared for you. And I need to stop repeating myself. You get my drift."

Oh.

Jesus.

I didn't know how to take any of that.

She might've seen my struggle, because she just mustered a smile. "Not trying to freak you out. I was trying to comfort you. I'm messing that up, too."

"No." I relaxed. I really did. "You're fine, and thank you. I think."

Her grin was crooked.

"Bailey."

We looked back. Ms. Wells was coming out of the door. She raised a hand. "We need to talk about your upcoming schedule. Come to my office next week."

I nodded, relaxing even more.

I loved this. Schoolwork. Talking about my schedule. A boulder of unease moved aside and my smile wasn't forced. "I will, Ms. Wells."

She grinned back, a small one, and her eyes narrowed on me a second.

Then Scott cleared his throat behind me. "We're holding up traffic, Bailey."

I shot him an approving look. He kept calling me Miss Bailey. I kept not responding unless he dropped the Miss part. My job was done.

"Be there in a second."

He moved for the door handle.

"What are you doing this weekend?" Melissa asked.

I thought about it. "I don't know. Kash hasn't mentioned anything. What are you doing?"

"I don't know if you'd be interested, but um, some of the others talked about going to the football game. I know we're grad students, but the game is a big one. Liam knows some of the players on the team. It's homecoming, too."

Crap. It was?

I hadn't paid attention. Life in our graduate hall was different than it was for the rest of the students. We dressed the same, but it was different with us. We were on the cusp of our next move into our future, into the jobs that we'd have for the next twenty years. Or so we hoped.

Since this summer, I was focused on family, on school, and on Kash. Nothing else got in there—except the longing to remember what it was like to be normal. It surged back up in me with a renewed fervor.

Homecoming.

Wow.

A football game. A college football game.

I never went during my own undergraduate years.

Suddenly, that was the *only* thing I wanted to do.

It would be different. We were in graduate school, but I wanted to go. I wanted that normalcy.

"You want to go? I mean . . ." She was scanning my face. "Our team is D1. It's not just a student thing, you know? People all over come for the games. The team is a big deal. We could make you incognito. I exchanged numbers with that Torie girl. She talked about 'doing you over' one time. She and her friend looked real savvy with hair and makeup. I bet they could make you look like a totally different person if they wanted."

God. I really, really wanted to go.

Feeling eyes on me, I glanced over my shoulder. Erik was there, his gaze locked on me.

I felt the hairs on the back of my neck stand up, but I didn't care.

I told her, "I want to go."

Her eyebrows shot up. "Really?"

"Yes. Really." I nodded, and I nodded some more. I really wanted to go. "Be at your place, tomorrow?"

"Yeah!" Her eyes were dancing. Her cheeks had flushed. "Game's at three. Come over at half past one. Plenty of time to get over there."

She was functioning as if I wouldn't have guards. I knew I wouldn't be able to give them the slip, but I didn't tell her just yet. Tomorrow.

"Great. See you tomorrow."

She gave me another grin before tugging her backpack over her shoulder and saying her good-byes. Veering down the sidewalk, she even waved to Scott, who only looked at me.

I approached the SUV. Before he opened the door, he said, "You know you can't go without us."

"I know."

He nodded. "I'll tell Mr. Colello. He'll start making plans."

That was the crux of my life. Now.

I couldn't go somewhere without security measures and protocols put in place. The only thing is that I didn't care at that moment. I was hoping to go incognito, get my guards to be as incognito as possible, and pretend I was normal for a day.

That was the hope. I was excited!

Scott opened my door—and I stared at Chrissy Hayes, sitting inside.

She put her magazine away and arched an eyebrow. "Hello, my daughter who has been avoiding her mother for way too long."

I was busted.

THIRTY

Kash

My phone rang at the same time that Matt walked into my office.

I hit the Accept button, putting it on speakerphone. "Yes?"

"Bailey just accepted her classmate's invitation to attend Hawking University's football game tomorrow."

I rolled back in my chair. "She did what?"

"Yes!" Matt pumped his hands in the air. "Finally my sister is doing something normal."

I glared at him.

He ignored me.

Scott continued, "She's supposed to be at her classmate's apartment tomorrow at one thirty. Game is at three p.m. The other male student knows some of the football players." He paused. "It's homecoming, sir."

Of course it was. Homecoming.

I scowled at Matt, who was still pumping his hands in the air, but at least he was doing it silently.

"Call the university. Start security talks."

"On it."

I hung up with him and amped up my scowl at Matt. "You could *pretend* to be concerned."

Matt waved his hand in the air, dismissing me, and dropped

into the seat across from me. He threw a leg up over one of the armrests, twisting his body so he was more sitting sideways. His arm went up on the back. "Whatever. Act all pissy. You and I both know this is a good sign. Bailes is getting normal again. A football game. That's good, Kash. Plus, I'm pretty sure my dad has season tickets for the company. They're always reserved. I tried getting them last year and it was a no-go. Some of the shareholders are greedy football alum from Hawking."

He was right.

Some of my scowl faded.

Shit. He was right.

"You couldn't get even one ticket?"

Matt smirked. "I didn't try too hard, but Hawking football is big."

"There's thirty different angles my grandfather could use to have someone hurt her there."

Matt's grin turned knowing. And wicked. "Like you're not going to call and secure a private box to help eliminate twenty-eight of those ways."

I sighed. My hand was itching to do it, but I knew I couldn't. Because unlike Matt, I knew the real reason she said yes to the game.

"She'll want to be in the stands."

He caught on, real quick. "You're right. She'll want to be as normal as possible."

Which meant I couldn't call for security protocols, but I wanted to. And I might anyway.

"If she goes in as normal as possible, word might not get to him until the game is done." Matt was following my wavelength.

Exactly.

My scowl came back. It just wasn't directed at him. "I don't like it."

"But you're not going to stop it."

Dammit. I wasn't going to stop it.

I eyed him instead. "Want to go to a football game tomorrow?"

That wicked grin popped back up. "Only if I can use the family's private jet to go to Aspen later. I know you can approve that."

"What?"

THIRTY-ONE

Bailey

"Mom."

She glared at me as I got inside the SUV. "Don't 'Mom' me. I've been 'Chrissy' for the last ten years. Don't try to manipulate me by being all sweet and lovey."

Yep. She was here for a fight.

And once I was settled and the vehicle was pulling forward, she started.

"You've been avoiding me. I don't like when my daughter who went through a recent trauma is avoiding me, and I don't care how big and bad your boyfriend is. A girl always needs her mama." She turned for the window, sniffling. "Or maybe her mama needs her girl? Either way, there was a whole bunch of need happening and my girl isn't picking up her phone." Those eyes turned glacial again. "Stop avoiding me."

Okay. I wasn't going to beat around the bush, either. "I know you're sleeping with Peter."

"That's none of your business."

"You're my mom. He's my dad. It's going to mess up my mind, and I avoided your calls because I didn't know how I felt about it."

"You know now?"

I nodded.

"Well?" Her eyebrow arched up. "You going to keep me in suspense? I had to be all ninja-like and sequester myself in your vehicle. You think that was easy?"

I hid a grin because man, I'd missed my mom.

"I don't want him to hurt you. That's what I decided."

She sucked in more breath, her head rising. She blinked a few times. "Damn. *Damn*." A pause. "You tell him that?"

I nodded again.

"When?"

"What?"

"When did you tell him that?"

"Uh." I had to retrace the days to my bathroom meltdown. "Monday."

Her eyes grew sharp. "He was here on Monday. Said you got upset. I was waiting all week for you to call, but my phone never rang. Not from you."

"I was out all week. I didn't go to school."

"What'd you do?"

I frowned at her.

"Right." She was nodding now, glancing back out the window. "You got that man of yours. With him all week. With him all the time, but I know you. I know my daughter and I know you've buried your head in your studies and in him. Am I right?" Her nostrils were flaring. It was costing her to say these words. "I know I'm right. I know you better than *anyone*."

"Yes. You do." I said those words softly.

"A mother knows her child. Always does, even ones that at some point had to become the adult in the relationship. Even ones who have a brain that's special, and especially ones with a mother who is up at all hours of the night worrying because she knows, *she knows* that that special child can't stop thinking about what happened to her, because she's got a brain that's on constant replay." She broke, her top lip trembling. Her voice grew hoarse. "Tell me you haven't been reliving what happened to you over and over again. Tell me that and I'll ease up on you a bit."

My mouth parted. "No." That's what she thought? I scooted forward, laying a hand on her arm. "No, Mom."

Her hand grasped mine, holding it tight.

"You were right the first time. I buried my head in schoolwork and in Kash. And I've been getting to know my classmates."

"Good." She swiped at her cheek, sniffled, and still holding my hand in a cement grip, she looked out the window. "Good. They're good kids?"

I knew what she was really asking. "They're normal."

They weren't like Matt or Tony or Chester. Or Victoria.

"You need normal right now."

"I'm going to the football game tomorrow." I curved up a corner of my mouth. "That normal enough?"

She barked out a laugh, still not looking at me, my hand still in a vise grip. "You never went before. Good you're going now. I'd like these classmates?"

I thought of Melissa. Liam.

"You would think Melissa was funny and you'd try to get me to date Liam."

A second laugh barked from her. "Good then." She glanced at me from the corner of her eye. "And that's not happening? You and this guy you think I'd want you to date?"

My smile turned soft. "No. It's not happening. I love Kash."

She closed her eyes, bending her head a little. "Right. You love someone whose grandfather is wealthy beyond wealthy and trying to hurt his grandson. He'll take aim through my daughter, and I'm not okay with that. I'm not okay with that!" Her eyes opened and they were piercing me. "I didn't keep you all my life without having a father only to have you smack in the line of fire. I am not okay with that."

"Mom." My throat was seizing. Emotions were clogging it up.

"I'll leave him. You leave yours. We'll go back to Brookley. The hospital's waiting for me to decide if I'm staying or coming back. You can remain at Hawking, like the original plan, but we'll forget them. We can still do it." Her voice was trembling. Her hand was shaking. "We can still go back. Let's go back, honey. Let's go back to being normal."

So I wasn't the only one struggling with the changes.

But it was too late.

She saw the look in my eyes and closed hers again. Her hand let go of mine, and she faced the window. "Right." Her head hung down. "Right."

There were no other words that could take away what she saw in mine.

She was scared. She wanted to run, but I couldn't. I loved Kash too much. I loved my siblings too much.

I scooted over to her, wrapped an arm around her shoulders, and pulled her to my chest.

I cradled my mom like she was my child, and she wrapped an arm around me, hugging me just as tight. I rested the side of my head against hers, and as her eyes remained closed the rest of the drive, I was the one who watched the outside world passing us by.

THIRTY-TWO

On game day, I texted Melissa I was outside.

She wasn't prepared for the vision she got when she came down to the SUV.

Me, in full Hawking garb. I was decked out in jeans, a gray Hawking hoodie with the maroon letters spelled out over the front, Hawking gloves, and a Hawking stocking hat.

Next to me was Kash, in jeans and a Hawking University black blazer. He had a Hawking ball cap on and pulled low, which made me swoon when I first saw him. The cap hid his eyes, but not that square jawline. And his jeans and blazer made me want to jump him. Kash was hot on a normal day, but he was sizzling dressed as a normal person. He even had a different posture, which I don't know if he was aware of doing, but it worked. His shoulders were lowered a little, bunched down, so his athletic frame still made the mouth water.

Still so damned gorgeous.

And we weren't alone.

Matt joined us, too. He went all out even more in Hawking apparel.

A maroon Hawking hoodie with the warm-ups that players wore before a basketball game, maroon colors and "Hawking" stretched up the side of his leg. He had a maroon stocking cap on, a Hawking maroon scarf wrapped around his neck, and he waved the Hawking colored pom-poms. Maroon-and-gray-colored fabric ribbons attached to two sticks of wood.

"Whoa."

The front door of the SUV opened and Scott came out, look-ing similar to us except he was in jeans and a gray sweatshirt. No Hawking letters anywhere. He would blend in with everyone.

Fitz was dressed similarly, too.

"Well, get in." Matt was impatient, waving a pom-pom at me. "We have a game to scope out, blend in with, and in no way at all draw any extra attention to ourselves." He waved that pom-pom again, giving Kash a wicked grin. "Right, bud?"

Kash scowled at him, lounging back in the seat next to me. "Keep talking, Matt. I'm sure we can do something else to make you 'blend.'"

Matt scowled back. His tone was amused, though. "Not fun, Kash. Not fun."

"Going to a game with two guards, not having a full meeting ahead of time with the security staff, is not my idea of fun."

I leaned into Kash's side.

He might be tense, but he was going for me, and we'd had a full conversation the night before about whether we should no-tify campus security or not. Somehow it was decided to go and try not to draw much attention to us. I didn't know if it would work, but we were going to try. Skating under the radar was the plan.

Matt, on the other hand, had no idea how to not draw atten-tion to himself. The pom-poms were a prime example. Melissa climbed in and took the seat next to Matt. She glanced to me. "Liam was going to save us seats by him and his friends."

"I thought his friends were on the team."

Melissa had never had Kash speak to her, and it was notice-able. Her eyes got big, and she froze a second. "I know. But . . ." She seemed to lose her train of thought. "Oh. No. He does, but he's friends with other guys, too. He was big into sports before his injury, so most of his friends are on the basketball team."

Kash cursed. "We can't sit by them."

Matt frowned at him. "Why not? You look like an athlete. I

have a 'trim figure' myself. And Scott and Fitz are tall. They'll blend. Especially with basketball guys."

"Athletes draw attention. That's what we don't want to do."

"I think it's perfect. Jocks usually hang in large groups, so when people are looking, they'll be looking at the players they already know. They'll skip over faces they don't know, and your face is half hidden with that hat. With how she's dressed, Bailey looks like all the other college girls that'll be hanging around the jocks. Her hair is hidden, so it's just her face they'd recognize her off of, and I'll make friends. People will think I'm just another jock that doesn't start. It'll be great."

"I still don't like it."

Matt's eyes flicked upward. "What a shock. We're still doing it and you know it. Deal with it."

Kash grunted. I didn't think he'd get over it, but Matt was right. We were still going to do it.

But he needed to cool down and not be so uptight, because people noticed him, and they'd definitely see his intensity. Like, now Melissa was firmly captivated with him, and I doubted she was aware of it. Her eyes kept returning to him, staying, and her face would get red before she jerked her gaze away. As we drove to the football stadium, it happened over and over again.

When we parked, Matt got out and glared at Fitz.

Fitz just lowered his head and grinned.

Scott laughed, clapping a hand on Matt's shoulder. "We're normal students. That means parking and hauling ass to the stadium, just like everyone else."

"You couldn't have dropped us off at the front and let us walk in? Lots of people are doing that, too."

Scott and Fitz both shared a grin with Kash.

"It was my call. We're walking. *Deal with it.*"

Matt just growled, "Asshole."

"Privileged schmuck," Kash shot back, his eyes sparking.

He was enjoying this. So was Matt. The two walked beside each other, sharing jabs. They were almost in their own world.

Melissa fell in step next to me. "Are they always like that?"

I was just as awed as she was.

Kash wasn't Kash right now. Or at least, he wasn't the guy who was worried his grandfather was going to swoop in and try to kill us. This was Kash how he must've been while growing up with Matt and the rest of the family.

He was more carefree.

Matt's hand reached out to punch Kash in the shoulder. Kash twisted, and caught him by his wrist. Matt said something. Kash returned with words, and my brother's head tipped back. A full laugh came from him, and Kash's head ducked, but we caught the side profile for a second. He was lightly grinning, and that vision swept through me. A rush of warmth flooded me.

I'd never seen this. Not once.

I salivated for more.

Fitz leaned in, saying quietly, "Yes." He glanced at me, and I knew he was responding for me. "This is their 'brother' dynamic."

Matt exploded with an *"Are you fucking kidding me?"*

Kash's head bent down, but we all heard him throw back, "Deal with it, Matthew. Fucking deal with it."

"Oh my God! Let it go!" But Matt was laughing.

He threw an arm around Kash's shoulder before Kash shoved him off, a soft punch to Matt's chest as he did. More laughter from Matt, and I could visibly see the stress melt from Kash's shoulders. They grew less rigid, looser.

I glanced back to Fitz. "Does Matt know *how* to not draw attention to himself?"

Fitz looked to Scott, who was fighting back his own grin. "He's never not gotten attention, so . . . no."

"Should I be worried about this?"

The two shared another look.

Scott's grin softened. "You'll be fine. You know Kash. He has three contingencies in place in case we need a quick getaway."

That eased up some of the sudden guilt I was feeling for making them do this. But thinking back, I realized I *wasn't* making them do it. I knew Kash would come, but Matt was the one who showed up without being invited. He already knew about the game, and he was the one who announced he was coming.

I was glad he did. I was thinking this would be a lot more fun with him.

Other people were walking around us, all going to the football stadium.

At first I tensed up, but only a few people checked us out. Those people shot to Scott and Fitz behind us, but Kash and Matt were drawing the most attention.

I saw what Scott said. Matt didn't know how to not get attention. Even him walking with his head high, his back straight, his pom-poms in the air, he was someone. They just didn't know who, or couldn't tell.

"He looks like a wealthy golden boy fraternity brother."

I glanced to Melissa. She'd been watching me, and she nodded to Matt. "Your brother. I can tell you're worried, but that's what the people are thinking when they see him. Your man is something else, but he doesn't want attention, and they're reading that. He's keeping his head down so they can't see him. They're going off his demeanor, and he's got a vibe that he's dark and mysterious, but somehow he's putting out another vibe that people need to not pay him attention. They aren't.

"Your brother, on the other hand, is something else. Fraternity rich kid. That's what they're chalking him up to being. And then they think Kash is one too, so they're getting attention. It's just not the attention you're worried they're getting." She nodded at them. "Guys like them, they're going to draw focus from people. Just who they are. Both are manipulating it into something else. Smart."

Yes. It was.

I remembered back to when Kash hugged me this morning, tucked my hair back into my sweatshirt, and said under his breath, "Fresh-faced student. Light. Nice. Eyes will skip over you, thinking you're another pretty face."

I'd been struck then by his words, but it made sense now. He was feeling out what "vibe" I was putting out, and he was right.

Innocent. Light. That's the aura Kash wanted me to give out, so with that in mind, I stopped worrying.

We had a game to enjoy.

THIRTY-THREE

Liam was waving us up. He and his friends took up a whole section, spanning five rows. They didn't fill out the entire row, but Kash was right. Athletes traveled in groups, large groups. Liam was in their third row when he spotted us. The grin faded when he took in Kash, then Matt, then Fitz, and lastly Scott.

Coming down the steps to meet us, he put his hands in his pockets. "I was expecting Liss, Bailey, and maybe a couple guys."

Kash stared at him. "Well—"

Matt popped his head up, grinning wide. "Deal with it."

He and Kash both laughed.

Melissa began giggling.

Liam was clueless, his eyebrows raised. He gave me a look. "You know the inside joke?"

I shook my head. "You don't want to know."

Kash cleared his throat. "If there aren't any extra seats, we can sit somewhere else."

Matt snorted. "That's code for either he'll bribe the people for their seats if Bailey wants to stay, or he'll maneuver us all into a box upstairs." He hopped up on the same step Liam was standing on, threw his arm around his shoulder, and squeezed Liam to him.

"We're here for three reasons," he said, and stuck a finger out. "One: because Bailey wants to be normal. She's been missing that phenomenon. Me, I was born amazing, so I don't know any other way." He held up a second finger. "Two: football. That says enough," he continued. Then he put three fingers in the air. "And the last reason: to drive Kashton crazy. He's tempering it right now. He really wants to throw his weight around, bash some heads, make some threats and move Bailey to safety, but he can't, because we're back to number one: Bailey. He's kinda nuts for her, so he's already primed. Our first meeting sucked, so I'm reintroducing myself. I'm Matt, Bailey's smarter brother."

Kash's mouth twitched.

Liam was slack-jawed. He took Melissa and me in. "He's for real?"

Melissa nodded. "He's been like this the whole ride over. I think this is how he is normally."

Matt winked at her. "Just wait till I get some liquor in me. I won't care if Bailey's here. You're going to be hearing some fabulous pickup lines." His arm still around Liam, he leaned toward Melissa and dropped his tone suggestively. "They'll be so smooth, you might learn what 'combustible climax' means." He winked. "If you get my drift."

Melissa groaned under her breath.

Liam made a gargling sound.

Kash stepped forward, his hand to Matt's chest, and pushed him upward. "Okay. Calm down, brother." He winked at me over his shoulder. "Let's find our seats."

Whoa.

Wow.

That wink . . . I was the one who just learned what a combustible climax was.

Melissa sidled close to me. "How do you handle that?"

I spoke, "In bed. As much as possible."

"Your brother?"

My head jackknifed to hers. "*What?*"

"I was talking about your brother." Her eyebrows pinched together.

"Oh!" Matt. I waved that off. "You'll either love Matt or you're going to hate him. Don't sleep with him and you'll enjoy him. But that's key. Don't sleep with him."

Liam had lingered, overhearing. "Solid advice."

"Looks like they found some seats."

An entire row was cleared when we got there, and Matt was already making friends with Liam's friends. A seat was left open on the other side of Matt, and Fitz went behind our row, dropping into that empty seat.

Matt went first. Kash. Me. Melissa. Scott on Melissa's side.

Liam moved around so he was in the row in front of us, right beneath Melissa and me.

His friends looked nice.

I didn't think they were graduate students, just a year younger than Liam.

They, in turn, were studying Kash and me, but Kash laid an arm around me, pulling me to him.

As he did this, my front to his side, he moved to my ear and said, "They'll stop paying attention to us. Matt will distract them in three, two, one—"

Matt started, "What do you guys lift? What's the average weight?"

Kash continued, without pausing, "Now all they'll know is that their computer friend brought another computer friend, a couple, Matt, and two other guys who don't seem too friendly. They'll talk to your brother because he'll make them, and they'll ignore the rest of us, except maybe one or two will give Melissa attention, wondering if their boy Liam is interested. If he is, we'll find out who are the good friends and who are the douchebags."

I slid a hand over his stomach, wrapping around his side. "What do you mean?"

"The ones who respect Liam will be nice to Melissa, but keep their distance. The douchebags will try to hit on her. They'll either do it at the game or wait till the after-game party."

"There's an after-game party?"

Kash lifted his head, cupping my face, and smiled down at me. His thumb traced my top lip. "There's always an after-game party, and because Matt's here, he'll control that."

I liked how he traced my lip. I tried to catch his thumb in my mouth. "How do you know that?"

He laughed lightly, evading my mouth. "Because Matt likes your friend and he's going to want to control who's in her space. He knows I'd rather take you home after the game, have our own after-game party." He moved more into my space. "And he knows Liam doesn't want Melissa around him, because what Liam's friends will notice, too, is that Liam is interested in your friend Melissa."

"He is? Wait . . ."

Kash's eyes sobered. "Matt wants to sleep with her. That's all."

I tensed up.

He smoothed a hand down my side, massaging at my waist. It helped loosen some of the tension. "So he wants to sleep with her," he continued, "but he won't, because he knows if he does he's basically just a predator. And that's what he wants to save her from with Liam's friends, because some of them are predators."

Air caught in my throat. "Does Liam know?"

Kash looked over my shoulder, observing a moment. "I don't think so. Some guys know. Some guys don't. He seems clueless."

I frowned.

He eased away, tilting his head, his eyes back on me. His thumb rubbed at my lip again. "But no one needs to worry, because your friend has eyes only for Fitz, when it's really Scott who's more interested in her. And both Fitz and Scott know this. Fitz is respecting him by staying away, and Scott isn't worried about anyone else because he knows he's the one who'll reel her in."

The air escaped me in a sudden rush. I glanced over my shoulder and saw it all in one look.

Scott was next to Melissa, the same grin he always wore on his face, as he watched her talking to Liam. She was nodding, smiling, but kept sending furtive looks down our aisle. I turned. Fitz pointedly had his eyes elsewhere, and Matt was still talking to a bunch of the other guys, but he was seeing it all, too.

I turned back to Kash. "You noticed all of this on the ride over?"

"No. I noticed this the second I met your friend."

Kash said I was smart, but so was he. Just in different ways.

"Well, I can say one thing for sure." I cocked my head back so I could really look into Kash's face. "My friend's gonna get a boyfriend soon."

Kash smiled down at me, I smiled back at him, and we continued to have our own moment. It was nice. Spending time at a game with my boyfriend and being able to just be with him. The end of the world wasn't coming. We didn't have an entire slew of bodyguards around us. There were regular people behind us. By the time the game started, I already knew it was worth it.

Matt made his rounds by the time halftime rolled around.

He moved from his seat, which was made easy because the guys kept leaving for the concession stands. Everyone remained standing the whole time, which also made it easier for Matt to socialize. So, by halftime, Matt was friends with all of the guys—and with some of the girls that were sitting in front of the guys. There were so many people, but I felt it was safe to say that if Matt walked on the Hawking University campus tomorrow, he'd be greeted as if he'd gone there full time for the past four years.

Liam and two of his friends mostly talked with Melissa the whole time. I joined in every now and then, but I was content to watch the game with Kash's arm around me.

Fitz and Scott watched everyone. They were still there to do their jobs, and only once were they relieved, when Erik showed. He took Fitz's spot and Fitz disappeared for a moment. He returned and Erik took Scott's place. When Scott returned, Erik conversed with Kash a moment before leaving again.

If anyone noticed this, no one said a word.

It wasn't until the fourth quarter started that a buzz began in the stands.

Kash's head was tilted down to mine. His temple was resting against my head. We were both watching the game, but his head had been half bent over mine most the time. It was how he watched the game, and I loved it.

Matt came back to us, his smile frozen. "Busted."

Kash's head immediately lifted.

Matt's eyes darted upward.

Kash looked and swore.

Right there, on the Jumbotron, was an image of Kash and me. I looked frozen in place. Kash looked ready to commit murder.

"We gotta go."

At his command, Fitz and Scott both stood, leaving for the aisle.

"What's going on?" Melissa asked.

Kash's hand was firm on my thigh. He was guiding me from behind to the aisle. He said in my ear, "We'll go up. We can finish the game in a box. She can come with us if she'd like."

"What about Liam?"

"Him, too. Five of his friends. No more."

Scott was craning over us, waiting.

Kash motioned. "Go up."

Scott nodded, and we began the climb upward.

I relayed what he said to Melissa and Liam. Immediately, both stood. Liam was turning toward his friends, but Kash wasn't waiting. His hand moved to the small of my back. He was right behind me. "Keep your head down. Don't make eye contact."

I did as he said, glad his hand didn't leave me. A few people called to us. A guy asked for money to save his house. Another guy cursed at us. There were others, but we ignored them all the way up to the main floor.

Once there, Hawking security was waiting for us. One of the

guys broke forward to talk with Kash. In that time, Melissa had followed us up. Liam, too. Three of his friends were trailing, and their whole demeanor from before was wiped clean. They were wide-eyed and looking at Kash and me with new interest. Matt seemed more reserved, and he moved next to me. "Since word is out, I'm making different plans now."

Melissa had heard and frowned. "Like what?"

Jesus.

Those two words, how she said them . . . we both heard it, Matt and I. And a glance at a stiff Liam? Him, too. Longing. Disappointment. Jealousy.

Melissa was interested in Matt, not Fitz now.

Matt cursed under his breath before saying, almost gently, "I was going to have people over to my place at the Francois Nova. Just a small shindig. But now I'm going to invite a couple more of my friends."

His gaze swept mine, and his was cautious.

Which told me who he was inviting.

"No."

He cocked his head back. "Hmm?"

"No." I was firm. "Not around my friends."

His mouth twitched. He did not like hearing that. "They're my friends, too."

"No."

Kash returned to my side. "What's going on?"

Eyes still on Matt, I answered him. "Matt wants to invite Tony and Chester to his party at the Francois, where my friends will be."

"No." That was from Kash.

Matt's nostrils flared. "I'm not remembering the moment when you two birthed me, made you my parents."

Kash laughed. "That a joke?"

Matt's eyes turned frosty, but he didn't repeat it. "I'll invite Guy, too."

"He's not much better around them."

Matt gave me a dark look. "He's way better and you know it."

I had it. "Invite Torie and Tamara. Only then will I allow it."

"Allow it? You *her* mom, too?" His eyes slid sideways to where Melissa was actively listening to everything. Liam was too, and he was looking pissed off.

Kash had had enough. He broke from my side, his hand going to Matt's shoulder, and he forcibly turned Matt around. They started forward. Everyone started forward; it seemed we were all waiting for Kash's move. We were shown to a private box a floor above. It wasn't at the top, but we had our own terrace.

We walked in.

Kash led Matt to the corner. Kash was saying something. Matt wasn't looking like he was enjoying it, and Kash wasn't looking like he gave a shit. He broke away, coming back. "He'll be fine. Your friends will be fine."

Matt glowered at me before moving close to pass me. He hissed under his breath as he did, "I would've made sure she was safe."

I said after him, "With Torie and Tamara there, I trust she will be."

He was going to the box's restroom. He stopped and glanced over his shoulder at me. "You could've come, too." His jaw clenched, and it hit me then.

This wasn't about Melissa. This was about me, because he assumed I wouldn't come.

My head shot up. "Maybe I was always coming."

He frowned, but his jaw unclenched. "Really?"

"Why not?"

His eyes moved to Kash, his meaning evident.

Kash sighed. "I said the whole day, Matt. I meant it."

The frown vanished from Matt's face, and he shot up. "Well, fuck that. I'm getting my drink on now." He changed paths, heading for the bar instead.

Melissa came up to me later, once everyone settled. "What was all of that earlier? Does your brother not have good friends?"

I paused for a beat.

Melissa was impervious to so much, but it was in a good way. I wanted her to stay that way, but she needed to know. Pulling her farther away from everyone, I told her the truth.

"Fitz is not interested in you."

Her face fell.

I kept on, "But Scott is."

Her face brightened. "Really?"

"And Liam is interested in dating you, too, while my brother wants to sleep with you." I didn't miss a beat. "Do not sleep with my brother. Just trust me. He's not head over heels for you." Hurt flashed, but I made sure she heard me. "It's not because of you. It's not even because of the last woman he had feelings for. He's got things in him that are blocking him from falling for anyone, so don't sleep with him. As for Liam and Scott, it's up to you. I think Liam could love you." I hesitated, looking at Scott over her head. He was frowning slightly in our direction. I added, "I don't know what to say about Scott, so that's on you."

With all that said, I stepped back to give her space.

She was floored—*floored.* Her mouth was hanging open. "All of them?"

I nodded. "Yes."

"Are interested?"

Another nod. Another "Yes."

"In *me?*" she squeaked, pointing at herself.

See. Obliviously cute. I hated taking that away from her.

I said, "I'm sure one or two of Liam's friends would like to sleep with you too, but don't fall for it. They're just doing it to be dicks to Liam."

Another squeak from her. "Oh my *God!*"

"Bailey." Kash was standing by the seats.

I said to her, "Now you know. Be smart about who you choose."

Melissa was quiet the rest of the game. Afterward, we were led to a private exit and left for the Francois Nova, since Matt said the after-game party was supposed to start immediately.

We got there, and it was fun at first.

And then . . . it wasn't.

THIRTY-FOUR

Kash

I was leaning against a wall, watching Bailey with her friends. Torie. Tamara. All three of them were focused on Melissa, who looked like a minnow swimming among sharks and knowing it. I almost felt sorry for her. Almost. Bailey and the other two were protecting her, but whatever was going on seemed important.

Word had gotten out.

It seemed the entire section we'd been sitting with decided they wanted to party with Matthew Francis. When we showed, they were already in the hotel lobby. The front desk attendants were in a fit, not knowing what to do, but Matt had been in his party mood. He said, "The more, the merrier," so everyone was allowed up.

A few more groups arrived, but Matt made the decision to shut down the open invites. No one else had been let up, instead Scott reported that the lobby was filled with Hawking University students.

"You pissed I invited my guys?"

Matt came over, a drink in hand, his eyes glazed. He was starting to sway on his feet, too. I was hoping this wouldn't be one of those nights.

I responded, "Yeah."

He flinched.

I glanced back to the girls. "You asked."

"I forget how honest you can be sometimes."

"Do you know yourself?"

He snorted, leaning beside me and watching the girls, too. "True, but I know you hold back with B. and others."

He was right.

"Tough love, brother. You earned it too many times for me to go back and tread water with you."

He got quiet. My point was made.

He echoed it with a quiet, "I deserved that."

I straightened from the wall and faced him. Taking his drink, I ignored his "Hey," and sniffed it. "Fuck, Matt. What's in here?"

"Vodka."

"Mixed with rum?"

He flashed a grin. "Mixed with whatever the fuck was behind the bar that would make it taste good. And what is this?" He motioned between us before he took the drink back, his head resting against the wall.

He knew me. He knew what was coming.

He tipped his chin up. "You know, it was fun hanging out with you today. You didn't have a stick up your ass."

I shot back, "You know, it was fun hanging out with you today, too. You weren't acting like a drug addict with a death wish."

He cringed. "Shit."

I didn't blink. "Fuck."

His gaze grew resigned, but he sipped his drink. "Okay. Lay it on me. Tell me what a fuckup I've been."

I scowled now, because that wasn't deserved. "When have I ever done that to you?"

His eyes fell to his drink.

He didn't respond.

"I'll take care of you. Make you leave a bad situation. Clean up after you. But when have I ever sat and lectured you? A few pointed words here and there, but shit, Matt. You deserved those. I'm not Peter. Don't put your father issues on me just because I've helped take care of you. And for the record, *brother*, I enjoyed to-day because you were part of the group. You were in there, help-ing. You had focus, a goal, and you were doing it because you love your sister."

A second flinch. A third. There was a fourth by the time I was done, and he stood there, his eyes unfocused as he grew quiet.

His face fell. Whatever was there, whatever attitude he was trying to fire up, crumbled. His head lowered. His drink too, so I grabbed it before it spilled. I handed it off to Scott, who was standing behind me.

Matt let loose a low and guttural "Fuuuck."

His head came up. His eyes closed, and a harder "*Fuck!*" came out.

I frowned.

"You're right. You're completely right and I'm an idiot."

Seeing eyes coming to us, I motioned to the side. "Let's head to your TV room for privacy."

Scott moved first, heading off to make sure it was open for us. Matt sighed, trailing behind.

Bailey tipped her head back as we passed by. "Everything okay?" Her hand moved behind her, palm up to me.

I caught her fingers with mine, sliding our hands over each other and pausing to kiss her forehead. "Everything's fine."

Melissa and Tamara let out audible sighs. Torie just grinned, her chest puffed up, and she gave me an approving look. I shot a pointed look from her to Bailey and back again. She got my mes-sage, clipping her head up and down.

She handed her drink off to someone else.

A few people were leaving the den, looking pissed off, but the expressions changed when they saw us coming. A few guys tried to say hello to Matt, and he replied, but halfheartedly. They looked to me, thinking about it. My eyes went flat. They didn't give me the same greeting.

Scott laughed behind me.

Going inside, I told him, "Just keep one of you in the hallway. I want the rest out there with Bailey."

Scott nodded, taking position at the end of the hall. The other guard returned.

"Connor came in, and a few others. They're helping to man the lobby."

That was good. "Thanks."

The door shut behind us, and I hadn't taken a second step inside before Matt was already going.

"I'm messed up. I'm so fucking messed up, Kash." He sank down on the couch, burying his head into his hands. His elbows rested on his knees.

I started forward to him, but he jerked back up.

He shot to his feet and started to pace. "I blame myself for what happened to Bailey."

My eyebrows went up. I hadn't expected that. "What?"

"Amanda and I started sleeping together, and because of her affair, her husband started stepping out. He was right there, ripe for Quinn to pick him up and start pimping him for her own fucked-up intents. But that was me. I set all that in motion. It's been eating me up. I don't know how to make it right, and I continue to keep fucking up."

He kept pacing.

I settled back, leaning against the wall.

"I wake up every morning, deal with my hangover, and swear that I'm not going to party again. I swear that I'm going to do something right, preferably for Bailey, but if not her, then for someone else. Ser. Cy. And I don't know what happens. I lose track of time. Or I get bored. I have no clue. Then I'm always, always at a bar or at Naveah drinking with the guys. You used to party with us. I know the guys don't want me to say anything, but they miss you."

That wasn't what I wanted to hear either.

It didn't matter. Matt kept going and pacing back and forth. "I'm not a drunk. I'm not an addict. Yes, I like both. I really like both, but I can stop. I did tonight. Shit's not too messed up. I mean, look at who's out there!" He swept his hand out, gesturing toward the hallway. "I don't want those people out there. I'm a lot of things, and I'll admit that I'm a bit of a dick. I don't know those people, but they're Hawking students. My sister's a Hawking graduate student, and my sister wants to have fun and be normal today, so hell. I'm throwing a fucking Hawking party for my sister. And she's having fun. It's the same reason you're here, chilling, even though I know you're itching to break some necks and kick everyone out. Bailey. We're doing this for her."

Now he stopped. Now he swung his head my way. And now his eyes were telling me I needed to say something here.

Fuck if I knew what.

I grunted. "You're right."

An emphatic nod, and he threw his arms in the air. He started pacing again. "I know! I know I'm right, and *why* am I right? Why aren't you pissed at me?"

"Why would I be?"

"Because I'm a fuckup! You should be pissed at me."

I put my hands in my pockets, rolling my shoulders forward. "I gotta admit, I can usually follow your thoughts. This? No clue. You blame yourself for Bailey being kidnapped?"

"Yes!" He cocked his head to the side. "No! I don't know. It sounds stupid, now that I'm hearing it out loud."

"Quinn's to blame for the kidnapping. Or if anyone else, blame me. I wasn't there. I knew shit wasn't right, but I still went off anyways. You boning Amanda Bonham didn't set that in motion, and I'm pretty sure Amanda boned you because her husband was already boning Quinn. So you were being used, in an odd, extra-marital affair way."

He froze in place, his eyes glued to me. "Holy fuck," he whispered. "You're right. You're so right. I'm as much a victim as Bailey—"

"No."

"I'm *almost* as much a victim as Bailey—"

"Try again."

"Amanda used me."

I nodded. "Better."

"Still, man." He raked a hand through his hair. "You don't know how much guilt's been racking me. I was going to try to get my life together."

"God forbid." My tone was dry.

"I know." He shuddered, then smirked. "I know you're being a smartass. I'm being serious—I mean about the victim stuff, not the other stuff. I really do need to get my act together." He expelled a snort that was half a laugh, motioning for the hallway again. "Bailey's younger than me and she's going to cure computer cancer within the year. What am I doing?" He gestured around the room. "I'm still throwing ragers in my penthouse floor that Daddy pretends is mine, just like how I don't really do crap at this hotel. The assistant manager is getting paid what a manager does for a reason, with extra to take the name demotion." His snort was only a snort now. No laugh. "I know whose idea that was."

"It was mine."

His head whipped back to mine. "You messing with me?"

I shook mine. "It was my idea."

He scowled. "Are you sure my daddy issues shouldn't translate to you?"

I grinned, leaning my head back. "Calm down. You weren't ready to handle anything real before." I leaned my head forward. "You are now."

He quieted.

"I think you need to, because you're slipping into old habits. One bender. Don't make this night your second. You had fun at the game with us. I know you didn't like a lot of those guys, but it didn't matter. You never paused or stopped. You distracted them so your sister could enjoy one football game. And now," I nodded to him, "you're slipping again. Don't slip."

His eyes were shining. He swallowed whatever he was feeling.

"Kash," he said in a hoarse whisper. "I'm a mess."

"Matt—"

A knock sounded on the door.

Matt cursed.

A head popped in.

Scott found me, but I was already moving. I saw the alarm, and that was enough.

I was crossing the room as he said, "We got a call. You need to go."

That was enough.

I paused in the doorway, looking at Matt. "Will you—"

He waved me off. "Go. I got her."

A dip of my head, up and down, but my feet didn't move. I was rooted in place.

"Matt," I called.

He looked up again, but he didn't say anything.

"Turn it off. Just think about Cy, about Ser, about Bailey. Think about them and you'll do fine."

As pep talks went, it sucked. I knew it. I knew he knew it, but it was the best I had in me. I felt he was searching for something more, but then we were moving down the hallway.

Scott was next to me. "We got a call from your guy. He said he'd brief you on the plane, but . . ." He hesitated.

I growled, "I don't have time for this—"

"You're going to have a guest on the plane."

Shit.

"Who?"

We'd gotten to the main room, and it seemed more people were in there. That meant people were crashing, but Scott wasn't looking at them. His gaze was pinned on Bailey as he answered, "Victoria."

That wasn't going to go over well.

THIRTY-FIVE

Bailey

More and more people were coming into Matt's penthouse floor, all Hawking students.

At first, I was loving it. The guards around me were blending and I was huddled up with Torie, Tamara, and Melissa, so it wasn't a big deal. I wasn't getting the attention.

That lasted thirty minutes.

Liam showed up, and he was lit. I thought he'd been here the whole time, but it was apparent he'd stepped out. The brown paper bag was my indicator. His eyes were dilated, his hair a mess, and his grin was sloppy. Those were my other indicators, as he came over to us. "Heyyy, my girls!" He threw his arm wide—not the one holding the booze. "These are my girls. Hey! Hey. Carl. Hey. Did you meet my friends?"

Carl was the guy sitting next to Liam during the game.

He was the guy who had conversed with Melissa almost the whole game. He was one of the two that seemed to be a good guy.

Carl was also sober, unlike his very not-sober friend Liam.

He grinned, though, seeming all chill. "Nice to meet you guys." His grin curved higher. "Again."

"*So guess what I did?*"

Liam had missed the "again."

Melissa and I shared a look, but I answered him for us, "What'd you do?"

He swung the brown paper bag forward, indicating me, before bringing it back and taking a long swig of whatever was in there. "I invited Hoda and the guys here."

The music could've stopped with a *screech*. The same effect crashed over our huddle. Even Carl's eyebrows shot up.

"Uh." He was the first to speak, scratching behind his ear. "Say what?"

Torie was glaring. "You did *what*?"

Tamara chided, "Watch yourself. She's going to go all Torie on you."

Liam frowned at her, cocked his head to the side, and narrowed his eyes. "Have we met?"

Melissa was sharing another look with me. I couldn't read her mind, but I felt it might've gone something along the lines of "*Your friend is about to* Torie *on his ass and I don't know what* Torie *means, but she seems super scary right now and I'm scared of her, so Liam better sober up real quick because he's gonna get his ass kicked.*"

Okay. She didn't say any of that. Her thoughts were probably more like "*Did you hear what he said?*"

Either way, I was right there with her.

Torie was about to kick Liam's ass, and he wasn't sober enough to enjoy it. The dude would be all sorts of remorseful in the morning.

"You did. I don't give a shit you don't remember me. You better tell me you didn't invite that bitch who sent out an image of my girl and her man in a private moment here? Where my girl is? Where her man is? And where her brother resides? Tell me you didn't do that."

Liam's mouth was hanging open. He was gawking at her.

Carl sighed, shaking his head. "Oh, man. Here it comes."

Liam said, "I'm usually chill, but fuck—you're hot."

Carl sighed again. "There it went."

Carl seemed like a good bud.

I poked him in the shoulder. "Hey." I nodded at Liam. "Get him out of here. He's inviting people who want to hurt me. I have guards around me for reasons, so that's not going to go over well."

He looked around.

I didn't know if he took in the guards or if he remembered them from earlier, but he nodded super-duper quick-like. "I got him. And for the record"—he leaned close—"he's only being this way because he saw how Melissa wants to bone your brother. He's in the feels, if you know what I mean."

Carl really was chill. I would've liked him in another universe. I nodded, stepping back from him. "Still not cool."

"I know." His hand came to Liam's shoulders, and right there proved how beyond Liam was, because Liam had no clue.

Then I felt a presence behind me, a split second before a hand slid around my waist.

A rush of heat swept me, and I knew whose hand that was. I knew whose chest I leaned back against, and I knew whose lips were coming to brush my cheek before rising to my ear.

I ignored everyone's attention.

"Hey," I murmured, turning my head so Kash's lips could find mine.

They did, and I wanted them to stay. They didn't.

A soft graze and he pulled back, but his hand didn't. He was tugging me away from the group. "I need a word."

That didn't sound good, but I was half-buzzed and too distracted to really take in how rigid he was, or how tight his shoulders were. He moved me into a corner with a semblance of privacy and turned his back to block anyone from watching.

"I have to—"

I didn't wait. I rushed out, "I told Melissa at the game all the guys who liked her, and I told her to steer clear from Matt. I didn't think she'd go for Liam. I really didn't. But I'm excited for her, no matter who she ends up choosing." I paused. There was something else, but I finally noticed the look in Kash's eyes.

Alarm pierced me. Everything else vanished.

"What's going on?" I gripped his hand.

"I have to go on a trip. I can't tell you any details right now, but I'll call you as soon as we land."

He was leaving.

I tried not to feel dejected.

I failed. A pin popped my balloon, and I was deflating fast. "Oh."

He frowned, his forehead resting against mine. "I'm sorry."

I closed my eyes. "It's fine."

He laughed lightly. "Don't lie to me."

A finger went under my chin, and he tipped my head up. I opened my eyes.

He said, "Not to me. Everyone else. Yourself even. But not me. Please."

I whispered, "I really liked being normal today."

His eyes softened. "I know you did." He lowered his head, his lips finding mine. "I enjoyed it, too."

"Boss." From Scott, behind him.

Kash tensed, but he gave me another kiss, this one harder, with more feeling, before he ripped his mouth away. A last kiss to my forehead before he folded me to him. "Be safe. Have fun. I'll come back as soon as I can."

Then he was gone, and I no longer wanted to be there.

Matt came up. "You okay?"

I shook my head. I turned to him, knowing tears were there that I'd never admit to and never let fall, so I moved into him. "I want everyone gone."

His arms closed around me, and a second later my brother barked over my shoulder, "Everyone out. Now!"

There were cries of protest, grumbles, a few curses, but they left.

My brother hugged me the whole time. Only my friends stayed, and I was including Carl.

I decided maybe I was wrong.

Maybe being normal was overrated.

THIRTY-SIX

Okay. I overreacted.

I mean, I really overreacted.

Kash had to go. It happened. It wasn't something to break down about, or wish the party to end. Though I hadn't realized I wanted to be there only because Kash was. I felt safe, and I could let loose. He was gone. The guards were present, but it wasn't the same.

Bottom line: I was missing him.

"There's talk about going to Naveah."

I was hanging out on Matt's deck, a blanket wrapped around me, sitting there and feeling embarrassed and sad. I was even more embarrassed about that. I looked up as Matt came out. My other friends would've come out, lingered by the couch, unsure where to sit because I was mostly sprawled over the entire couch.

Not my brother.

He picked me up, sat, and put me against him so I was half leaning into him. He rested his arm on the back of the couch. "How you doing?"

"Wondering why I got emotional earlier," I admitted, looking down, picking at the blanket in my lap.

His arm squeezed me against him before returning to the couch. "My guess is it's because you were having fun, you were a bit tipsy, and Kash told you he had to leave, when I'm sure you and him were looking forward to other activities tonight. Activities I don't want to hear about, by the way."

I grinned. "That's probably why."

"No reason to be embarrassed."

His arm fell to squeeze around my shoulders. "You got some interesting friends in there."

I lifted my head. "Dax and the guys show up?"

"And a chick who security didn't let through."

I lifted my head farther, tilting to see him.

He said, "She's at the front desk. That's the farthest she got, and she's insisting she's got something important to tell you. Only you." He raised an eyebrow. "Is this the bitch classmate that showed up with my ex Saturday night at Naveah?"

His ex?

Oh!

Camille Story.

"I forgot you dated her."

"Not thinking I did. She's a lot different. I hardly recognized her, to tell you the truth." He winced. "To be honest, it was more like a few drunken hookups. I called when I was wasted. She opened her door and legs. That sort of thing."

"I'm thinking you made an impression."

"Maybe. Or she targeted me because she already had an agenda. Either way, her bestie is downstairs pleading to talk to you."

I didn't want to go, but I was going to go.

And I knew I was going to hate going.

But I was still going.

Squashing a groan, I stood.

Scott and Connor had gone with Kash. Of the main guys I knew, they had left back Fitz and Erik. I took them in, noting, "Isn't this your normal time off?"

They shared a look, bookending me on the way to the elevator.

Erik cleared his throat. "We're getting double time, but we'll be relieved in the morning."

Time. I'd forgotten the time. It was a little after nine. It felt like it should've been after midnight, but I guess that's how it went when you started the festivities at a football game in the middle of the day and then kept going.

"You want us to come with you?" That was Matt, but Torie didn't ask. She bypassed him, stepping firmly into the elevator as it opened.

She wasn't alone.

Melissa came behind her, Tamara bookending *her*.

Liam, Carl, Dax, Shyam, and a few other guys from class followed, too.

They were about to get on the elevator, but Erik held up a hand. "No more. Next elevator."

The doors were closing when Liam shot a hand up. "Don't kill her."

No one said a word inside.

The door closed.

We descended into the abyss of hell.

I might've been overreacting again. I didn't care. I grinned.

"This is the same bitch from Naveah?"

I didn't have to answer Torie.

Melissa did for me. "Yes, but if she's here, then there's a good reason she's here."

That got my attention. That got everyone's attention.

Melissa kept on, "She wouldn't come, especially to your brother's place and to your dad's hotel. Hoda feels bad. Kash handed her ass to her"—Look at Melissa, she was picking up our speak!—"and she feels bad, but she's been trying to figure a way to make it up to you. If she's here, this is her making it up to you. Trust me." She ended with a *harrumph* and a nod. Her hair had a little bounce to it.

No one said a word. We were mostly in shock, or I was guessing.

But then there really wasn't anything to say. Whatever Hoda was here to say, I'd listen. With that in mind, as the elevator opened again and we walked out to a still seriously packed lobby, I found her in two seconds. She was at the front desk, an arm resting on the counter. Her body was half-turned to watch the lobby, but her head swiveled toward where we were. Our eyes met, and her body jolted. Her arm even scraped against the counter, getting the front desk attendant's attention.

He looked at her, saw where she was looking, and clambered to get out from behind the desk. "Mr. Colello said—"

Erik stepped in. "We got it. Is there a private room nearby?"

The attendant stopped talking, taking me in, and Hoda, who was migrating around the desk toward us. Hotel security was standing by her, but seeing that it was okay for her to approach, he went back to the front door.

The elevator pinged behind us. Matt, Liam, Carl—the whole group—spread out around us.

Hoda took them in, gulping.

The attendant snapped to attention again. "Mr. Francis, sir!"

Matt moved forward. "They need a conference room, and I want all lingering students out of the lobby. They either need to be a guest or know a guest, and it's okay for us to make them produce a keycard. If anyone gripes, send them my way." My brother touched my arm. "My sister has to have a meeting. What room's available?"

Well, hell. We just saw Manager Matt.

I liked it.

We were shown to a conference room. All of us traipsed inside—and I mean all of us. Seemed Hoda wasn't getting a one-on-one but a one-on-twenty-*ish*.

She took it in stride. I had to hand that to her.

"Okay." She smoothed her hands down her sides, her eyes darting to take in everyone. "Wow. Okay. I didn't realize I'd get an actual audience."

Matt growled, moving to stand in front of me. "My sis can hear your words, but you talk to me. Got it?"

I couldn't see her anymore, but she whispered, "Got it."

Liam was still drunk but looked like he was attempting to

pretend to be sober. He and Melissa, and Carl, since he was an extension of Liam at this point, all stood between Hoda and the rest of us.

"What's up, the Hodes?" From Liam.

His pretending wasn't working.

Melissa shot him a frown and mirrored Matt, standing in front of Liam. She reached out to touch Hoda's arm. That I could see.

"I told Bailey you wouldn't be here unless it was important, and you don't want to hurt her anymore."

Matt's back straightened, stiffening.

"Yes. Right." Still a whisper from Hoda, until she cleared her throat. Her next words came out more clear, stronger. "I messed up. I was jealous and insecure, and I was educated on the error of my ways and realize how stupid I was. So"—a deep breath—"I wanted you guys to know that I didn't reach out to Camille. She found me."

What?

I stepped around Matt. "She found you?"

Hoda nodded, looking sick. "She came to Naveah. I wasn't the one who put that picture of you and Mr. Colello out to the blogs. That was her. But it was me who got the picture in the first place. She, um . . ." Her eyes darted to Matt before tearing back to me. She was twisting her hands together. "Thinking back, she targeted me. I mean, it sounds weird saying it, but I think that's what she did. She used to come in when I was working. She looked different each time, too. I thought she was trying out new wigs, but now, seeing how Mr. Colello reacted to her, and"—her eyes darted to Matt—"your brother too, I realized that there was longer history there than I knew about."

"She broke the story about Kash and me."

"I know." She bit down on her lip, her eyes downcast. "I'm sorry."

"What do you mean, she targeted you?" Matt interjected.

She looked up, her eyes widening. "Uh. Just that. She was friendly with a few of the staff, then somehow she started always being in the bathroom when I was. We laughed, joked that it was meant to be. We were supposed to be friends, but she knew I was on the IT staff there. We became friends. We, huh"—another visible gulp from her—"we used to meet up at our apartments. Sometimes we went to a movie, but mostly it was just gabbing like girlfriends do. She likes to drink wine and talk."

Hoda's eyes found mine, silently pleading. "I just thought she was being a good friend to me. I didn't realize she had an agenda, but she steered conversations toward you, about Kash. She took the pic from me. I confronted her about it, but she said she was helping me out in the long run. She insisted that that pic would keep you from coming to Hawking. I didn't know how it would stop you, but she was adamant it would."

A very, very bad thought was coming to me.

A truly bad and horrific feeling. It was so bad, I tasted acid in my mouth.

I swallowed it back and kept listening.

"I don't know how to make it up to you, except I've been sticking around her."

"You *what?*" Melissa snapped at her.

That was surprising.

Matt thought so too, sharing a look with me.

Hoda flinched, turning to Melissa. "It's not what you're thinking. When I got kicked out of my apartment, I've been staying with her. I was thinking I could stick around and, if I heard something, I could let you know. I mean, she thinks I'm firmly anti–Bailey and Kash, so it could work out perfect."

Matt moved into me, brushing against my side, and I was feeling what he was thinking.

She had access to Camille Story's apartment, to her actual lair. She was behind enemy lines.

"She's got a room in her apartment. She locks it up, keeps the key on her, and it's not a normal lock. It's like a dead-bolt lock, and she's even got a keypad just for that room."

I glanced over. Erik had his phone to his ear; his eyes were speculative.

I'd bet a million bucks he was relaying word for word to Kash right then and there, which I felt like a kick in my stomach if he was. Kash was available twenty-four/seven to the guards but not to me. That wasn't sitting well with me. There were other bad tastes going on with me, too, and I needed to block all of them out. If I didn't, my head would explode.

"That's why I'm here."

God. Hoda was shaking. She was so scared.

I felt a wall loosening inside me.

She spoke right to me. "We were watching the game on TV today when the camera showed you guys. Two seconds after that, her phone started ringing, and man . . . Her eyes lit up. She looked like she won a Pulitzer Prize. She took the phone, sprinted for her room, and I heard a few words before she sealed herself inside. She answered the phone with 'Hello, Quinn.'"

Ice blasted my insides.

Everything that'd been getting riled up—dead. Total deadness inside.

Quinn.

Matt swore next to me. "No fucking way. No way."

Hoda frowned, her eyebrows pulling together. "That's what I heard."

"We know." I surged forward, touching her arm to reassure her. "He's saying that about Quinn." I tried to say more, but the words shriveled up in me.

Quinn had been on the phone with Camille Story.

That'd been the sick feeling before, but I hadn't wanted to give it time to grow.

"Quinn was behind those articles. Your face. Kash's identity coming out. She was goddamn behind—" Matt broke from the group, his face furious, and he started pacing back and forth in clipped and almost frenzied steps. "I can't." His voice was strangled. "I can't be here. I can't be in the same fucking city as that bitch. I stay here and I will do major damage, and I know Kash has things planned. I can't get in the middle of it." He stopped abruptly, turning to Erik. "Is that Kash?"

Erik nodded. He started to hold the phone out, but Matt was across the room in a flash. He took it from him before it even cleared away from his ear.

"I need that plane now. I need to physically be far away from that bitch, or I swear to God I will—" He stopped talking. He started listening. A second later, his eyes turned to me. His voice sounded hollow. "Okay. I'll do that." He handed me the phone. "He wants to talk to you."

I took it and moved to a corner of the room. "Hey."

"You okay?"

"Yeah. I mean . . ." No. But . . . "Yeah. You know about everything?"

"Erik was relaying it." Kash's tone got super scary cold. "I need you to hear me. I will handle this. Quinn's trial is being moved up. I'm told that her lawyers are scrambling to bring it forward instead of stalling, which means she's got something planned. Knowing that, knowing these new developments, I need you to keep Matt contained. He can't go on a bender and he *really* can't go anywhere near Quinn. She'll use it against the family for her case. I don't think we can send him away alone."

"I know."

"He asked to use the jet earlier to go to Aspen. Go with him. And," he hesitated, "I need you to take all of his friends, too."

"*What?*"

"Matt needs to be distracted. If he goes only with you, he'll obsess about Quinn. He won't be able to help himself. He'll see you and he'll remember what Quinn did to you, and that's not good for him. If you take your friends with, he'll do the same thing. Your friends don't distract him enough. So I need you to take his friends. And you need to go now."

Was I hearing him right? "You want my friends to go?"

"Take everyone. I don't give a fuck. I just need Matt distracted and unable to get to Quinn. I don't want him to strangle her."

Right. Distract. No strangulation.

I could do that.

"Okay." I turned around. Everyone was watching me, and it was my turn to gulp. "We're going to need a second plane."

Kash didn't laugh. "Give the phone back to Erik. I'll get it all taken care of. And Bailey?"

I paused. "Yes?"

"I'm coming back to you, but it'll be a day or two."

A day or two. "We have school on Monday."

"You guys can skip, or I'll make some calls. See if you can work remotely from Aspen."

"Okay," I said, knowing I should be fine. Right? All would be fine. Kash would take care of it all. I just needed to distract my brother. A bad idea came to me on how I could make sure he was distracted. A really bad idea.

Matt looked like he was on another level of wanting to rip heads off people, so maybe the bad idea wasn't such a bad idea.

I swallowed.

Kash prompted in my ear, "You good? Just have everyone go to their places, pack a bag, and head to the airport."

I swallowed again, feeling a knot in my throat. "Yep. Totally good. On it."

"I love you."

"I love you back."

We hung up, and knowing this was such a stupid, stupid idea, I handed Erik his phone back. I asked Matt for his, saying I needed a number for Kash. He gave it to me, and I texted Fleur and Cedar.

Want to go to Aspen?

Such a bad idea.

THIRTY-SEVEN

The airport didn't know what hit them.

We were all standing on the sidewalk outside O'Hare, waiting, as group after group showed up.

Matt. Tony. Chester. Guy. All of whom had been quiet at Matt's party. I kept forgetting they were there, but they were. Then my group: Torie, Tamara, Melissa, Liam, Carl, Dax, Shyam, and three more of the guys. Hoda. She was in the classmate crew.

When everyone arrived, three vans pulled up. We were all loaded inside.

We were driven to a private section of the airport, and everyone piled out. We were led into a private sitting area, and that's when my bad-idea-surprise was waiting inside. Cedar and Fleur were all smiles to the guys, all chilly attitudes to the girls—except to me. With me, they were just wary.

Matt pulled me aside, wanting to know what the hell I'd been thinking.

I told him the truth. "You need distracting. I don't know who's more distracting than those two girls."

He scowled. "They're bitches."

"Exactly."

The idea, though horrible for me, did have merit, and Matt was seeing that now.

He still scowled at me. "You know they're going to torture you."

I nodded. I was already tired and it hadn't even started. "I know."

Then he softened, drew me in for a hug. "What'd I do to deserve such a good sister?"

I grinned. "Our father likes to have unprotected sex."

He barked out a laugh, letting me go. "No doubt. I didn't inherit the unprotected sex part, but I think I got my weakness for women from him."

"Matt." I hit him in the chest.

He shrugged just as an airport staff member approached the group, saying our plane was ready to board.

Matt sighed behind me. "I asked to use the jet, but we got too many people."

"Poor Matthew Francis, having to fly on a commercial flight." We were led onto the plane first, taken in to cut in front of the entire line of passengers waiting at the desk. They'd put us on a big-ass plane. Most of us were in first class. The rest of the group was put in the Economy Plus section.

"Miss Francis. Mr. Francis." The flight attendants were all bright smiles. Now I got why we were getting the special treatment. I hadn't forgotten, but at the same time, I *had*. Taking one of the seats by the window, I swung in and leaned forward to Matt, who'd taken the seat in front of me. "I've been so wrapped up in who Kash is that I forgot who Peter is."

Matt threw me a look, a slight tug at his lip. "We can get sequestered away from the real world sometimes. Makes it easy to forget."

Tony dumped his bag onto the chair next to Matt but kept going to a back seat.

Melissa took the seat next to me.

Torie and Tamara sat next to each other, but I saw, once we were in the air, that Tony was next to Tamara and Guy was next to Torie.

I texted Kash.

I feel like I'm on a school trip.

I waited, but no response.

Maybe he was somewhere he didn't have reception.

I wouldn't think about it until later.

But later would be too late.

THIRTY-EIGHT

We were taken to a resort, where we broke off into two separate large cabins. Both attached to a main building housing the kitchen and eating area, along with a game and media room and a larger living room with a massive fireplace. The two separate cabins each had a smaller kitchenette area and sitting rooms, but it was obvious that the main building was where everyone was supposed to hang.

Dax and Melissa assumed that one cabin would be guys, the other for the girls.

Nope. Didn't happen.

One cabin was Matt, Tony, Chester, Guy, Fleur, and Cedar.

The other cabin was Dax, Shyam, and the three other guys. Melissa went with them, and she gave Torie a pleading look, so that's how Torie and Tamara ended up in that cabin, too. Hoda trudged behind them.

I started to head after them, but Matt hooked an arm around my neck and tugged me with him. "Nope. My sister stays with me." That was how I ended up in their cabin.

Liam and Carl took a room that was the most in-between both cabins as could be. There was one sleeping room in the main building, tucked in the back hall, and that's where they tossed their bags. It made sense, too. Carl wasn't fitting in with the computer group. He'd taken up with Guy if Liam was with our classmates.

A lot of people.

I was forgetting the whole reason we'd come on this trip

until Matt came to my room and leaned up against the doorway. He folded his arms over his chest, his head cocked to the side. "Thanks for doing this."

I paused in my unpacking. I was more grabbing a change of clothes, but everyone was "unpacking," so I felt that was the appropriate thing to do.

"For doing what?" See. I'd forgotten.

He frowned at me. "For helping to distract me. Quinn being out, and her having her hooks in Camille. That makes me all ragey. I want to be like Kash and bash someone's head in, but I can't. Not with those two." He gave me a dark look, coming in and shutting the door behind him. "So my question to you: what are we going to do with them?"

I paused. And gulped. Unease trickled down my spine.

"What are you talking about?"

"No way am I letting Kash have all the fun. Camille Story, that's on me. I fucked her and ditched her. I primed her to be all vengeful. And Quinn, that's partly on me, too. Us being here, that's helping me keep a clear head, but no way am I sitting on the sidelines. I want my hands dirty."

Yep. Another gulp.

This wasn't good.

I sighed, letting go of my bag and turning to face him more fully. "Matt," I started, speaking low.

"No." He spoke over me. "No way. Quinn tried to hurt you. She wanted to end you. I get the Calhoun part; that's on Kash to deal with. But Quinn and Camille—we should get a piece of that pie, and I'm thinking Kash isn't going to include us, so that means it's on us. What are *we* going to do to handle them?" He motioned between himself and me on the "we" part.

I had to gulp a third time.

A different feeling took root, an excited feeling, an anticipatory feeling, a predatory feeling. It was slow, but it was spreading. Oh yeah.

I think I was liking this a whole lot, probably more than I should've.

I whispered, "Team Batt?"

My brother gave me another dark look, a wicked gleam, and I shouldn't have liked how he flashed a triumphant grin, but I was feeling everything he just said.

He gave me an approving nod. "Oh yeah. Team Batt." He held out his hand.

I wasn't sure what to do with it, so I reached out, opened it, and shook it.

A funny look was on his face, but then he nodded and pulled his hand free. "Okay. I was going with the fist bump. A sibling handshake works, too." He raised an eyebrow. "We're doing this?"

We were doing this.

"I can hack 'em."

He frowned. "I don't know if we should do that. That can be traced, can't it?"

I opened my mouth to respond, but the door swung open and I realized it hadn't been shut the whole way.

Hoda stood there, pale. "You can hack?"

Shit.

"Crap."

Matt shared my sentiment.

"Yeah."

She gulped now. "Did you hack me?"

Um . . .

Her eyes bulged out. "You did, didn't you?"

Another question I felt was better off not being answered. I looked to Matt with that one.

He gave me a pitying look back.

Yeah. He wasn't helping.

She took another step inside. "What did you do? With my stuff, what did you hack?"

Oh wow. Now *that* was the question I couldn't answer.

I coughed, looking away.

"Oh my God," she whispered under her breath. But she was thinking and frowning. "Nothing changed. I never got an alert. I should've."

I just drew in a breath and held it.

"You didn't change any of my passwords. You didn't get any of my social media taken down. There were no extra charges on my accounts. What—what's the point of hacking if you weren't going to do anything with it?"

She was assuming I couldn't still get in there, but that made me wonder if I could do the same program with Quinn, or at least with Camille Story's program. Hoda was another computer person, but something was telling me Camille Story would be the more anal and paranoid of the two. She probably had programs set in place, and I wouldn't know that unless I was actually at her computer.

That gave me an idea, and that meant truth time was about to happen.

I wasn't sure if I wanted to deal with the fallout, but I was calculating that Camille Story was a bigger problem than Hoda. At least right now she was.

So.

Here we go.

I spoke clearly. She needed to hear everything. "I'm still locked into your system." I didn't wait to see the shock, or the alarm. I pushed past that, saying further, "And I hacked everything. Your social media. Your email. Your school account. I even got into your online journal, and the second and third backup journal you have there. Your drive. Your online drive. I got it all."

Her entire face was hanging on the floor.

"I can monitor anything you do. Your bank statements. All of it. So here's what I'll do. You get me into your apartment, into that back room, with an entire evening sitting behind Camille's computer, and I'll pull out of everything of yours. All of it. It'll be like nothing happened. I don't know your passwords. My program doesn't need to know those to get in. I'll take my stuff all down."

Her eyes were glazed over, but she was fast adapting. "For one night sitting behind Camille's system?"

"Her entire system. The motherboard. I need access to that room, and I'll take it from there."

She visibly swallowed. "How are you going to—I mean, she has an entire system just to load up her laptop, and that's the one I can see. I can't even imagine what she's got on her computer."

I glanced to Matt. He was watching us like a hawk.

"That's for me to handle. Get me a night in there and you can watch me pull out of your stuff."

Her eyes narrowed on me. "I can't see you in there?"

She was referring to her accounts. I shook my head. "No."

"Damn." Her eyes clasped shut for a second. She sounded defeated. "You're the genius in the program, aren't you? The one that's above the rest. I knew there was one, but I couldn't tell who it was." She laughed to herself. "I thought it was Dax, but I wasn't sure. He got an A-minus on the last quiz."

Yes. So scandalous. An A-minus.

Matt snorted.

Hoda glared at him.

He shrugged, smirking at her.

She glared again, but really, the effort was lost. He didn't care.

He felt moved to share. "I'm in a different league, girl. Scare down, not up."

She scowled, but some of the heat was gone. "Whatever." She nodded at me. "I'll get you in."

Score! "Okay."

"But I want to watch you pull your stuff out of my programs."

Not a score. "Sounds fair."

But that last picture of Kash and me in the hallway . . . I was waiting for the right time for my revenge on that one. We came to a truce, but not about that last picture. Hoda would find that out in due time.

This was the moment in the conversation where she should leave.

She didn't. She remained.

Matt and I waited.

A beat later, her head lowered, and what I assumed was the real reason she was in my room came out. "I wanted to thank you for letting me come on this trip, and I got an email from Ms. Wells. Goa was cc'd on the same email. They've approved us to all sync in for class tomorrow."

Crap. I'd forgotten.

Matt started laughing. "Kash was busy."

Kash was—or someone who worked for him.

Erik was standing in the hallway and I directed my question at him. "You're getting paid triple overtime, right?"

He flashed me a grin. "We're being compensated, yes. Mr. Colello treats his employees well." His gaze slid in Hoda's direction, and there was a burn there.

She flushed.

"Hey!" A knock sounded, but Torie had already announced her presence. She stepped in, took in Matt, Hoda, and me, and grinned. "Looks like an interesting party in here."

Matt lost some of his smirk. "What are you doing in here?"

Her eyebrows pulled in at his tone. "Relax. Food's ready. I was sent up to let you all know."

He clipped his head in a nod.

Torie added to me, "I'll let everyone else know."

"Thank you."

She left, and Matt had had enough. He shot Hoda a pointed look. "Get gone. I wasn't done talking to my sister."

Another flush, but this one was redder. Her mouth tightened. "Right." Her eyes found mine, but she didn't say anything more, and she only raised her hand up in a halfhearted wave. She left, too. Matt followed her to the door, shutting it so even Erik couldn't overhear.

He didn't make me wait.

He turned and announced, "Okay. So. I'm going to fuck either Fleur or Cedar this weekend. I'm assuming that's why you invited them, for me."

He would've been right, but I hadn't been thinking that. Not exactly.

"I wanted you to know. It's not a slap in your face, but I'm not coupling up with anyone here, and I either fuck, get blitzed out of my fucking mind, or raise holy hell to distract myself from doing what I really want. I'm trying to play it smart, so that means I gotta fuck. And a lot. I'm probably going to do them dirty."

I winced. "You do not need to share all of that. Trust me."

"I am trusting you, that's why I'm telling you. If they get in your face about something, just know the real deal. It's just fucking. That's it. I'm not going to be nice to them. There'll be no promises from me. They'll know the score is straight sex. I'm giving you a heads-up."

"Great."

Another clipped nod from him. "So I'm going to go."

"Right." And to be a smartass: "Thanks."

He shot me a grin before opening the door and saluting Erik. "She's all yours to guard."

He was gone and Erik was still standing there. He looked at me through the opened door. "He's in a mood."

Yes. Yes, he was.

I was missing Kash all of a sudden, more than I had been before.

I wanted him to call me. I wanted him to fly here. I wanted him to crawl into bed with me.

I wanted to be standing in his arms right then and there.

But I wasn't, and that was just how the cards fell.

THIRTY-NINE

Kash

I had a gun pointed at my face, and I was not happy.

We flew from Chicago to Greece, one layover, and I had to endure Victoria the *entire* flight. And now, an hour into our arrival, Griogos Maragos had a gun six inches from my forehead.

I moved before anyone else could.

I saw the gun barrel and then red, just a whole ton of red. The next instant I was standing over Griogos's body, his gun in *my* hand and *his* barrel six inches from *his* forehead.

He lay completely still, his usually dark tan an uncharacteristic pallor, and an odd smell that told me he'd pissed his pants was filling the room. That all flashed in my mind, but I simply did. Not. Care.

"You point a gun at me?" I growled, bending down, pressing the end of the muzzle against his skin.

"Kashton!" he choked out, throwing his hand up as if to ward off a bullet. "Please. Don't. I have family."

"I'm aware." I pushed it harder against him, hoping I broke skin. My nostrils flared. I wanted to smell his blood in the air instead, but he just stayed there, frozen, pissing himself. "I came over here as a courtesy visit. I could've sent men to do my bidding, but I brought your granddaughter with me. I wanted her to hear how fucked you are." I ground the gun barrel into his forehead again, and this time a trickle of blood seeped out.

Satisfaction.

"Now, tell her."

I was jumping the gun here. Pun not intended.

I didn't care. I got word twelve hours ago how heavily in debt Griogos was to my grandfather.

"Does your granddaughter know she has another aunt?"

Victoria gasped. "What?"

"You used his companies to traffic women for my grandfather." Not asking. Telling.

Griogos started weeping. "Please. Please! Don't—"

"You've been doing it since Victoria was a baby, and the only time you tried to stop was when her father begged you to find another transport company."

"He's going to kill my *oikogéneia*. Please. I am begging you." A hiccup. More sobbing.

His family. He really thought I believed he cared about his family. He hadn't once looked at his granddaughter.

"So you went to my grandfather and you said the same words to him. *'Please. I am begging you.'*"

He flinched, his head moving under my gun barrel as he was giving up. He was folding.

"He blackmailed you with a video of you with an underage prostitute that you had trafficked over to the States for him." Now I asked, because he had to say the words. Victoria had to hear him admit his guilt. "Didn't you?"

He had moved to lie on his side, his knees pulled to his chest. He was in a fetal position.

His head was down. His eyes closed. He almost had a blissful look on his face.

I straightened, still holding his own gun but pointing at him from a distance. "Tell your granddaughter the truth."

He opened his eyes.

He whispered, "You don't get it. Your men are good, but they're not that good, because my granddaughter already knows." Now he looked at her, a deep apology flashing over his face, mixed with sorrow and regret. And shame. So much shame that it lined his every word.

I turned.

Time slowed.

I felt a shift.

Something was coming.

A curveball.

I didn't want to see when I looked, but I couldn't stop from looking.

There. On her face. Guilt.

Victoria knew.

Griogos kept talking. "She didn't know all of it, but she knew enough. Enough where it wasn't only her aunt that I was prostituting."

I looked back to him.

God. Victoria.

I had touched her.

I took her to bed.

I asked her, "Me?"

Was she a set-up?

Pain flared in her eyes, but she dipped her head down. A small nod.

His eyes moved to mine, a clearness in the middle of them. "Your grandfather came to us two years ago, said you would be coming for him soon. He was a step ahead. He's always a step ahead."

"Don't, *o pappoús mou*," Victoria whispered, her own tone broken.

Jesus.

My insides turned wooden, and I maneuvered so I was facing both of them, with the gun still on Griogos. She was on her knees, shaking her head, pleading with him. Not me. She had one hand outstretched to him, and she implored him again. "Don't, *o pappoús mou*. Please don't."

"I have to. He has to know. He's right. His grandfather cannot win, not any longer." He sat up, ignoring the gun, and reached for her.

She went to him and he folded her in his arms. Her head was cradled to his shoulder and he smoothed her hair back as if she were an infant. He rocked her back and forth, crooning into her ear, "It's for the best, and then you will be free. He will not let Calhoun hurt you."

"No! *No!*" Her hands fisted into his suit jacket and she tried to shake him. Her head was violently shaking side to side. "*No!*"

He cupped her face, stopping her movements, and his thumbs rubbed back and forth over her cheeks. He was trying to soothe her again, but Victoria kept screaming and shaking and rocking, and nothing was working on her.

She had snapped.

"No!" She turned on me, a feral look in her eyes. "You don't hurt him. Got it?! You don't hurt my grandfather!" With that, she launched herself at me.

I grunted.

Her body hit mine, but I swept her to the side.

Balled fists started hitting me. "No! Don't hurt him! No!"

One of my guards came forward, and plucked her away from me. His arm went around her waist, her back to his front. Her fists were still swinging. She was kicking out. Her entire body was twisting, trying to break free.

Her screams were hysterical and hoarse at the same time. "I'll hurt you, Kash! I'll hurt her. Don't touch my grandfather. Don't—"

I should've expected this, bringing her with me, but I couldn't have.

They tried to use her to set me up. I should've seen that. I hadn't.

That was my mistake.

Griogos looked up at her, a different pleading look in his eyes, and I motioned for one of the guards.

I snapped, "Take her out of here! Now!"

They took her. One wrapped his arm around her neck. She was still trying to break free. He applied pressure on her neck, just enough so she would lose consciousness.

When she fell silent, he caught her body, lifting her up.

"Take her back. Put her on a commercial flight to Chicago. Get her out of my sight."

I turned to Griogos.

I was going to kill this man. I hadn't decided before. I had hoped to use him, maybe turn him for my own purposes, but not anymore.

"Finish. *Everything.*"

I had lost all patience.

He nodded, his head hanging down. "As you know, Calhoun's been watching you all your life. He knew the kind of man you were becoming. That you were rallying to fight him. He has underestimated you in some ways, but in others, he was far ahead of you. My daughter was supposed to befriend Quinn Francis. My granddaughter was supposed to befriend you. She was to do more than that. She was supposed to seduce you. In an ideal world, Calhoun wanted her to marry you, to have you fall in love with her, and she was supposed to use her influence over you to bring you back into your grandfather's control. If nothing else, she was supposed to find dirt on you so he could blackmail you. But nothing worked."

"We did date."

"You shared nothing with her. You had sex with her. That was it. Calhoun wanted video of it, but she wouldn't do it. She refused and we suffered because of it."

He nodded again, just two bounces. His voice was clear. Resigned. "I have a USB drive in a safety deposit box. I'll get you access to the box."

A darkness was forming in the depths of Griogos. It hadn't been there before.

Anger. Fury.

Griogos was starting to rally against Calhoun, now that he had been defeated, now that he knew there was no going back.

His next statement proved my guess was right. "You take that USB drive. You take what I have on it, and you use *that* to destroy your grandfather. You do it, or he will murder all of my family. He already took one of my daughters. He targets the women. I have sons. He hasn't touched my sons. You must kill Bastian, Kashton. You must. It's the only way to be rid of him. The only way."

He was done. I could see the final look in his gaze.

There was no more, so I had a guard bring his phone over. "Call your banker."

He did.

We were given his passcodes.

He recorded a good-bye voice-mail to Victoria, then called his daughter.

After all of that, after we made sure any security surveillance was turned off and destroyed, I had the guards leave, so that only Griogos and I remained.

He had moved to a couch, but now he stood. He faced me. He nodded, his eyes giving me permission. "You must. You know it. If you don't, then I will."

I started to put his gun back on the table, but he stopped me. "*No!* You have to. You must be the one. You must."

I had never done this.

I lifted the gun.

Peace came over his face.

He closed his eyes.

FORTY

Bailey

Something was wrong.

The first day in Aspen had been fun.

Some of the guys went snowboarding while some of the girls stayed back for wine. But in the evening, people had split off into groups. Matt's group took the main sitting area, with shots being passed around, rap music blaring. Tony somehow found drugs to score. He pulled those out, too.

Also, everyone was coupling up.

Torie was on Guy's lap.

Tamara was on Tony's lap.

Matt disappeared early on with Fleur and Cedar, and everyone seemed to know about the threesome that was currently happening in his room.

My friends had retreated to the small living room area of their cabin. I checked in, saw Melissa and Hoda laughing in the corner with Liam and Carl. Dax and the guys had their computers out. They were buzzing about a new video game that had come out on Friday.

I went to my room, ignoring the sounds and smell of sex coming from Matt's room, and curled into my bed with my phone in hand. I'd sent Kash a few text messages, and called, but he hadn't responded.

And now it was dark and this feeling . . . I'd felt this feeling all day long. It sat on the bottom of my stomach like a boulder. I kept wanting to remove it, to shrug it off. Nothing.

It wouldn't move, and now whatever it was had come to fruition. And it wasn't good.

I knew. I just knew something bad had happened.

I sat up, seeing it was close to midnight my time.

Grabbing my phone, my heart pumping in my eardrums, I hit Kash's name. Then waited. Then held my breath.

A second later, "Hey."

God.

God.

"What happened?"

He didn't respond, not right away. "I'm heading to Berlin. I need to get something. After that I'm coming to you."

"What happened?"

"Bailey."

That made my heart even worse. I heard the pain, the longing, and I heard how he was keeping it all locked down, all to himself.

"Kash."

He sighed. "I got things to tell you, but I can't over the phone. I don't know who's listening."

Shit. I couldn't say anything to that.

"I want to help you."

Another sigh, this one sounding warmer, if that was possible. "I know, and that means everything to me. Trust me. Once I'm done here, I get what I need, I'm coming to you. Nothing's going to stop me."

I whispered, clutching that phone so tight. "Okay."

That phone was my lifeline to him. I knew he was going to go, but I didn't want him to.

"You okay there? Anything happen with Matt or your friends?"

I eased back down in bed. He'd moved on to other conversations so I could relax as much as I could. "Yeah. You know what Hoda said, but the rest is all fine. You got us an extension so we can Skype into our class tomorrow? That was sweet of you."

He was silent a beat.

"I didn't do that."

"What?" I sat back up, my heart starting to thump hard again.

"I didn't. All I did was relay to Peter that you and Matt needed a trip out of town. He said he'd take it from there, so . . . My guess: your father made two calls. One to his executive assistant, for her to arrange everything for your trip, and if it was needed—and it sounds like maybe it was—a second to the head of graduate programs at your university. Them getting a call from someone who is about to donate seventy million to their school, I'm sure it's no skin off their noses to have a couple grad students Skype into a class for a day."

I eased back onto my bed. "That's nice of my dad."

I expected him to say something in return, maybe something funny, or even just a "babe." He didn't. My alarm began to spike for a third time in that conversation.

He was quiet again, just a split second. "How about your friends fly back tomorrow night but you stay? I'll come to you, and mention it to Peter, so it could be a family trip, too."

Now my heart really was pumping.

My hands even got sweaty. "Yeah?"

"Yeah."

I was *seriously* missing him. "I wish you were here."

"Me too, Bailey. Me too."

I whispered one last time, "I love you."

"I love you, too."

He hung up, and I ached.

FORTY-ONE

Knock!

Knock!

Those were more like *Pound! Pound!*

I rolled over, grabbed my pillow on the way, and let it loose. The door was opening just as my pillow was in the air, and *smack!* Right in Matt's face.

I grinned, my head on the other pillow, and one eye opened at him. "Score." That came out as a croak.

I was tired.

I didn't want to look in the mirror. I was sure the bags under my eyes would be down to my mouth line.

He rolled his eyes, bent, and grabbed the pillow. Tossing it back on my bed, he crossed his arms over his chest. "Got a call last night. Got an update on new plans, too. Aspen was supposed to be my getaway, and you were supposed to come along for the ride."

I tossed back my blankets.

Matt quickly averted his head, throwing up a hand. "Oh, God. Warn a brother next time. I don't need to see you in your pajamas."

"Relax. I slept in sweatpants and a shirt."

I walked past him for the bathroom.

I could feel his glare on my back. "With no bra. That's not an image I need to see of my sister."

I paused. He was right. But I'd been cold in the middle of the night and had pulled on a sweatshirt. I yelled that, too. "I'm in a sweatshirt, moron."

"Oh. Whatever. Listen, um . . ."

I used the toilet. Flushed. Washed my hands. I was waiting during all that time. I could hear his voice through the door, but he'd stopped talking. My alarms started going off, and while drying my hands I pulled the door open and stepped into the doorway. He was there, his head tipped back, one hand on his jaw as if he had no clue what to say next.

"Matt."

He looked at me. Yep. I'd been right. His eyes were tortured.

I sighed. "Kash is right."

The torture slid away to concern. "Kash is right about what?"

"I have baggage from being kidnapped by Quinn. Bad enough where it's hard for me to go to the house to see my siblings. There's the constant undercurrent of war going on between Kash and his grandfather, a war that Kash keeps me out of, but he hasn't in a lot of ways. But both those things are going on right now, added to whatever happened last night—"

"What happened last night?"

"Plus, Quinn is out of jail, and she's connected to a certain blogger who hates us, and I'm sharing all of this to express how much my plate is full. You're standing in my room, hesitating, and I can't handle anything more, so spill. Whatever it is, we'll deal with it now, because I cannot carry any more, and I cannot stress how serious I'm being about that fact."

"Right." His hand fell away from his jaw. He faced me squarely, rolling his shoulders back. "I was with Fleur and Cedar last night when Fleur's phone lit up. She didn't answer. Cedar's phone blew up right after, and she answered." His eyes went hollow, for just a second, then hardened. "Victoria was on the phone. She'd been with Kash. In Greece. They went together."

Hit.

Hit.

Hit.

Three hits, all right after another.

I drew in a ragged breath. "Oh."

"Kash called me, said he'd talked to you, but he didn't say anything about Victoria." He hesitated again and was wary. "Did he say anything about her to you?"

What?

Victoria?

Suddenly, I felt my insides squeezing. Hard.

"No." That word scraped over my throat to get out.

"Right. Well, she's coming here, and she's *mad*."

"What?"

He shook his head. "Fleur, Vic, and Cedar have been around us and the guys all our lives. I know you don't like 'em. I know you have reason not to like 'em. And I know they're stuck-up bitches, and the only reason they're stuck-up is because all of their families are old-money wealthy. That's a different circle, if you get my drift. You. Me. Our dad. We're not in that circle, but those girls are. Chester is. Tony and Guy, they aren't."

I was waiting.

"And Kash is most definitely in that circle. I'm sharing all this to help you understand why we put up with the girls. Some of it is power and connections. Some of it is because their families know our families. Some of it is because, when you hang with someone for so many years in a row, since you were all in first grade and on—those are friendship roots that don't get cut so easily."

My throat was getting raw. I knew he was winding to the point.

A stark sadness flashed in his eyes. His mouth tightened. "I usually treat those girls like trash. It's fucked up, and I'm not justifying my ways. It's a response to how bitchy they can be at times. I used 'em last night, but that's not been anything new. Fleur, Cedar, even Victoria, back in the day—they aren't sluts, but they do have healthy sexual appetites. They trust us guys, hence the reason why they get around, but it's only our group.

"I'm sharing all this because they iced me out last night, and that's not good. You need to understand the significance of them icing me out. They've never iced me out before. I don't know how the cards are going to fall with the guys, but if the girls iced me out, something happened with their families or Victoria's family. I'm sorry to lay all that on you, but when you walk down there for breakfast, Victoria is here, and I have a feeling you and I both might be walking into a bloodbath."

Dread took root in my legs, anchoring me down.

My tone was dull even to my own ears. "I called Kash last night. Had a feeling something happened. He said he couldn't talk about it on the phone because he didn't know who was listening. This is bad."

Matt was frowning. "This is bad."

I tried to move. I couldn't. I was still anchored in place.

"You going to be okay?"

"Yeah." That cost me, too. "I'll be fine."

I think . . .

"Okay." I wasn't looking, but I could feel his concern. "I'll wait for you in the hallway."

That was sweet.

My brother waiting to have my back . . . or no.

I looked just as he was leaving. "Matt."

He paused, looking back.

I flashed him a grin. "Team Batt."

His eyes warmed, but he didn't return my grin. "Team Batt. All the way."

Now *that* was sweet.

He went out to wait, but it didn't take me long to finish changing. If we were walking into battle, a part of me was absorbing Torie's and Tamara's ways. I dressed like a warrior.

Okay, I didn't really. They would've worn leather pants, black corsets, and they would've had their hair greased back or in braids like a Viking.

I just put on black leggings, but they had a leather strip that went down the side of my leg. I paired that with a black hoodie sweatshirt that wasn't baggy, not at all. It stuck to me like a second skin.

And my hair . . . I couldn't do the grease look, but I could do the braids. I had two braids on each side of my face, so I was half Viking right now.

It took me longer than I thought, but Matt didn't gripe when I opened the door. He just took me in and noted, "Ready for battle."

"Ready for battle."

There was no guard outside my door.

I never questioned it until later. I never thought to.

That'd be my first mistake that day.

FORTY-TWO

When I walked into the breakfast area, the groups were split down the middle. My cohort was on one side and Matt's was on the other.

Matt rounded behind me and stood in the middle.

Cedar and Fleur were in the middle, like us.

A very angry Victoria was in front of them.

I swallowed, seeing Victoria.

Her eyes were bloodshot. Her eyes almost matched her hair, which was wild and messed, and she had an unnatural pallor to her skin that I knew wasn't healthy.

I wished I had pushed Kash more to fill me in on what happened. I had a second for that thought before her eyes snapped to mine, and I knew two things at once.

One: she wasn't well. She had a crazy look in her eyes.

And two: she was here for me.

"He likes to fuck hard."

She launched. That was her first attack.

I had time enough to suck in my breath, fortify my insides, because I knew more assaults were coming.

Matt growled, "Not cool, Vic."

She ignored him, sweeping around him. The air around her got even chillier. "He likes to make you come first, maybe two times, before he lets loose, and when he does, you are the only person in the world to him. That's how he makes you feel, isn't it?" Her eyes were so cold. She drew back, her head high, as if she were holding court. "That's how he made me always feel. I missed him when he tossed me aside. You get addicted to him. He does that. Makes you feel that intoxication, that high, and then he pounds you with pleasure, and he pounds you so hard you just gasp for more. Then he tosses you out, and it's freezing out there."

The others started to rally now.

Torie and Tamara pushed to my side.

Torie started to step forward, "Listen—"

I held a hand up. No matter what, I needed to handle this. Me. Not them.

Guy and Chester came forward, standing on the side.

Guy said to Matt, "What the fuck?"

Matt's eyes flicked once to Guy before returning to Victoria. "Whatever happened between you and Kash is in the past—"

An unnatural laugh rippled from her.

It was unsettling to see.

"I'm not talking in the past." She tipped her head back and let out that laugh, and an icy shiver trailed down my spine. Her eyes came back to me. "Unless we're talking 'the past' as in twenty-four hours ago."

She waited.

A beat.

Her words penetrated.

They penetrated hard, and I stumbled back a step.

I felt kicked in the chest.

A *whoosh* came out of me. I lost air, and the force was emotional, but it staggered me.

Pain ripped through me like a thousand knives sticking in, all at once.

My vision blurred.

"Matt," Torie growled in warning.

I shook my head. I was hurting, but I had to hear this. I didn't know why. I just did.

"He fucked me hard. He flew me to Greece, making me come

over and over again on the plane. And it didn't stop there. He was insatiable. What have you been doing?" Another sick laugh from her. "Or maybe I should be saying, what *haven't* you been doing? What's the problem, Bailey? Not enough for him? Or maybe it's something else. I bet it's something else."

Her voice dropped, softening. She was trying to be gentle.

The look didn't fit on her face.

It was a farce.

Victoria was hard, angry, and bitter. Her attempting to be pitying was a farce. She looked like the Joker.

I reeled from what she was saying.

Kash *was* on a trip.

How would she have known that unless she went with him?

"Or maybe it's like mother, like daughter? You were his side piece, just like your mother was for Peter Francis."

"That's enough!" From Tamara this time. "Shut her up! Shut up."

"Victoria," Matt growled next to me.

Victoria ignored Tamara, her eyes going to Matt. Some of that pitying look dwindled. "It's the truth, Matt. You know it. He stepped out on *your* mom with *her* mom. How can you stand next to her knowing that? That her mom helped destroy your chance to have two parents—"

"SHUT UP!" He was in her face, his hands in tight fists, but he was holding himself back. Barely, though. "You know that wasn't the deal with my mother. And as for Bailey, you should stop while you're ahead, because in two seconds she's going to pull her head out of her ass and she's going to remember the world stands up, not down. She's going to light into you and you're going to be nothing but a sniveling piece of shit on the floor."

She shook her head, another laugh. "You're sweet for thinking I can still feel anything like that." She moved past him, coming toward me, almost swaying in a smooth manner.

She ignored how Matt shifted, too.

She added, "He must not have told you. I'm not surprised. He was like that with me. He didn't tell me things. Always working. Always having some battle to handle. And yeah, he was as obsessed with Calhoun back then as I imagine he must be now. It's all a joke, you know. You do know that, right? I know Calhoun. He does have some bad business colleagues, but the man himself is a sweet grandfather. All he's been doing is trying to get close to Kash."

No.

I hissed, drawing air in.

That pierced me. Hard.

"I can see that Kash has you believing the lies, but it is all truly a lie. Calhoun just wants to know his grandson." She leaned in, her face so close to mine. I felt her breath. "Except for how he was with me. It was almost a frenzy, as if he hadn't been touched in years. That's how much he needed me. I think he just needed a hole that wasn't yours. He plunged in and he kept going. He wasn't even seeing me; his need was making him blind to who he had underneath him."

"You're such a bitch." From Matt.

I couldn't speak.

I couldn't move.

She was pounding me, over and over again, and I couldn't move to stop it.

I wanted to think she was lying . . .

But . . .

Was he tired of me?

He hadn't called yesterday, until last night, but I knew something happened.

My stomach heaved.

"What hurts the most?" She was snapping at me, but also taunting in the same tone. "That he fucked someone else? Or that he was so blind in his need to fuck someone else, he didn't care who it was?"

She sliced me open with the last two questions.

Girl.

I heaved again, but in relief.

Finally.

That voice in my head wasn't mine. It was Chrissy Hayes. It was me. It was all of the Hayes women, and I knew what else she was about to say to me.

You shut that fucking bitch up now. Even if you're questioning your boy, you don't take that shit from her. You don't take that shit from anyone. Never let 'em see your insides. She doesn't get to have the last word. She doesn't get that pleasure. It's yours. So take it. Now!

All the crap Victoria threw at me, flinging it in my face, slid to the side. No matter what she said, no matter if it was true or not, it didn't matter. Not here. Not in this battle. Because my inner Hayes was right.

This bitch was not going to win.

"Shut the fuck up." From me.

Matt sighed beside me. I could almost feel his relief, his and Torie's, and Tamara's.

Victoria started to roll her eyes.

"No!" I snapped, catching her chin.

The move shocked her. Her eyes widened.

I had touched her. Not good, but I went with it.

I squeezed her instead. I pinched her chin, just a tiny bit, and I grilled her. "You have lost. Whatever Kash did to you, you're here. You're bitter. You're angry. And it makes you look ugly, so that tells me what you're saying is a lie."

I felt strength pouring into me with every word I said, because the words were true. I mean, I still didn't know about Kash, but she was being ugly and bitter, so, true. The Kash question was on the back burner for now. I'd deal with that later.

It was as if all the Hayes women were with me, filling me, pumping me back up, helping me say what I needed to say because they saw it for what it really was. She pulverized me, but I was swinging back.

"You were already forgotten before I even came into the picture. You know it. Your friends know it. The society pages know it. Whatever happened this weekend—*if* he needed to fuck you— you wouldn't be here unless something went bad. You wouldn't be throwing it in my face. No, no." I sidled closer to her, letting her chin go. "You're here to hurt me, so that only tells me one thing. That you lost, and you're here to cause as much damage as possible on your way down."

I stepped back.

I expected a comeback.

I got nothing.

She wasn't crying. There was no break there. That told me I was right. She was already broken. Kash had done something to shatter her.

Matt must've seen it too, because he said quietly, "Leave. Now."

Victoria laughed.

She actually laughed, but like before, it was still sick. It was also a destroyed laugh, coming from someone not put together right.

It was alarming.

"With fucking and utmost pleasure, Matt. I got what I came for. Now that your precious sister knows who she lets between her legs, I'm taking my girls and we're flying back. Do not attempt to call us when we're there. We are through. Our families are through. When we get to Chicago, we are enemies from here on out."

She swept out, but some of the fierceness had left her.

Cedar and Fleur wavered, glancing at the guys, who were locked down. Their faces were set, their jaws were hard, and each was facing off against them, their feet a shoulder length apart. Their hands were in fists at their sides, and they were heated.

"Cede! Flow!"

Cedar cursed, then went after their friend. She dragged Fleur behind her.

I felt Torie and Tamara at my side.

"You okay?" Torie asked.

I couldn't answer. I didn't know.

Tony clipped out, "What the *fuck?*"

Guy was cringing. "There's going to be a trickle-down effect. Cedar's dad is giving mine a shit ton of business this fall. Word gets out and people are seeing who's on each side, I can see Cedar's dad pulling out. He's a pussy when it comes to his daughter."

"Same with Fleur's family."

Tony added after Chester was done, "My own grandfather's not happy with Kash. He fucked her and tossed her. It pissed her off enough where she flew all the way out here to impale a knife in Bailey and then twist it—yeah. This is going to be bad."

Matt had had enough. He rounded, his nostrils flaring. *"Are you kidding me?"* He jabbed a finger in the direction the girls had fled. "One: Kash isn't a cheat. Two: he hates her guts. Three: I'm the brother, so it's all gross to me, but I have to say that Kash and Bailey do not have a problem in bed. Four . . . Do I still need to keep going? Because if that's not a flyby, trying to hurt someone close to Kash because it's obvious he did something to hurt her, then I don't know what is.

"And fifth: Do you all fucking know who you're talking about? Have you forgotten? It's Kash, and he's not in our leagues anymore. Hasn't been in for a long-ass time. He's not even in the pros right now. He's in the hall-of-famers and you all know it. Tony, I highly doubt your grandfather is going to walk away from Kashton Colello when I know he was begging him to be saved just a month ago. Kash's family defines 'old money,' so you all better shut up and start remembering which side of the line you *should* be on."

He wasn't done.

He turned to me, gentling his tone. "Those were bald-faced

lies from her. I know you said you knew that. I know you called her on it. But I need to make sure you really know it."

Her words had hurt, but I nodded. I bit down on my lip. "I know."

"Wait for Kash."

Another nod. "I'll wait for Kash."

He let out some air, only then looking like he could still breathe. "Good."

But I had lied to him.

I didn't know about Kash, and I didn't know how to process that.

I was feeling all sorts of feelings I shouldn't have been feeling.

I didn't shut it down.

That was my second mistake that day.

FORTY-THREE

We sent everyone to fly back, except Matt and I. The two of us alone stayed back.

We were sitting down for dinner when they hit the door running.

Cyclone burst through, full-out sprinting for us. He dropped his bag by the door, and then he was first in Matt's arms. I was next. His little body was squeezing me tight.

I was melting.

"Bailey!" His arms still around me, he leaned back. "I've got so much to tell you. You were right about AI being the next big thing. All the guys in my advanced class worked on a project together and we made an AI rock."

I stared down at him.

First, I was marveling at how adorable he looked, no matter that he was shooting up in height and his face was beginning to grow more. Second, I had missed my little brother something fierce, and now his arms were around me. And third, an AI rock?

"What?"

He squeezed me before jumping back, his cheeks red and his eyes excited. His hands were waving all around the air. "Yeah. I mean, it can't talk, but it can move. We tell it to do things and it'll move there. Like, one guy told him to get him a soda from the fridge and the rock actually went to the fridge."

Oh my God.

They had possessed a rock.

I just blinked at him, not sure how to respond.

Matt chuckled next to me, but then Seraphina was running through the doorway, too. She went to me first, burying her head into my shoulder and neck. And wow. Cyclone went up an inch, but Seraphina had shot up at least two inches.

No. No. No. They needed to stay little. They couldn't grow. I wasn't having it.

But she stepped back, a shy grin now coming over her, and she turned, stepped, and buried her face into Matt's chest next.

His face softened, and he hugged her before she turned back to me. "I have a lot to tell you."

"Good." Good! I still had a mission to hack the mean girls who might be giving her crap. I needed to do an interrogation later, because I had promised Kash last summer that I wouldn't hack my siblings . . . again. But I was looking her over, and she looked good.

She looked more than good.

"Ser," I whispered, feeling all the emotions clogging my throat. "You are beautiful."

She was stunning!

Her hair was longer, a little lighter, and that made it shine even more in the light. Her face had a natural, healthy glow, and her lips were the cutest shade of soft pink. Her eyes were dancing, and there were no shadows in them. They were clear, focused, and glistening as much as Cyclone's were.

I pulled her back into my arms for another hug.

At that time, *Marie* came through the door, along with my mother. Both were carrying bags and wheeling luggage in.

I didn't question any of it.

I didn't question why Marie was back, what brought her back. I would, just not now.

I didn't question why they were bringing in the bags. I never thought to. And then Marie was coming toward me with a fierce expression set on her face. Her mouth was firm, determined, and I was bracing myself.

She grabbed my shoulders and jerked me to her.

My face reared back, or it would've been right in her bosom.

She held tight and I felt her nod against my head. "I've missed you. You been gone too long. It's ridiculous."

I looked over her shoulder, saw my mother fighting a grin, and hugged Marie back. As soon as my arms closed around her, her whole body shuddered, and she held on for another beat before shuffling back. She sniffed and almost threw her arm up, wiping the back of her arm over her eye. "You have stuff to work out. You work it out with your family. Got it?"

I was grinning.

Same Marie.

"Got it."

She clipped her head in another nod before turning and yanking Matt to her, too.

It was a whole repeat, almost verbatim, but they faded as my mom came to stand in front of me. She'd lost some weight since I saw her last. That wasn't good. And there were bags under her eyes. And the spark, her feisty spark, wasn't there. It was, but it was less. It had faded.

So, very not good.

I noted all that, said not a word, and she tugged me to her for a hug, just one that wasn't as tight as Marie's.

She whispered in my ear, "Payton didn't come. Martha thought, if anyone got a picture, she looks too much like Quinn. It'd set off a whole new round of tabloid gossip and theory."

Ooh. That was brilliant.

I stepped back. "Good thing Peter has that publicist on retainer, huh?"

Chrissy grinned back, but like everything else I noted, the usual spunk wasn't there.

My heart took a dive.

This wasn't good, so very not good.

I hesitated, but then started. "Mom—"

Another arrival swept inside, and when I say "swept," I mean he really did sweep.

Peter came in, loaded to the teeth with bags. He had bags on his shoulders, on his arms, a strap was hanging from his actual teeth. And he was shoving two large bags forward with his legs.

Matt snorted before going to help his dad.

Chrissy sighed. It was faint, but I heard it, and she moved to my side, keeping an arm around my back.

I'd missed my mom's public displays of affection. I'd forgotten how a hug from her made the morning dread go away, or a cuddle on the couch settled me in my belly.

Though now her body was aligned next to mine, her head to my shoulder, and I was pretty sure I was giving her all those effects right now. She seemed to be settling, and her arm got heavier around my waist as the guys finished bringing in the bags, then stopped and hugged each other. It wasn't a man hug. It was a full hug.

Well.

The flare that was normally in my mom seemed to have moved.

Peter's face was lit up.

Like Seraphina, I'd never seen my father more alive and healthy and happy. A bright, wide smile. His teeth seemed more blinding, matching the whites in his eyes as they were dancing, too, and scanning the room. He found me. His face melted, warming, and in two steps he was across the room to me. He caught me up, pulling me from my mom, and his hug was almost as strong as Marie's. Almost. It was a close second.

He lifted me off my feet, shook me just a little, affectionately, and set me back down.

I heard Marie whisper in the back, "*Dios mío.*"

"You and Matt being here, calling for a family trip. Best idea ever."

Wow.

He was beaming at me, literally beaming.

He made a face, pulled me back, and his hand smoothed down my hair. He bent his head and whispered to me, "You're looking a lot better than the last time I saw you."

I convulsed at this, my arms jerking, and I was hugging him back just as hard as he was holding me.

"I was so worried about you that day, and Kash came in." He tipped his head back so he could see me better. "I thought I looked at Kashton as a son, but that day . . . that day he truly became a son to me. He put me in my place, because I was so worried, but he didn't do it to be mean. He did it because I was getting in his way to getting to you. And Kash, as you've probably noticed by now, has no patience when it comes to anything getting between him and what he needs to do to take care of his loved ones. That boy—" He cursed softly, laughing lightly. "'Boy.' He's not a boy anymore. That man loves you. I know I've messed up in the past and I've got a lot to make up for, going forward, but I couldn't be as proud as I was in that hallway. I was terrified because my daughter was hurting, but I was also proud, and just filled with so much love. All the crap I've done in the past, one thing I gave you was him. I shouldn't take the credit, but I'm going to." He framed my face with his hands. "I love you, Bailey. I need to say it more often, something I'm doing with the others, too."

Okay.

Kash.

That was another something I was going to tackle later, when he was here. Then I would know what I was supposed to be feeling. Right now, I wasn't so sure. But that wasn't for the here and now between Peter and me.

He set me back, putting an arm around my mom's side and pulling her to his side. Both of them surveyed me, and I saw I'd been wrong.

Chrissy was content.

The feisty flare I'd been used to wasn't there, but it didn't need to be there. She was at peace, and I had never, never seen my mom looking like that.

I was floored.

What had been happening at the house this last month?

Chrissy laughed. "She's not used to seeing me like this."

Peter grinned, his head tilting down to rest over the top of hers. "We've struck our daughter speechless."

A gargle left me.

I sputtered.

I couldn't. I could *not*.

Who were these people?

"Come on, honey." Chrissy took pity and broke free from Peter's hold. She came to me, her arm sliding around my waist, and she walked me up the stairs. "We're going to have some much needed mother–daughter time right now."

"Can I come?"

We paused.

Seraphina had skipped to the bottom of the stairs where we were. She was holding her iPad, her eyes all lit up and hopeful.

Chrissy tensed beside me.

I was the one who took pity now. "Give me a bit, Ser. There are some things Chrissy needs to talk to me about, so come up in thirty minutes? Yeah?"

She shot me a grin back. "Yeah! See you in thirty. Mother–daughter–sister time."

I was melting. Full-out. My knees were going to become one with the floor.

Chrissy chuckled in my ear, her arm tightening around my waist. "Let's go." And once we were up a few steps, another chuckle. "You're becoming such a softie."

I shot her a look. "Like you aren't? I barely recognize you."

Then we were in my room. The door closed behind us and Chrissy headed for the couch. I perched on the end of the bed and we stared back and forth.

Hayes women did not like to get into heavy discussions—at least not with each other.

Chrissy sighed, scooting to the edge of the couch and sitting with her shoulders up, her head up, as if she were taking tea with the English queen herself. I half expected a teacup and saucer to appear and her little finger to curl in the air.

Me, I grabbed a pillow, because my gut was flaring and I wasn't sure what was coming my way.

This.

This, whatever Chrissy was about to say, was why half of her spark was gone.

I knew it, and I didn't want to know it, but then she said it.

"We're in trouble."

See. There.

I so fucking didn't want to know it.

I shoved down a knot and nodded. "Okay. Tell me what's going on."

A tear slipped from her eye.

"I'm in love with your father."

FORTY-FOUR

That was not what I'd been expecting.

"Say what?"

"I'm in love with your father." She waited, as if she'd made a huge announcement, like she had gotten the codes for the nuclear weapons and was filling me in on the secret. Granted, I wasn't sure how I was feeling about this either, but it wasn't the end-of-the-world stuff I'd been dealing with lately.

"Okay."

Her eyebrows shot up, and fast. "Okay? *Okay*? That's all I get? Just 'Okay'?"

I scooted back more firmly on the bed. Another one or two exclamations like that and I'd be falling off the bed. "I mean, I know you were sleeping with each other. You came to me, offering to go back to Brookley. I could tell you were scared. I didn't really analyze it, but now I can see why you were scared." I motioned to her. "Because you were falling in love with him."

Thinking about today, I added, "And if he hasn't said the words, it looks like he feels the same."

Her mouth thinned. "Your very nonresponse response is pissing me off."

I grinned. "I told him to treat you right, Mom."

The "Mom" did it. Her lips parted, then curved up.

I continued, "You either cut and run, which is what you suggested, or you dig in and start growing roots. I didn't go, and you never ran, so yeah. It makes sense that's where you're at now, just as long as he treats you right." I was stepping back into our more normal roles, because I took on the motherly tone. "I'd highly suggest counseling. For both of you."

"Why?" Her eyes got big.

"Because he has a problem with women. You both should do counseling. It's a smart idea to work out the bugs before really getting too deep." But she was already too deep, and I clamped my mouth shut, *really* getting it now.

She'd said the l-word. That was deep for us Hayeses.

"We're in counseling. I thought you were saying for a specific reason."

Oh, whoa again.

"You're in counseling?"

She nodded. "We've been for a month. It's the only way I'd commit to anything long term—besides, you know, the sex."

Cringe.

"Mom." I closed my eyes.

"What? You just talked about it yourself."

"Yeah. In a very clinical way. Hearing it from your mom, and the little happy sigh at the end of that word, was not what I needed to hear."

She was smiling. She didn't care.

Maybe it was a point I didn't need to fight about. I still didn't know how I felt about it. I was assuming I'd watch, over the next day, to see, and then think on it. But I really didn't need to think on it. They were moving forward, and anything I had to say wouldn't be heard anyway. So yes. I was just going to keep quiet and observe, then pick up the pieces if or when it fell apart.

I'd decide then if I'd hate my father or not.

"Okay. So . . ." Subject change. I heard her get more businesslike. "Tell me what's going on. Why are we out here?"

I knew what she was asking.

"We're up here because I wanted to hear about whatever's going on with you."

I was being a smartass.

Her face went flat. She cocked it to the side. "Don't smart me. I'm not asking why we're in your room, and you know it."

I laughed. "We came out here to distract Matt. We found out Quinn was in contact with someone he knows, and if we stayed in Chicago, he would've done something stupid."

At the mention of Quinn, Chrissy Hayes's flare came back, full force.

There was a tic on the side of her neck, and her vein was sticking out. My mother just became the Terminator.

"Mom?" I was treading lightly here.

She growled, a full, bearlike growl, and shot to her feet. She began pacing. "I hate that bitch. You don't know, Bailey. You have no idea. The games she plays with those two little ones, I could just wring her neck."

I sat back.

Not good.

"She's playing games?"

She kept pacing. "Calling them collect, only talking to them if they answer. Marie came back last week. I still don't know why she was sent away. He won't say, and no one else is talking— Marie either—but if she answers, or Theresa, the bitch hangs up. That was when she was still in the county jail. Now she's out, it's a whole lot worse. She's calling to question them about homework, what they're eating, when they're going to bed. Who they see during the week. She's not questioning them in a mom way. She's interrogating them to control them. She found out Ser's private tutoring with that other Quinn, two-point-oh, was canceled and she blew a lid. She started yelling at Seraphina, not at Peter. I was in the room when she took the call, and Ser folded. These big tears came to her eyes and she went to her knees, Bailey. Her knees. If I ever wanted to murder someone, it'd be Quinn."

Ser on her knees and crying was going to haunt me forever.

I had questions, fervent and panicked and slightly hysterical questions, though I knew they could be for another night. Like why was Peter allowing this? What were the conditions of the case where she could call her children? What were his lawyers doing to get her back behind bars?

But this.

It hit me, rocking me in place.

This was why Calhoun had posted her bail, to set her free on her family and the little ones. To hit us where we would bleed the most.

He was a bastard, a dirty fucking ruthless and calculating bastard. Mom wanted Quinn, and I wanted him.

"I'm sorry."

She *pffted* at me, still pacing and flicking her wrist in my direction. "Not your fault. *So* not your fault. It's all hers. And your father, I keep telling him the divorce needs to be done now, but it's not happening. She was going to sign. He told me it was done, and then nothing. She changed her mind, and now her lawyers are playing all these games. And the trial. Don't get me started on that, either."

"Wait. Trial?"

I suddenly got serious—very, very serious.

"Chrissy." I stood slowly from the bed. "What's happening with the trial?"

It was my trial, about me, and why did she know and I didn't?

A wave of panic started to push in, but I held firm. I shoved it back. I wouldn't let myself go there, not here, not with my family here.

She stopped, her face going white. "*Dios mío*," she whispered. "I messed up."

I pulled out my phone, bringing up the news websites, but there was nothing. There was no mention of Quinn and a pending trial date.

I blacked my screen and gripped my phone tight. "I thought trials like that take forever."

Chrissy wasn't talking. She stopped. She was only staring at me.

That panic was pushing back, crawling inside of me again.

I swallowed over a knot. "Mom."

But then there was a tentative knock at the door, right before it opened, and Seraphina stepped inside. She was holding her iPad, an uncertain expression on her face. She'd changed clothes so she was in leggings and a large sweatshirt. Her hair had been braided behind her, too, with a few wisps falling to frame her face.

She looked so beautiful, like a real angel.

"Can I—Did I give you enough time?" Her eyes were darting between Chrissy and me.

I wanted to ask for more time. I needed to know about Quinn. But I saw how Seraphina's hand had bunched her sleeve over both hands. One sleeve slipped half-down on the iPad, over the corner. The other hand was wringing the doorknob.

She bit down on her lip.

My time could wait.

I held open my arms. "Now is perfect. Come here. I want to hug you again, and then you need to tell me everything about your friends and school."

It was the right thing to say.

As I sat and listened to Seraphina for the next hour, Chrissy sat with us, and both of us just listened, because it wasn't lost on either of us that Seraphina was chatting away.

Seraphina had never just chatted.

Things were good, or things were getting there, and I felt something shift from my shoulders. Calhoun aside, Quinn aside, hoping Peter wouldn't cheat on my mother aside, everything else would be fine.

I truly thought that, for the first time since the night a stranger slapped his hand over my mouth and told me I was going to be kidnapped.

This would be my third mistake that day.

Peter burst through the door five minutes later. "Where are the guards?"

"What?"

Seraphina stiffened next to me on the couch.

Chrissy sat upright in her chair.

He glanced back, then to me. "I asked Matt, but he said the guards weren't around today. He assumed they were on the perimeter." His mouth firmed a second. "They're not."

Oh—

I whispered bleakly, "I thought the same thing. I didn't even notice." They'd been gone since I woke up. Kash had called once to let us know he was boarding a plane from Berlin. He'd be arriving around one in the morning.

I looked at the clock.

That was six hours from now.

There was a pounding, the sound of a stampede, coming down the hallway. A guard came to a stop, looked at us, then jerked Peter away from the door. I didn't recognize this one.

I was on my feet in the next instant.

"Bailey—"

I whipped around, but pointed at my mom. "Stay with Seraphina."

She looked alarmed, but she did, taking my place on the couch and scooping Ser into her arms—a Ser who was suddenly shaking almost violently.

I stepped out in the hallway.

Peter cursed, but he moved to shut the door behind me.

He and the guard descended on me.

Peter spoke first. "They found the night guards. They're dead."

I lost my breath.

I started to fall, but no.

I stopped. Kash wasn't here. He couldn't ride in and save the day. I shared a look with my dad. It was up to us. I was trying to translate that to him, and he nodded. He got it.

The guard continued, "All the other guards are gone. We can't reach any of them. The ones usually assigned to you were told they got a day off. None of them showed. I just got ahold of Erik—"

I fell.

Totally. I couldn't stop myself.

Erik. Oh thank God.

Peter grabbed me, hauling me up, and I was surprised at how strong my dad was.

The guard kept on. "And Fitz. They thought it was weird to get that text, so they called in, and as far as we can tell they were directed to a dummy operator. You know what that is?"

I shook my head.

"It's what scammers set in place. They hijack the call, direct it to their partner, and if they know all the proper protocols, then they can con whoever is on the other end of the phone. Erik and Fitz were conned. They came in. We're looking at their phones. It seems their phones got swiped. They were given copy-cat phones."

Oh jeez. He didn't need to fill in the blanks. I knew exactly what happened.

Their phones were copied. Stolen. Replaced. The security pro-tocol would look the same on their phones, but the actual line would be sent somewhere else.

I was shaking my head. "When they check in, they must have codes or something to identify themselves? The guards calling in and the security headquarters they're calling into. Right?"

"They did. They called in and were given the passcode from yesterday. Both called in early in the morning, so they didn't question the same code, just thought things were lax since Mr. Colello has been overseas since Saturday."

But . . . why?

The guard got a suddenly bleak look on his face. He lowered his head, his eyes intent on me. "We are down guards. We need to move, and me saying that means we should've moved before we even arrived here. We need to move that fast."

I didn't notice the guards.

I'd been distracted with thoughts of Victoria and Kash together all day.

I ignored the feeling of impending doom.

And I let myself believe that everything was going to be fine.

Three mistakes. Three grave mistakes.

A guard suddenly came barreling from around the corner, waving at us and shouting, "*Get inside! Now!*"

We didn't get the chance.

The ground shook beneath us, and the windows exploded over us.

FORTY-FIVE

Kash

The second we touched ground, my phone started blowing up.

I glanced at the number calling and my world shifted.

Ignoring how my phone kept buzzing from all the notifications streaming in, I answered.

"You're kidding me calling me from this number."

He laughed.

I stopped, knowing.

My grandfather had done something.

A sick, twisted sensation sidled right alongside that feeling. All of that happened when I heard him laugh, as we were stepping off the plane and I saw my security staff already waiting for me at the car parked on the tarmac.

"I left her for you."

Her. Not my mother, whose number he was calling from, which I had programmed into my phone as "Mom" and which I transferred over each time I got a new phone, because a part of me couldn't bring myself to delete it.

He wasn't referring to her. And I wanted him dead. Not now. Not in the future. I wanted him dead eighteen years ago.

Why the fuck had I been waiting so long?

I stopped, head bent, phone to my ear, and I was aware that my guards paused just beyond.

I grated out, "What did you *do?*"

"I left your girlfriend for you. I wanted you to feel what I felt, losing my little girl. She pulled away from me. It was slow at first, then she moved away, and then she completely stopped talking to me. That's what your girl is going to do to you."

God. What had he done?

"She's going to blame you, you know. If she doesn't at first, it'll slowly come out. It'll build. Day after day. A little more each day. She won't reach for you. She won't respond when you kiss her. She'll flinch when you touch her. She'll lie there, dead, like a corpse, when you fuck her. And then she'll pack her bags one day and move out, and that's the day she'll tell you that she blames you because, grandson, it is your fault."

"*What did you do?*" I roared, my hand gripping the phone so tight I was surprised I didn't break it.

But he laughed.

He only laughed before he said, so fucking smug, "I broke her. That's what I did."

Then . . .

Dial tone.

FORTY-SIX

Bailey

Déjà vu.

I was experiencing it. Not shock. Not grief.

I didn't know who they were. The two police detectives had introduced themselves after I'd been checked out of the hospital. Because of who my father was, because of who I shared my bed with, they decided the paramedics weren't certified enough to clear my health, to let me go to the police to give a statement. The top doctor at the Aspen Medical Center had been called in. He looked over all of us, or *most* of all of us.

They cleared me and I was brought here. The detectives explained that they didn't want to walk me through the events in a sterile environment, so here we were.

Another dark room. A single table. No windows except the two-way mirror. But I wasn't at the Phoenix Tech headquarters; I was at the Aspen Police Department. And it wasn't Bright and Wilson sitting across from me.

Like I said, déjà vu.

"Can you tell us what happened?"

No.

God.

I closed my eyes.

They had come in, set a recording device on the table, and pressed Record.

They would make me tell them, but everything was hurting me. Everything. Little knives had slipped under my skin and were burrowing into every organ, every vein, every ligament, every cell, and they were destroying me from the inside out.

"Miss Francis." That was Detective 1.

"Hayes," I rasped out.

"Excuse me?" Detective 2 leaned forward.

They would call me by my name.

"My name is Bailey Hayes."

"Right." They shared a look.

Detective 1 tugged at his collar, his pen tapping a nervous beat on the table, before he cleared his throat. He scooted his chair closer, and here we go again.

"Can you take us through the events that happened at the cabin your family was renting?"

I wanted to laugh.

He was framing it as a question, as if I had a choice. I had no choice. That was a lie. They would make me stay. They would make me tell them what happened, even though they knew, even though there were security cameras, even though I knew the others had all given their own accounts. But mine. They wanted my words. Me. Because this had happened because of me.

I was the target.

Those knives were in my throat. All of them surged through my body, attaching and piercing me. They didn't want those words to come out.

I drew a breath, feeling the knives sink in even further, tighter. And as if I were tasting my own blood—or maybe it wasn't mine—I started.

"We were in the hallway—"

Detective 2 mirrored his partner, putting his elbows on the table. His shoulders hunched forward. His head inclined, and he read from the paper. "It says here that you and your mother and your sister had been talking in your bedroom. Is that correct?"

I swallowed my own blood.

Those knives wouldn't stop cutting at me.

I whispered the word, "Yes."

"They'd only arrived thirty minutes before that?"

Another whisper, this one quieter. "Yes."

"You and Matthew Francis, your brother, though you don't have the same last name, had been at the house all day?"

"Yes." Barely a sound from me.

"That you guys hadn't noticed there were no security guards on duty that day?"

Three mistakes.

I could barely answer. "Yes."

Detective 1 took over, his tone one of disbelief. "Why hadn't you noticed? Seems you would've, you know, since according to everything the others have said, you travel with guards all the time."

"I was distracted."

"Right." Detective 2 shuffled his papers, pulling out a different file. "Your brother mentioned that a Victoria had flown in and 'went at you like a starving wolf.' Those were his words."

My breath was ragged.

"Yes. She said some things that got in my head."

"That she had slept with Kashton Colello, your boyfriend?"

"Yes."

"But you think it was a lie?"

"Yes." A hiss from me.

"And you think she only said that to you because she wanted to hurt you?"

I gritted my teeth. "Yes."

"So there's no chance Kashton Colello actually slept with her?"

"No."

They stared at me, falling silent.

They shared a look.

Neither expressed anything. Both faces were hard, guarded.

Detective 1 reached under the pile of files and pulled out a piece of paper. He showed it to me. "Do you know who Griogos Maragos is?"

MILLIONAIRE DEAD! MAFIA CONNECTED.

I read the headline. "He's a millionaire that's dead." I nodded at the paper. "Says the Mafia did it."

They both frowned before Detective 1 looked at the printed article from an online newspaper. He chuckled slightly before taking the paper back and putting it under the pile once again. "Are you aware that Griogos Maragos is Victoria's grandfather?"

My chair shifted.

I didn't move. My chair didn't actually move, but it shifted nonetheless. I was looking at them sideways, upside down. "What?"

"He was found dead in his Greece home, and after we reached out, shared that his granddaughter had made a visit to a residence in our district, and that there'd been an attack there twelve hours later, they were willing to share a few facts. Seems there's some travel logs saying that your boyfriend and Victoria flew to Greece this weekend. Victoria also flew straight to Aspen, while your boyfriend took a flight an hour later for Berlin. Can you tell us how this is all connected?"

Calhoun.

It was Calhoun.

I was reeling, but something had happened. Something bad. Kash couldn't talk over the phone. He was going to Berlin.

I couldn't let myself even think about Victoria.

He knew.

He knew that he'd have to take that trip, and he hadn't given me the heads-up when it was actually happening.

Why?

Jesus.

Why?

To protect me.

Not to lie to me.

To keep me in the dark.

And he'd only do that if . . .

To protect me.

Because he knew he was going to do something illegal, something bad. I looked to where that paper was again, the Greece story, and I brought it up in my mind.

MILLIONAIRE DEAD! MAFIA CONNECTED.

I had skimmed the first few paragraphs, though I hadn't read them. It didn't matter, with my mind, and I was reading them now.

"That article says it's believed to be a self-inflicted gunshot."

They shared a look. Detective 1 grabbed the article and pulled it out.

They didn't think I could've read that fast, or that far down. I told them, "Fourth paragraph. Second sentence: *'Greece authorities broached the home of Griogos Maragos. His body was located with a self-inflicted gunshot wound. He is believed to have ties to the Bennett Family and the Makarov Family, Mafia families from Russia and Calgary. He is also known to have associations with Calhoun Bastian, a billionaire—'"* I stopped and locked eyes with both of them, ignoring their surprise. "Want me to keep going?"

Detective 2 coughed, folding his hands together on the table. "How about we talk about what happened at your cabin tonight?"

Jesus.

No.

Please no.

I shot back, "How about we keep talking about a death on the other side of world?" I couldn't stop it. Dammit. A tear slipped out. My voice broke. "Because that's way easier for me to process than what you're asking me to tell you, which you already know."

Pity flashed in Detective 1's eyes.

Finally.

I felt an ease in the pressure on my shoulders.

"Okay." Even his tone gentled, and that did wonders. But no. So no. More tears were sliding out now, and I hated it, because it's one thing I felt I shouldn't do. We Hayes women . . .

Seeing those tears, he said, "Look, we need a statement from you on the record. You have to tell us something, so as much as you can, just walk us through what happened."

Two breaths.

Two pauses.

Two heartbeats.

And I started.

"We were in the hallway. They told us the night guards were gone and the day guards had been told not to come in."

The ground shook beneath us, and the windows exploded over us.

"They blew up the garage and then began shooting into the house."

"Get down!"

"My dad threw me on the ground."

Bang! Bang!

"The guard with him began to exchange gunfire with whoever was shooting from outside."

"Bailey!"

"My mom started screaming from inside the bedroom."

"Are you okay? Are you okay? Oh my God. Bailey. Are you okay?"

"My dad started patting me down, making sure I hadn't been shot."

"You have to get in that room."

"He dragged me into the room."

"Oh my God, Bailey! Thank God. Oh, my baby."

"My mom crawled over to me and wrapped her arms around me."

Sobbing.

"She was rocking me back and forth."

"Ser, honey. Honey. Sweetheart."

"My dad went over to Seraphina, and he was trying to calm her down."

Bang! Bang! Boom!

"The gunfire suddenly stopped, and then there was another explosion. It felt like the ground was breaking apart underneath us."

Detective 1 said quietly, "One of your father's guards blew up the propane tank on the property. He killed four of their men in that explosion."

I hadn't known. I knew now. And *good.*

I let that process, then I was back in that room.

Footsteps were stampeding. Yelling. Shouting. "No, no—" Bang!

"They got inside and they killed the guard that was in the hallway."

It happened so fast after that. It'd been a blur.

The door was kicked open.

"My dad must've shut the door. I don't remember when he did that, but they rushed inside."

I had to stop.

The room was swirling around.

My chair felt like it was tipping over.

I grasped the table to keep my balance, and I kept talking, but I sounded drunk, even to myself.

"They were wearing black masks."

Like when I'd been kidnapped. Like Arcane.

I had razor blades in my throat. I swallowed, talking, my tongue scraping over them.

"My dad didn't have a gun. None of us did."

They rushed inside.

"Hey!" Peter stood up. His hand shooting out. "You can't—"
Smack!

"They knocked him out."

"Aaah!" Bloodcurdling screams punctured my eardrums.

"Seraphina was screaming." My voice was so low, so quiet. I could barely hear myself. "She was so scared."

I was being shaken, but it wasn't me.

"My mom was still holding me."

My voice gave out.

I couldn't keep going.

A hand touched mine. One of the detectives said to me, "Take your time."

Now they were being kind. Now, when they knew what I had to say.

"They—" I swallowed my blood, and I pushed forward, because I was a fucking Hayes and that's what we did. "They pointed the gun at me."

"No! NO!"

"My mom shoved me behind her, and she stood up."

I couldn't. I just couldn't.

"Seraphina was so scared by now, but she was whimpering." I could taste my tears. The salt slipped into my mouth, mingling with my own blood. "She peed herself, she was that scared."

"Miss Francis—"

"I'm a fucking *Hayes!*" I pounded on the table, not knowing there was a *snap*, not knowing that both detectives stilled, both had heard it, and both looked at my hands. Neither said a word. "Call me by my name!"

"Miss Hayes—"

I rushed out, because I wanted this to be done, "They ignored Seraphina." I was grinding my teeth so hard. My fists were grinding into the table at the same time. I never felt that pain, not at all. "They shoved my mother aside, pointed their guns at me. Three of them were in the room by now, and then they pulled the trigger."

Click. Click. Click.

I flinched now, remembering. "They purposely emptied their barrels, and when no bullets came out, one of them laughed. He said, 'Remember that sound, 'cause it won't happen the next time. That's your gift from him.'

"Then one used his gun to hit my mother across the face. They grabbed her, dragged her behind them."

"No, no, no! Mom!"

"They kicked me aside, barred the door, and we could hear my mom screaming the entire time. They had dragged a security guard's body in front of the door."

I didn't tell them how heavy the guard's body had been, or how my hands had been shaking because I was suddenly too weak to push his body and that door open.

I didn't tell them any of that.

"When I got into the hallway, they were dragging her to their vehicles outside. All of them were loading back up."

No.

I locked down.

I stopped feeling.

I was no longer in my body, and I watched myself from the corner of the room as I sat there.

"They took my mother to their vehicle, then turned to the house. They made sure I could see. I will never forget him. I will never forget his eyes. He shoved her to the ground, to her knees, put the gun to her head, and he pulled the trigger." I saw myself flinch before finishing. "They killed my mother."

The detective sitting closest to the recorder reached over and hit Stop.

There was a commotion outside my interrogation room.

Shouts.

The door burst open and Kash was there.

He took in the room, then snarled. "This is over." One step, a hand to my arm, but I was already pushing back from the table. He took me out of there.

I still watched all of this from the corner of the room, detached from my body.

I didn't come back to myself until we were in the back of an SUV. Kash's arms were around me, and he was saying into my neck, "I'm so sorry, Bailey. I am so sorry."

I returned to his comfort, and to the next impending wave of doom, except that this wave was mixed with grief like I'd never experienced before.

And I didn't want to experience it, so I left my body once again.

FORTY-SEVEN

The world didn't know him.

It would.

He knew, striding through an airport in Bangkok, Thailand, that everything would soon change.

Everything.

The blood that ran through his veins, who his mother and father had been, and who had kept *him* in hiding all these years, it all gave him that power.

Just like the other one.

But he didn't grow up like that one. Not at all. Not even a little bit.

He boarded the plane, his bag over his shoulder.

The flight attendant watched him. Interest and attraction sparked in her eyes as she took in his cognac-brown eyes, but she awarded him a professional smile. "Mr. Chase Bastian. Welcome aboard. I'm certain you will love Chicago."

He nodded, taking his seat. "I'm sure I will as well."

ACKNOWLEDGMENTS

A big, huge thank-you to my publisher! To my agent. To Crystal. Amy. Tami. Chris. Serena.

A big, huge thank-you to the ladies in my reader's group. To all the bloggers who have posted for me and supported me. To Social Butterfly.

It's been a long road from that first phone call with my agent, then with Monique, and now I'm writing the acknowledgments for the second book of The Insiders trilogy.

I hope you enjoyed *The Damaged*, and I hope you keep trusting me. ;)

ABOUT THE AUTHOR

TIJAN is a *New York Times* bestselling author who writes suspenseful and unpredictable novels. Her characters are strong, intense, and gut-wrenchingly real, with a little bit of sass on the side. Tijan began writing later in life, and once she started, she was hooked. She's written multiple bestsellers, including the Carter Reed series, the Fallen Crest series, and *Ryan's Bed*, among others. She is currently writing to her heart's content in northern Minnesota, with an English cocker spaniel she adores.